LOOKS ARE DECEIVING

LOOKS ARE DECEIVING

BILL VANPATTEN

INPUT AND MORE

Cover design by Michael Rehder.

Interior design by Phillip Gessert.

ISBN 9798737025731

Printed in the United States through Amazon Kindle Direct Publishing.

ALSO BY BILL VANPATTEN

Seidon's Tale
A Novel

Dust Storm
Stories from Lubbock

The Whisper of Clouds
Stories from the Windy City

Ángel (IN SPANISH)

Elena (IN SPANISH)

Daniel (IN SPANISH)

Cuentos cortos (IN SPANISH)

For Terry, Paul, and Russ

• • •

—*Isn't this a surprise.*

—*I'm not here for a social visit.*

—*What are you here for?*

—*I want you to give me some insight. Tell me what I don't know.*

—*You know what happened.*

—*True. But there's more. I want to know what's in your head.*

—*My head?*

—*Yes.*

—*Have you talked to anyone else?*

—*Not yet. I really just want to talk to you.*

[pauses]

—*Okay. Where should I start?*

—*Anywhere you want.*

[pauses]

—*Then I'll start with the first...the first victim.*

• • •

CHAPTER 1

W HO WOULD HAVE thought a routine bike ride in late June would entangle me in murder? But then, it was my own fault for getting involved. I just couldn't help myself. Chalk it up to being in the wrong place at the right time, plus my insatiable curiosity and my inability to walk away.

I pedaled along Avenue 28 on my way toward downtown Mañana. My short legs spun round and round while my body pumped out sweat in a feeble attempt to cool me off. I had established a fifteen-mile loop that was just enough to keep my doctor from telling me to do more cardio. At the age of forty-nine, I had to work to maintain even an average physique. Fat was a genetic predisposition in my family, along with dark hair, brown eyes, and a height ceiling at five feet six. No Gay Pride–float body here.

I turned right onto a side street that would add an extra half mile to my route and allow me to make a U-turn behind the Regent School. As I zoomed along, my nose twitched. I'd caught the scent of something foul. At first, I wasn't sure what it was—then, bam! I recognized the stench of uncooked pork sausage left out in the garbage for several days in the summer heat before sanitation came by to pick up the bins. I caught some movement out of the corner of my eye.

In the field, a flock of a half dozen buzzards had their heads buried in something. From the number of them, whatever it was must have been large. I had to investigate. I'd been like that since I was a little kid. I possessed a curious nature, and unsolved problems were magnets for my constantly snapping neurons.

Against my better instinct, I braked to a stop. I turned my bike around and pedaled back to study the scene. The flock of buzzards was about one hundred feet from the shoulder of the two-lane road. One of them lifted its crimson beak to eye me, flesh dangling so that it looked like a feathered zombie. The bird tossed its head back, gobbled its mouthful, and then went back to the task of rendering the carcass with its buddies.

I pulled my bike off the road and onto the edge of the field. The late-June sun hurled down angry heat as I gingerly sidestepped the drought-ridden grasses and scrawny wildflowers that sprung from the packed and dusty earth. The buzzards shifted from side to side and made little gurgling noises on my approach. One of them flapped its wings and took flight, aiming right at me. I screamed, not in a manly way, I admit, and ducked as it flew past my head—the fetid smell of its feast emanating from its body.

For a split second I contemplated returning to my bike, hopping on the seat, and continuing my cardio workout. I could've just called animal control to report something out in the field. That would have been the smart thing to do.

But damn my curiosity!

I took another step toward the flock. Then, as if some far-off signal had reached their ears, the buzzards flapped in unison and took off, leaving their meal and me in a cloud of San Joaquin Valley dust. I coughed as I continued my approach.

Then I spotted it.

A human hand.

It jutted up from the low-lying dead brush, one finger

curled slightly upward, as if signaling me to come closer. I inched my way toward the hand—and then...

Oh shit.

I vomited.

CHAPTER 2

I STOOD BY the edge of the field as the police and forensics team arrived. A fortysomething man with peppered hair and the hint of a beer belly approached me. Dressed in a dark-blue polo shirt and khakis, he gnawed on a toothpick, which he plucked from his teeth and tossed to the ground.

"You Will Christian?"

"I am." I extended my hand and he grasped it.

"Lieutenant Joseph Reed." He removed his sunglasses and revealed blue-gray eyes, rare among humans, almost preternatural. "Could you show us the body?"

I walked him over to the grisly scene. "You'll excuse me," I said as I stopped about ten feet short. "I already tossed my cookies once." I pointed to a particular spot. "I wouldn't step there if I were you."

He ignored my comment and traipsed over to the body, a team of three men and one woman following him. I looked on as two guys marked off the area with stakes and then wound police tape around each one, stretching it across to signal a crime scene. Another guy set about taking pictures, while the woman squatted next to the body.

"Looks like some kind of blunt-force trauma," she said. "See here on the side of the head?" She pointed with nitrile-gloved hands. "This section is caved in. I'm guessing the skull is completely fractured." She stood up and moved around, then pointed to the area around the head. "The ground should be soaked with blood."

Lieutenant Reed nodded. "He was killed somewhere else, then dumped here." His voice was flat, and he didn't move as he studied the body.

"Exactly," the woman said. She sized up the remains before her. "The buzzards have done some fine work, but I think our witness over there saved us a big headache if he scared them off."

The lieutenant looked at me and then walked over. He pulled out a pad and a pen.

"Mr. Christian, I need to get some information from you."

"Sure."

He took my address and phone number, then asked me what had happened. I recounted every step I took, every detail, even about the buzzard that flew at me—although I omitted the scream. He listened and I watched as his smooth hand scribbled on the pad. I noticed a gold wedding band.

"So, you didn't touch the body or get near it?"

"I told you," I said. "As soon as I saw that pecked face, I lost it. I walked back to my bike and called 911."

He reflected on this. As we stood there, a red Ford F-150 pulled up and parked on the side of the road. A tall man in a classic cowboy hat stepped out and headed for us.

"Hey, Tim," Lieutenant Reed said. The other man stopped short, about three feet from us.

"I saw the unit as I was driving," he said. "I was headed over to The Palms for some work."

The Palms was the local gated community, built as part of the large golf course complex some twenty years prior. I lived there, around the corner from my sister, Laura.

"What's up?" the other man asked.

"Looks like a homicide," Reed said. "Bash to the head."

The man whistled. "Doesn't sound like Mañana."

"Right?" The lieutenant mopped his brow with the back of his hand. "We don't see foul play like this around here."

I stood there, waiting. When no one said anything, I stepped forward and stuck out my hand. "Hi. I'm Will Christian."

The man looked at it, waited a beat, and then took it in his. His grip was vise-tight, offering one of those handshakes that some straight men use to signal their masculinity. I gripped as strongly as I could in return, but his hand was almost twice the size of mine.

"Tim Shakely," he said.

"Tim is my cousin," Reed added. "He's a local. Lived here his whole life."

I looked at the lieutenant, then back at Shakely. One thing I'd learned in the several years I'd lived in Mañana was how proud the natives were. If you were born and raised here, you wore it like a badge—and you reminded others that no matter how long they lived in this town, they were transplants. Smaller-town living.

"My dad was a cop," Shakely said.

"Hired me," Reed added. "Uh oh." He jutted his chin toward a van that had just pulled up. "Fresno is here."

Mañana and the nearby cities of Merced and Madera were too small to have television news, so Fresno stations covered local events of any interest. I watched as a reporter stepped out of the van along with a cameraman. They surveyed the area, apparently looking for a suitable spot to set up. Then the reporter marched over to us. She was dressed in a navy-blue pantsuit but wore Nike running shoes. Evidently, she came prepared to walk out in these fields, and then I realized that field reporters are seldom shot below the waist. Maybe she wore those shoes all the time for comfort.

"Is one of you the officer in charge?" she asked.

"I am," Reed pulled a badge from his pocket and flashed it at her.

She proceeded to ask him questions. He answered carefully and kept some information from her.

"I can't speak to that."

I thought she might ask Tim or me if we knew anything, but instead, she and her cameraman moved off to set up their shot with the forensics team and the crime scene in the background. She began speaking into the camera. Within five minutes, they left.

"And Mañana gets its three minutes of TV fame tonight," Reed said as he watched the van disappear down the road.

"I thought Harold Fennel got you that," I said.

The two men looked at me blankly.

"He's from here. The author of *What Goes Around Comes Around*. They made it a movie. You know, with Bette Davis and Olivia de Havilland." Still no response. "Congratulations, gentlemen, you pass the straight white male test." I smiled.

"I don't know what all that means, but you'll have to excuse me," Reed said.

I turned to see that the woman who had been examining the body was calling to him. He told me to wait, as though my curiosity would let me do anything but stay. He trudged over to the taped-off area. I redirected my attention to Shakely, taking in his lanky boot-clad frame, dressed in faded Levis and a long-sleeve button-down shirt. He reminded me of a fiftysomething version of Jake Gyllenhaal's character from *Brokeback Mountain*.

"What are you lookin' at?" he asked as he spat onto the dirt.

I was caught off guard. "Oh, nothing, really. I just didn't expect cowboys in this part of the country."

"I'm not a cowboy." He wrapped his words in disdain.

"That's some belt buckle you got there," I said, maneuvering the conversation to something else. I jutted my chin at his waist.

He kept his gaze on me. "Yeah. It was a gift."

"I've never seen turquoise like that before. It's really...well, it's really blue. Makes your eyes pop."

He stood there, thumbs anchored into jean pockets, staring at me. Just then, Lieutenant Reed returned to join us.

"Man, what a mess." He shook his head. Off in the field, the forensics team was bagging the body.

"I gotta get back, make my report. I may call you later with additional questions," he told me. He turned to Shakely. "Let's have a beer later."

"Sounds good," Shakely said.

The lieutenant made way for his car, climbed in, and headed down Avenue 28.

"So, you and Lieutenant Reed are cousins?" I asked.

"I'm married to his cousin." Again, I picked up a hint of contempt in his words.

I shifted from one leg to the other. "I get the feeling you don't like me."

"Why wouldn't I like you?"

"I don't know. Maybe you don't like gay people—or short, half-breed Latinos."

Once again, he spat on the ground. "I couldn't give a shit. I just get the sense you think you're better than everyone else. Let me guess. Big-city guy. Highly educated. Maybe early retired. Moves here because the cost of living is lower."

"Yes. Yes. Yes. And no. I moved here to be near my sister."

He seemed to think on this—his turn at taking me in. I watched as his gaze went down to my running shoes and then back up.

"And I don't think I'm better than anyone," I added when his eyes met mine again.

He nodded slightly. "So you say."

He turned and headed back to his pickup. I watched as he pulled out, the tires crunching on the gravel and dirt, spewing up a small windstorm of debris. I covered my mouth and nose.

"Well," I said to no one, "he's not getting on my list for the next dinner party."

CHAPTER 3

FTER MY RIDE, I showered and then texted my sister.

Coffee? Got big news

She replied "yes," and ten minutes later I walked into the Starbucks off Highway 99. Because I frequented this place to work on my laptop in the afternoon, the staff all knew me.

"Hey, Will!" a number of them shouted amid the whir of blenders and the hissing of milk being steamed. I took in the familiar aroma of roasted espresso beans and called out a "hi" back to them. Laura was waiting for me at a corner table.

"You haven't ordered yet?" I asked.

"I was waiting for you. Get me what you're having, but have them add a shot of whipped cream."

I made my way to the counter and Bobby—a slightly chubby twentysomething—scooted over from a sink where he was rinsing a blender. He wiped his hands on his green apron.

"Your usual?"

"Yeah," I said. "But also make one for my sister and add some whipped cream."

"Got it." As he punched my order into the digital screen in front of him, he asked me how my day was going.

"I found a dead body," I said, trying to sound nonchalant.

"What?"

"Yep. Over on Avenue 28. Had to call the po-po."

"Dude! Are you shitting me?"

"Dude, I am not shitting you."

He turned and said something in a low voice to a fellow employee, and so began the whisper campaign among the rest of the staff. I watched as lips moved and eyes widened. I envisioned this scene multiplied throughout the town as word spread like a virus.

When I reached for the coffees, Bobby said, "Any details?"

"Just watch the news tonight. Or in your case, check your phone."

I knew that kids his age tended to get all of their info from websites or social media. For Gen Z, TV news was as foreign as fried grasshoppers from Mexico. I settled in with my sister.

"So what's the 411?" she asked as she licked at the spiral of whipped cream floating on her coffee. "You hook up with some guy?"

"Not this one. Not even Viagra could have gotten him up."

As I told her the story, my insides churned again at the image of the buzzard-pecked body. In my head I could hear the gobbling noises of those birds, the buzzing of flies. My coffee suddenly tasted bitter.

"You're not kidding, are you?" my sister said.

I made the universal sign of cross-my-heart-and-hope-to-die.

"Do they know who the victim is?"

I shook my head. "I'm sure they'll identify him by tomorrow, unless his family or friends have already reported him missing and the cops put two and two together."

"Wow." She sipped on her coffee. "A murder here in Mañana. Well, that's gotta give you something to write about."

Ever since I'd left a university career to start a new career in writing, my sister had offered ideas—everything from romance novels to self-help books. But the last thing I wanted to think about right now was writing about murder. I needed to change the topic, get the image of that kid out of my head. I squinted as I looked at her hair.

"I think you're getting grayer. You should do something about that."

"Like you? I'm not that vain."

"Vanity has nothing to do with it, although I do like that magazine a lot."

She shot me a *ha-ha* look.

"I keep the gray out so that I can continue to attract men," I said.

"So your smarts and charm aren't good enough anymore?"

"You're married. You don't have to look good."

She grimaced.

"You know what I mean," I said, my tone halfway between apology and jest.

Although my sister was only seven years older, her penchant for sun and outdoor activities like (gulp) camping and fishing had layered her face with more wrinkles than she should have at her age. With the extra pounds she carried and the salt-and-pepper hair that crowned her short body, she looked quite a bit older than I did. Once at the supermarket, the clerk made the mistake of calling her my mom. Before she could blow up, I escorted her by the arm and out the sliding doors.

"He was Latino," I said.

"Who?"

"The dead guy. And he was young. From the little I glimpsed, I'd say early twenties."

She studied me for a few seconds, as though trying to ascertain what was going through my head. "You think it might be a hate crime?"

I shrugged. My sister and I both identified as Latino even though we were only half and looked more gringo than our cousins. It always surprised everyone to hear me speak Spanish and to talk about my Mexican grandparents. "There are all kinds of Latinos," I would remind such people. In contrast, the largely Latino staff here at Starbucks displayed classic features like olive or brown skin and faces crafted from several centuries of Spanish blood stirred into the indigenous gene pool. It occurred to me that most of them were around the same age as the victim I'd found earlier in the day.

"Be sure to watch the news tonight," I said to Laura, my thoughts lingering on the Starbucks crew. "There might be additional information."

A male voice boomed from the counter. "Why don't you go back to where you came from?"

I craned my neck to see what was going on. A tall medium-built man with graying hair and matching beard was pointing a finger at Bobby. A red ball cap sat perched on his head, the white lettering unmistakable: *Make America Great Again.* A lot of people are fooled by the blueness of California on electoral maps. Conservative pockets pepper the state like jalapeño slices on a bed of nachos. Mañana, while nestled in a district that reliably went Democratic every national election, has its fair share of right-wingers who'd die before they'd ever vote for a person with a *D* after the name. This place was smack in the middle of the state's agricultural belt. It was like Kansas, without the wheat fields—and no Dorothy and Toto for entertainment.

"I'm not sure what you're talking about, sir," Bobby said. He was visibly shaken.

"You come here, pump drugs into our kids, ride it out on welfare. You need to get the fuck back to Mexico."

The place had gone tomblike. All eyes were focused on the scene at the counter. I stood.

"Careful," my sister said.

"Call 911."

She slipped outside as she dialed. I headed for the counter, my insides a mix of wariness and anger. "What seems to be the trouble?"

The man was breathing hard. I smelled booze. Bobby looked at me, eyes wide.

"This ain't your business," the man said.

"Well, sir, if you notice, everyone's gone quiet while they watch you. You're making it public business." I spoke calmly, but I could feel my heart rate ticking up.

He surveyed the store. Most of the dozen people present kept looking. Only a few dropped their heads to avoid eye contact.

"Bobby," I said, "why don't you tell this man where you were born."

"At—at Madera Community Hospital," he said.

"And your parents?"

"My mom was born in San Jose. My dad in Los Banos."

I turned to the man. "See, sir? There must be some case of mistaken identity here. This nice young man who works so hard for his money waiting on people like you was born right here in California. So were his parents. And where were you born?"

The man's face reddened, and his hands curled into fists. I stiffened. But before he could take a swing, I heard the whoosh of the fly blaster as it shot air over the opening doors. Lieutenant Reed had just entered, accompanied by a uniformed officer. My sister followed them as they marched straight over to us.

"Mr. Christian," Reed said to me, taking in the situation. "Something going on here?"

"I don't know, Lieutenant." I turned to the man. "Something going on here?"

He unclenched his fists. "No. I'm just getting some coffee."

"Bobby, get this man his coffee, will you?" I said. "And it's on me. Oh, and make sure it's in a to-go cup."

The man's expression radiated with the rage bubbling underneath. I tilted my head and smiled. Bobby passed him a tall black coffee. The man grabbed it and stormed out. All eyes followed him.

"You okay?" I asked Bobby. He gulped and then nodded.

"Anybody want to tell me what the hell just happened?" Reed asked.

"Oh, just a little misunderstanding. I think we're fine now. Thanks for coming by."

"You know, Mr. Christian, that guy had a good five inches on you and at least fifty pounds. You need to be careful."

"I appreciate your concern. But now I'm wondering about my little discovery this morning."

Reed arched an eyebrow.

I looked at my sister, then back at the lieutenant. "I think you might have a hate crime on your hands."

• • •

It was a lot easier than I thought it would be. The kid died before he knew what happened. I'm not even sure he saw me coming. I snuck up from behind and then bam!

[slams the table with his hand]

Have you ever heard a skull crack? Crack is a good word. Just saying it. Cuh-raaack. That's what it sounds like. Cuh-raaaak. Like your head is one big egg.

[pantomimes with hands]

I only needed to strike once. He fell face forward and even in the dark I could see the blood seeping out into the dirt. That was over by the Berenda Reservoir. No one goes by there at night. Who uses that reservoir anyway? It's all locked up. But I only used that spot once. Can't be too sure, and you have to play it safe.

[pauses]

I'm sure the shrinks think it was so easy for me because of my dad. They always want to know about your family, your upbringing. They poke around to find out the underlying causes of your actions. Mostly to find out if you're crazy or not.

[chuckles]

I'll tell you what I told them. I'm not sure my father ever really wanted children. He spent a lot of time on the road, with his work, driving trucks. He wasn't a bad man, don't get me wrong. Never beat us. Never said unkind things. He hardly ever drank. He just wasn't there much. I think out of a given month he might have been home for a week. And when he was, he was always too tired for us. My mother divorced him when I was ten. You see, I learned to detach, let go. All those times he'd leave us. That was practice for when my mom finally left him. I never really missed him.

[pauses]

And for the record, daddy issues didn't make me kill anyone. You know why I did that. I'm just saying that in order to take someone's life, you have to be able to detach, not to care. Comes in handy in my line of work. Well, what I used to do anyway.

[pauses]

So not caring is important. When I took out that first kid, I didn't feel a thing.

• • •

CHAPTER 4

T HE EVENING REPORT proved to be what I'd expected: a bit sensational and lacking in detail. The reporter used typical news language while she looked into the camera: "apparent homicide," "unidentified victim," "young Latino male," "information should be forthcoming in the next few days." I wondered whether they'd follow up on the story or if, as Reed had said earlier in the day, it was just three minutes of fame for Mañana. I thought of the earlier incident in Starbucks. I recalled the expression on Bobby's face, how he was taken by surprise, clearly unsure of the gin-blossomed, MAGA-hat man's intentions. Mañana was about 40 percent Latino, and while our little Central Valley hamlet seemed peaceful enough, I knew that racism coursed through this country's veins like cheap vodka in a drunk's bloodstream.

The next day I ventured downtown to the police department. Given the size of Mañana, it was a modest one-story cement-block building the color of dried putty. I pushed my way through the glass door and headed to the reception window—a bulletproof plate of glass with holes that allowed me to speak to a ununiformed receptionist. She looked up at me with makeup-heavy eyes.

"May I help you, sir?"

"Yes. Could you tell me if Lieutenant Reed is around?"

"May I tell him what this is about?"

I leaned in and lowered my voice for effect. "Just tell him

the guy who discovered the body is here." I winked and took a seat.

The area lacked color: cinder-block walls, a dull linoleum floor that had seen better days, and a bulletin board peppered with outdated announcements and Amber Alerts. I'd expected to hear radio calls and a dispatcher voice from behind the window, but the place was eerily quiet. A morgue would have been more cheerful. A door to the side of the reception opened, and Reed emerged.

"Mr. Christian." He extended his hand. "How can I help you?"

"I was wondering if you had identified the body."

He gestured with his head. "Follow me."

We passed through the same door he'd just come out of and he ushered me to his office. It was a small space, certainly not like those you see on cop programs such as *Law & Order*. His wooden desk was piled with folders and documents, and behind him were several low stacks of cardboard boxes that I surmised were filled with additional files. Displayed on the wall were a handful of certificates: his college diploma, police academy diploma, various commendations. Photos of a woman and a boy sat perched on the desk. I picked up the one of the boy.

"Your son?"

He nodded and grunted a "yep." I noted the same steel-colored eyes.

"Looks like you."

He plopped into his swivel chair while I sat in one of the two chairs that faced him.

"Why are you interested in the identity of the victim?" he asked.

I shrugged. "Well, we kind of have a relationship, you

know? I found him. I chased the buzzards away. I almost threw up on him."

I was holding back. There are some things you don't tell a stranger, especially your true motivations—and while the lieutenant was not exactly a stranger, he wasn't a friend, either.

He leaned forward and opened a file. "Sergio Ramírez. Age twenty-two."

"Local?"

He nodded.

"Any address?"

"Mr. Christian, I get the sense you are snooping."

"Like I said. We have a relationship. Actually, I'd like to pay my respects to the family."

He mulled on that, pursing his lips.

"It's a Latino thing."

"But you're not Latino."

"Looks are deceiving, Lieutenant."

"Yes, yes, they are."

Reed eyed me, perhaps wondering just who I was and if I had some hidden interest in this case.

"You know," I said, picking up one of the photos on his desk to examine it, "the internet's a great tool. With the name, I can probably locate his family anyway." I placed the photo back on this desk.

He looked down at the file and read out loud an address. "You need me to write that down?"

"No. I have an excellent memory."

I stood up to shake his hand. Before he grasped it, he spoke.

"This is a homicide. Someone out there murdered this boy. Remember that curiosity killed the cat."

"Yes," I responded, "but if I recall, the cat had eight more lives."

I shook his hand and then turned toward his office door. I could feel his gaze following me as I left.

CHAPTER 5

OUTSIDE THE SUN beat down as I made my way to the car. Another ninety-eight-degree day was upon us. Dust and smog hung in the air, obscuring any view of the Sierras in the distant east. I got in, cranked up the AC, and headed several blocks north to Stockton Street.

This part of Mañana was old compared to the newer development where I lived on the other side of Highway 99. The houses here were all modest one-stories, some with chainlink fences and barking pit bulls, others with well-manicured front lawns and tall trees, but all slightly frayed at the edges. When James Ryan founded the town well over a century before, he christened it Mañana, believing it would be a gateway to tomorrow in the Central Valley. I doubted he had ever envisioned a major highway splitting the city in two that reflected different times in its history.

I pulled up in front of the address that Reed had provided me. The house was painted a light yellow and a few cement steps led up to a front porch. In addition to several faux Adirondack chairs, I noticed a child's bike and a coloring book. I knocked. A teenage girl answered. A small boy was at her side, clutching her thigh.

"Excuse me," I said. "I understand this is the home of Sergio Ramírez. I've come to pay my respects to his family." I smiled at the boy, who promptly released his grip on the girl and darted into the recesses of the house.

She eyed me, then called out to her mother in Spanish. A woman with red, puffy eyes approached. She was about my age, a little on the plump side, with short dark hair that hinted at turning gray. She carried a wad of Kleenex in her hand. The smell of vanilla votive candles trailed behind her, and I imagined somewhere in the living room they'd set up a small altar to honor her son.

"Yes?" she said, her voice hoarse.

I switched to Spanish. "*Señora Ramírez. Siento mucho la molestia.*" After I apologized for my intrusion, I told her I was the one who found Sergio's body and that I'd come to offer my sincere condolences. Then I told her who I was. "*Soy Will. Will Christian.*"

She dabbed at her eyes with the Kleenex. "*Gracias,*" she croaked. "*Pero no podemos recibir visitas ahora.*" They weren't receiving visitors.

I explained that I understood but that I was hoping she would speak with me. I told her I wanted to find out what happened to her son.

"*Pero no es policía.*" She said this almost as a question: you aren't the police.

"*No. Pero el asunto me tiene preocupado.*" I let her know that I was concerned.

She shook her head and said she was sorry, that she couldn't talk anymore. She closed the door and I heard a chain lock slide across the other side followed by muffled sobbing. As I turned to leave, I caught a glimpse of the teenage girl peeking through the window behind pulled curtains. Our eyes met and then she gently let the cloth in her hand drop into place.

• • •

BILL VANPATTEN

IN MY CAR, the image of Sergio's mom hung before me as I
drove—her red-rimmed eyes, the lack of sleep that I could
see there. I imagined the grief she must have been experiencing. The death of a child had to leave a wound inside a
parent that would never heal. On top of that, he had been
murdered. I wondered if she thought it was a hate crime, that
her son had been a target simply because of his skin color and
last name. I thought about MAGA-hat man at Starbucks and
poor Bobby. A mixture of anger and sadness pushed at me,
and I tightened my grip on the steering wheel. I clenched my
teeth. It was a bad habit, and at night I had to wear a bite
guard to keep from wearing my molars down and waking up
with lockjaw.

I looked at my dashboard. The clock read three thirty. A
little early for a drink. I pulled into the Save Mart parking
lot, thinking that some light grocery shopping would divert
my attention. I always liked supermarkets. I remembered as a
kid I'd go with my grandmother. Her English was limited so
I'd be her official translator, just in case. She taught me how
to look for the best tomatoes, the nicest avocados, the sweet-
est peaches. Whenever I wander a produce section, I'm taken
back to my childhood.

As I picked over some apricots, I noticed a new guy setting
out fresh greens. He looked to be in his early-to-mid forties,
good-looking, dark hair, Latino. He was about my height, just
a tad taller, and had a decent build. His short-sleeve shirt
revealed muscled arms as he sliced open a box of lettuce. I put
down the fruit I'd been inspecting and casually walked over.

"Are you new here?"

He flashed a smile. "Yes, sir. I transferred from one of the
Madera stores." He held out his hand. "José."

I smiled in return. "Will." A few beats of awkward silence

ticked away. "I know pretty much everyone in the store, so I thought I'd introduce myself."

"I'm glad you did. It's always nice to get to know people."

I caught something in his eye—a silent twinkle maybe, or even a look of expectation. It was the visual contact that sometimes passes between gay men. We look at each other differently than straight men do. I've never been able to put my finger on what it is, but it's there. He continued to smile.

"Well, maybe I should let you get back to work."

"Yeah, maybe. I guess." He smiled again as he stood there. "You know," he added, "zucchini is on sale today. Check 'em out."

I glanced at the neatly laid out veggies and resisted making a comment about their size and shape or even tossing out one of my usual quips, such as, "Well, that's not the kind of zucchini I had in mind." His smile did not waver.

I threw caution to the wind. "If you're ever up for a drink or something, let me know."

He didn't hesitate. "I'm off at five."

I slipped in a pause for dramatic effect. "Meet me at The Fairway."

He looked at me quizzically.

"It's over at the golf course. Ask your coworkers."

I turned and smiled to myself as I walked away, knowing that he was probably checking out my ass.

Thank God for cycling.

CHAPTER 6

THE FAIRWAY WAS a local establishment on the golf course adjacent to my gated community. It was a typical restaurant and bar, far from a dive but certainly nothing fancy. Well, maybe fancy for Mañana. The interior walls were brick and the tables were made of rustic oak, offering a warm feel, but you could see wear and tear on the trim, and the chairs were metal versions of what you might buy for your patio. Silverware rolled up in paper napkins waited for customers on all the tables along with water goblets turned upside down.

The door to the left of the restaurant led to the bar. I entered at five and took a seat at a high-top. I sniffed something like bleach. The tables and stools must have been wiped down recently, but I noticed they'd missed the windowsills. Didn't they ever look for crumbs there? Mandy, a large-breasted streaked blonde with a nascent baby bump, strode over.

"Hey, Will. The usual?"

"I'm going to wait. Someone's joining me."

She pounced. "Someone? Or *someone*?"

"Don't you have wine glasses to polish?"

She cackled and made her way back behind the bar. It was a Tuesday and I counted only three people seated on the stools at the counter where Mandy was pulling a beer from the tap. They were the usual types I tended to see here at happy hour: T-shirts, jeans or shorts, ball caps. Interestingly, no women—and the men all sat with plenty of space between each other, the way straight men do. I never understood that. I'd made some great friends sitting at restaurant bars in Chicago, where I'd lived for seven years before moving back to California. I found it easy to talk to strangers, plopping down beside them, striking up a conversation. But then, I've never been worried if someone thought I was gay.

As I waited, I reflected on what had happened. Had I stumbled across a hate crime? Why Sergio? Who was he? And then I thought about how he had died so terribly. The pain must have been incredible as his skull caved in. The bar dissolved before my eyes and images of Sergio's buzzard-pecked body floated before me. I heard the buzz-buzz of flies. My stomach turned on itself. A voice brought me back to reality.

"You thinking of me?" José stood there, smiling with perfect Colgate teeth.

I shook my head. "Oh, hi. Sorry. I was daydreaming."

He gestured at the empty table. "You waited for me."

"Sure did. What kind of impression would I have made if I'd been halfway through a drink before you arrived?"

He chuckled as he sat. "I don't know. I already have a good first impression of you."

Mandy made a beeline for us. "So, what can I get for you gentlemen?"

I let José order first.

"What's your best Chardonnay?"

She mentioned one from Paso Robles and José went with that.

"Nice. You have that in common with Will." She turned and headed back to fetch our drinks.

"I take it you're a regular."

"This is Mañana. It's easy to be a regular when this is the only decent bar we have. That is, unless you like dives filled with bad karaoke singers and truckers pulling off 99. I can take you to one of those, if you prefer."

He chuckled. "Maybe another time." He sat across from me.

Mandy returned with our drinks and set them down on cocktail napkins. "Let me know if you'd like something to nibble on."

Just then the bar blared with country music. I winced at the loudness of it.

"Let's sit on the patio where we can hear each other," I said, almost shouting.

José followed me, and we found a table for two in the shade.

"This is nice," he said as he took in the view of the golf course dotted with palm trees and errant geese. "How long have you lived in Mañana?"

"Just over two years."

"You from California?"

"Native. I'm from Santa Clara, but I was living in Chicago before I moved back. And you?"

"I grew up in Madera. I tried San Jose for a while but that didn't work out."

He looked down at his glass and I guessed there was a story there but not one that he wanted to tell—at least not yet.

"Yeah, sometimes things don't work out," I said, "but only in the short term. They always work out in the end." I thought of Sergio lying in that field. Things certainly hadn't worked out well for him.

He nodded. "True." He took a sip of his wine, then looked at me. "You have family here?"

"My sister." I told him my story—how my parents had divorced when I was fourteen. My sister was older, so she had already gone ahead and started her own life. My mother turned around and married an expat from the UK.

"You don't sound fond of him."

"He was an asshole. The day I turned eighteen I came home to find all my belongings bundled up in Hefty bags and a lock installed on my bedroom door. He'd put up a sign: 'You're an adult now. Go fend for yourself.'"

José made a face. "Oooh. Harsh."

"Karma got him in the end."

"How so?"

"My mother got cancer over ten years ago. But it had spread so quickly she didn't last a year after the diagnosis. My stepfather barred my sister and me from the property after my mom died. I heard he'd piled up my baby shoes, my sister's Communion gown, and a bunch of other personal items and burned them in the barbecue pit."

José tilted his head. "So, what was the karma?"

I pulled one side of my lip up into a smile as I leaned in. "He cooked some ribs on that firepit the following week and choked to death on a bone."

José whistled.

"Before my mother died, she told me that my sister and I had to take care of each other. So, I finally moved back to California and now live down the street from her." I brushed a pesky fly from my forehead.

We chatted some more. José's last name was Torres, and he had just become the new store manager. He'd gone to college, studied psychology, and started a master's degree in counseling. But in the end, he just didn't want to study anymore. I suspected there was more to the story than that. He was impressed that I had a PhD in linguistics.

"The scientific study of language," he said. "Not a lot of you out there."

I jerked my head back. "I'm impressed. I have to explain to most people what it is."

He shrugged. "I took an intro linguistics course in college." He swirled his wine around in the glass. "And you left academic life two years ago to write full time and to come live near your sister?"

I nodded and said, "Yep."

"Wow. I like you even more now."

"Thanks. I call myself a writer now but, to be fair, I'm an aspiring writer."

"How's it going?" he asked.

"Slow. I spent my first year here working remotely for my position in Chicago. I didn't really start writing until this spring. Most of the time I do freelance work editing, doing webinars in my field, or consulting."

We continued talking, getting some of the basics out of the way such as age, favorite vacation spots, food likes and dislikes. When José found out I was a half-breed Latino he asked me if I'd heard about the recent murder.

"Heard about it?" I said. "I found the body and called the police."

"What?"

I told him the story. It surprised me that I was talking about it with such nonchalance when earlier the grim image of Sergio had haunted my thoughts.

"So you think it's a hate crime? Against Latinos?" he asked.

I shrugged. "I don't know. But given what's been happening in this country, I wouldn't rule it out." He mulled on that. "Hey," I said, "let's talk about something more uplifting. Tell me about your family."

"My mom and dad still live in Madera," José said. "I have an older brother who lives in LA and a younger one who's career military."

Mandy pushed through the glass door that led to the patio and made her way to us.

"You two okay on your wine? Ready for another?"

I looked at José and his mouth pulled down while cocking his head. "Sure, why not?"

"Okay, Miss Mandy. Two more."

She winked and disappeared, only to return not two minutes later with fresh glasses.

"I kind of had them half-ready," she said. She spoke to José. "He always has two. No more, no less." She left us.

"I like you," José said with a smile.

"Thanks. I'm a likeable guy." I lifted my glass. "We didn't toast before. Here's to new friends."

"And maybe more," he said, our glasses clinking.

"Boy, you don't beat around the bush."

"If I recall," he said, "you asked me out."

I feigned surprise. "You think this is a date?"

"I sure hope so."

I examined the contents of my glass, pretending to inspect the color. "Well, just so you know, I never kiss on the first date."

He smiled. "Maybe I can change that."

"Only if you buy my drink."

He laughed out loud. "What if I buy you dinner?"

"You'll just have a bigger bill, that's all."

He laughed again. "I really do like you."

All thoughts of the day—the murder, Lieutenant Reed, Sergio's mother—were as distant as the smog-shrouded Sierras.

I smiled and looked into José's big Hershey-colored eyes.

● ● ●

I know what you're thinking. It's easy to kill someone if you sneak up behind them. Maybe you think that at heart I'm a chickenshit, that I couldn't look them in the eye. Let me ask you this: How would you kill someone?

[pauses, studies me]

I thought so. You can't answer because you believe you'd never kill anyone to begin with. Bullshit. You want to know the truth? Almost everyone is capable of killing. Just watch someone fly into a rage and you can see it in their posture, their breathing, their eyes. The wife who kills the cheating husband. The kid who opens fire on his schoolmates. The soldier who takes out a twelve-year-old in the Middle East. Killing is all around us. We carry it inside, like a recessive gene. Go look up homicide rates and I'll bet you'd be surprised. So, don't think you're special. You're like everyone else.

[pauses]

Every killer has his own style. Some kill up close. Some far away. Some come at you from the front. Some come at you from behind. Some like to cut and carve. Some like to strangle. Some like the feel of a gun in their hands. Some will just bash your head in.

[pauses, leans toward me]

So, I'll ask you again. How would you kill someone?

● ● ●

CHAPTER 7

OKAY, SO I lied. I wound up kissing José good night after dinner. It was a perfectly chaste kiss. Lips and just a hint of tongue. I didn't want to seem too eager. He hinted at wanting more, but I told him we needed to get to know each other. Truth be told, I was excited. When I was younger, I would have jumped at the chance to invite someone like him home. With age, I'd learned to temper my desire, not to be too quick on the draw with men. But there was something about José I really liked. Maybe I needed to relax my self-imposed constraint. When I got home, I called my sister.

"I met someone," I said.

"So soon after a murder?"

"I found a body. I didn't kill anyone."

"Okay. Spill."

I gave her the highlights.

"All right," she said, "I know how you are. You are quick to fall for guys. You don't always take your time." She paused and in the background was the unmistakable sound of a bag of potato chips being ripped open. "I want to meet him," she continued. "You need me to check things out for you. If you had before, you wouldn't have been married to that asshole for twelve years."

That "asshole" was my ex, John. We'd met during my first teaching position in Illinois. I fell madly in love and went about the blissful life of partnership. When I turned forty-two, he slammed into a midlife crisis head on.

"I found someone else," he said one evening. He was so matter of fact, he could have said he was going to the store to buy milk or that the gas bill had arrived.

I stopped what I'd been doing and stared. Finally, I gulped and eked out a "Who is it?"

"No one you know."

That no one I knew turned out to be a twenty-one-year-old undergrad. And boom! Just like that I joined Bette Midler, Goldie Hawn, and Diane Keaton in *The First Wives Club*. Talk about a cliché. After we separated, everyone made it their duty to tell me all the stories of his cheating ways, and that he had been going after younger guys for years. I don't know if my sister would have picked up on his duplicitous nature or not, but I wished someone had—or at least my friends had told me. I fell into a slump after the split, and for almost three years I couldn't even date anyone.

So, meeting someone like José who was interested in me and not someone half his age buoyed me. I didn't want my sister to put a damper on it.

"Give me a couple of dates before I throw the meet-the-family thing at him, will you?"

I could hear her crunching on potato chips. "When are you going to see him again?" she said between mouthfuls.

"Tomorrow. And stop eating on the phone. It's rude."

"I'm hungry. Shut up."

"The least you could do is make a sandwich. The chips are so fucking loud."

"Where'd you guys go?" she asked.

"To The Fairway. Where else?"

Crunch. Crunch. "You tell him about the body?"

"It came up, yes." For a split second my mind wandered toward my earlier encounter with Sergio's mother. I really wished I could have talked to her.

"Well, I want to meet him soon," my sister said.

"Okay." I told her to say hi to Amanda, her wife, and hung up. I thought about José and how odd life can be. One day you discover a dead body. The next you discover a potential boyfriend.

• • •

THE FOLLOWING DAY I got up early, as usual, and worked all morning. At noon, I packed it in and headed off to the gym. Our local workout joint was not big, but it had everything a person needed, from cardio to free weights to machines. And, because Mañana is a small town, you tended to see the same faces at the same times during the day. As I entered, one of the regulars, Lanny, signaled to me with his meaty hand as he mouthed something I couldn't make out. He often spoke sotto voce to me, letting everyone else know the conversation was not for them. When we first met, he lowered his voice to ask me if I was gay.

"Why are you whispering?" I asked him.

"Well, you know, we're talking confidential stuff."

"Lanny, I'm gay, not in the CIA."

He chuckled at my response and took an immediate liking to me, saying that if anyone gave me trouble to let him know. Lanny was a Mañana native, born and raised, and a retired firefighter—and he looked like one. He could easily have carried me over his shoulder on his six-feet-two frame. I walked over to him.

"What's up?"

"Is it true?" he asked in hushed tones.

"Is what true?"

"You found that dead kid."

Yep. The word had spread. I nodded.

"Terrible, terrible thing," he added.

I agreed and gave him the shortest version I could of what had transpired two days prior. Of course, Lanny had opinions about everything and everyone.

"Reed is a good guy. Known him for most of his life. He'll get to the bottom of this. Of course, it had to be a Latino kid."

"What do you mean?"

Lanny leaned in as he lowered his voice even further. "There are some real racists in Mañana. Pains me to say it 'cause this is my hometown."

And for the next five minutes I heard him talk about how everyone on the city council was white, how it took years for the police force to hire even one Latino officer, and how The Palms was built on the other side of 99 far from the town's concentration of brown people. Sometimes my patience wore thin with Lanny because it was hard to shut him off. But this time I stayed put and listened. He was strengthening my idea that Sergio was the victim of a hate crime. Maybe he had insight that would be useful.

"You know, I have lots of Latino friends."

"And at least one gay one, too," I said.

He pulled his head back, not sure of whether I was poking fun or just making a statement. Then he smiled.

"You're one funny dude."

I patted him on the shoulder and headed to the cardio area to warm up. As I passed through, I made a mental note of all the people in the gym. Well over half were visibly Latino. Some were in their twenties—like Sergio had been—and now that the news was out, I wondered if any of them worried for their safety.

I did.

CHAPTER 8

AFTER I CLEANED up, I headed for Starbucks. José wanted to meet during his break, and when I arrived, he was seated and waiting for me, a tall coffee in front of him.

"Sorry," he said, "but my breaks are so short that I didn't want to lose time."

"I know. I get it." I maneuvered into the seat across from him. "I'll get my coffee later."

"I had a great time last night," he said.

"Me too. I told my sister about our date. She already wants me to introduce you."

José cocked his head.

"Don't worry. She just wants to do the usual. You know, interrogate you."

"Oh, I'm not worried. I'll charm her pants off. I'm just amused that you're already talking about me."

"You should see my diary."

Just as I said this, a teenage girl emerged from the restroom alcove. She sported long, dark hair, and like many girls her age she wore jeans and a form-fitting T-shirt. I recognized her immediately. She had answered the door the other day at Sergio Ramírez's house and had peeked out the window as I left.

"What is it?" José said.

"Huh?"

"Your eyes are locked on something behind me."

I quickly explained.

"Oh," he said. "Do you want to talk to her? You can. I have to get back soon, and I'll see you tonight for dinner anyway."

"You know, I think I'm falling for your kindness."

"Wait until the first time I wake up next to you. I can be grumpy."

He winked, got up, then leaned over and kissed me. I heard Bobby and a couple of others call out, "Woooh," from behind the counter. I don't embarrass easily but I could feel my face blotch with red. I waved them off as José walked out. When I turned, the teenage girl stood in line looking at me. I got up and waltzed straight toward her.

"Excuse me," I said, "but I remember you from yesterday. Are you related to Sergio?"

"He's...was my brother." Her voice was soft, lilted with grief.

"I'm so sorry for your loss. I was the one who found him."

"I know. I heard you talking to my mother."

"May I treat you to whatever it is you're having, and will you speak with me for just a few minutes?"

She pondered this, then looked over at Bobby.

"He's a good guy," he said to the girl.

She turned back toward me and said it was okay. We ordered and within minutes were sitting back at the same table that José and I had occupied.

"My name is Will Christian."

"I remember. I'm Julie. Well, Julieta."

"That's a pretty name. Nice to meet you. Again, I'm so sorry. This must be very hard for you."

She nodded as she brushed away the beginning of a tear with the back of her hand.

"I was wondering, do you know if your brother had any

problems with people? Maybe someone who didn't like Latinos?"

"No." She sipped on her iced tea through a green plastic straw. "I don't think so. He was a happy guy. He talked to everyone, and everyone seemed to like him."

I searched her face. I sensed she was holding back; there was something more.

"Julie, I know the police are on this case, but because I found your brother I feel...well, it's weird. I feel somehow involved."

"That's kind of you." She gestured over her shoulder. "That guy that was here. Is he your boyfriend?"

Her forthrightness surprised me just a bit. I offered a weak smile. "Well, I'm hoping it turns out that way."

"My brother—he was gay, too."

I pulled my head back just a bit. I had not expected this. "He was?"

She nodded.

"And did your parents know?"

She shook her head. "I think my mother has suspicions, and now I'm worried it will come out in a way that Sergio never intended. That was his story to tell, and now a murderer took his life *and* his dignity away." Her voice had risen in pitch, and she pursed her lips. I reached for her hands.

"Let me know if there's anything I can do. If you think someone like me can help your parents understand their son better, I'm happy to help."

"Bobby was right. You are a good guy." She half-smiled.

"Thank you."

She got up and excused herself, saying she had to pick up her little brother from piano lessons. I gave her my phone number and told her to call or text me anytime. Unexpectedly, she leaned in and hugged me.

"Sergio could have used someone like you." Then she dashed out the door.

I reflected on what she told me. So, Sergio had been gay, but his family didn't know. But she did. Probably typical. Siblings would confide in each other about their lives before they'd tell their parents anything. I finished my coffee and made my way out. In the parking lot, I spotted Lieutenant Reed. He and his cousin, Tim, had just pulled in. They got out of Tim's truck dressed in shorts and polo shirts that read *Mañana Little League*. Each had a ball cap perched on his head.

"Nice to see you," Reed said, a toothpick twitching in his mouth. Tim nodded toward me, his expression implacable but at least not hostile. He leaned up against his truck as he stuck his thumbs into his shorts pockets. I took the plunge.

"Tim, I want to say I think we got off on the wrong foot the other day. I apologize if I acted out of turn."

He eyed me and then shrugged. "I was having a bad morning. Business related."

"Friends?" I stretched out my hand. He shook it. Reed simply looked on.

I glanced at the bed of the truck and saw a half dozen baseball bats secured with bungee cords, a dozen or so baseballs bound up in a fishnet bag, and a handful of mitts. Reed must have caught me looking.

"Tim and I coach Little League," he said, indicating the equipment with a chin jut. "We're off to an afternoon practice."

I nodded in approval. "That's pretty cool."

"It's a nice break from what I do during the day," Reed said.

In spite of those steely eyes, I could see what he meant. He carried some kind of weariness. Mañana may be a small town, but I was sure he'd seen all kinds of trouble over the years—domestic disputes with battered spouses, robberies, bar brawls with bloodied noses. Hell, even the year before, a woman in The Palms tried to run over her husband in the driveway. Enough of those situations and you get tired of people. And now, murder haunted our town.

"Are you pursuing the possibility of a hate crime?" I asked.

Reed pulled the toothpick from his mouth. "We're pursuing all possibilities."

I glanced at Tim, who crossed his arms and studied his cousin's expression.

"Well, we've got to go," Reed added. "Batting practice starts soon, and we want to grab a couple of iced teas to take."

As they entered the store, I reflected on my ten-year-old self. I never took up Little League. Instead of sporting equipment, I held fast to beakers, chemistry experiments, and, of course, reading. It was hard to believe now that I was such a loner as a kid. I'd have to ask José if he ever played ball. Something told me he probably had and that I was dating a former high school jock. I found that hot.

I got in my car, but before I closed the door, I realized I could have told Reed I'd learned that Sergio was gay. Could his murder have been related to that? I shook my head. For some reason, it seemed better to keep it to myself for now. Reed was the investigator. Let him find out. Besides, José was coming for dinner later—and against my better judgment, I'd invited my sister over for drinks.

CHAPTER 9

A S I HEADED down Avenue 28, Eric—our community's landscaper—waved to me from The Palms' entrance. He and his crew were busy reconstructing a faulty irrigation system. Eric was a tall and burly guy with a scruffy beard who tended toward being taciturn—except with me. I admit I once had a slight crush on him, but he was as straight as the lines painted on a highway, so those feelings didn't last long. I was too old to pine like a schoolboy. I pulled over and got out of my car.

"Hi, Will. What's up?" he said, a big smile emanating from below his Ray-Bans.

"Just on my way home. Saw you and thought I'd stop. How's it going?"

"Making progress." He took off his hat and mopped his brow. "You won't believe the shoddy job they did originally. A real mess. We just finished laying all the new pipe for the irrigation pump we had to install."

I looked over and saw the three men loading old metal pipe they must have dug up and replaced. Images of Sergio's bashed-in head invaded my thoughts. Could a metal pipe have struck the fatal blow? I shuddered on the inside and forced the images into the recesses of my mind.

"Hey, Eric, I was curious. Any more trouble from Stan?"

Stan was a resident of the community who had a profound dislike of Eric. He'd allegedly harassed Eric's workers for being Mexican, which seemed odd to me. What landscaping crew in California wasn't populated by Mexicans? I wondered what kind of resentment ran through the labor community because of the percentage of Latino workers. Could someone be harboring a murderous grudge? Someone like Stan? Someone like the MAGA-hat guy at Starbucks?

"Well, I haven't run into him lately," Eric said.

I simply nodded. "I'll let you get back to work."

He said goodbye and then trudged over the tilled dirt toward his workers. I hopped back in my car. On my way down the main street inside our gated community, a silver-haired man pulled out of a side street in a golf cart going as fast as he could. I swerved to avoid him. He pulled hard to the right and his golf clubs went spilling out onto the street. I stopped to see if he was okay. Without addressing me, he made his reaction clear.

"Goddamn it!" He picked up two metal-faced drivers from the gutter along with a putter. He inspected them for damage. "Shit!"

He reattached the golf bag to the back of the cart while muttering a few more epithets and then climbed into the cart. I waved him on, and I took one last look at those golf clubs as he drove away. They jostled in the bag, clanging against each other. I pictured the swing of a club against someone's head, contemplating the kind of damage it might do. I shrugged the image off and put my car in gear. I let my thoughts turn to the evening ahead. José was going to meet my sister. She had pushed for this and I'd given in.

What was I thinking?

• • •

JOSÉ ARRIVED AT five thirty and surprised me at the door with a bouquet of flowers. He leaned in and kissed me. I felt a spark fly from my lips down to my toes. Jesus. How could I have been falling for this guy already? Or was it just that I'd been alone for so long?

"I've got some Chardonnay chilled," I said as I led him to the kitchen area.

"Perfect." He looked around. "I love your house. It's so LatinoSouthwestern, almost."

"Thanks."

Over the years, I had accumulated a good deal of art from all kinds of Latino and Spanish-speaking artists. Visitors commented that my house looked like a gallery. In addition, I'd decorated with furniture pieces from Santa Fe, Mexico City, and elsewhere. I gave José a brief tour, pointing to this painting and that painting, hoping to entertain him with stories behind each purchase. I wanted to impress him, to be sure, but I also wanted him to see more of the Latino side of me. I had just met him that week, and if anyone had forced me, I would have admitted I thought there was something special about him.

"And this one here started it all," I said, indicating the canvas hanging above the fireplace in the family room. "It was the first piece I ever bought."

José walked over and examined it, as though he were at the Prado or the Louvre.

"It's called *The Girl Who Loves Coyotes*," I continued. "The artist is renowned in New Mexico. Can't go into a dime store there without seeing her art on greeting cards."

He turned and surveyed the room. "You've done well for yourself."

I shrugged, trying to be modest but at the same time still

wanting to impress him. "I had several textbooks that sold really well. Made me lots of money in royalties. Plus, I was fully vested at my university after twenty-two years, so I was able to leave with a pension and benefits at my tender age."

He looked around. "I take it your sister isn't here yet."

I shook my head and offered him the wine. And as if on cue, I heard the ADT alarm ding as the front door opened.

"It's me!" Laura called out.

I gulped down some wine and sucked in a breath. José looked at me quizzically.

"She's going to grill you," I said.

Laura swept into the room with a baguette and a bottle of wine in her hand.

"Where's Amanda?" I asked.

"The usual. Intestinal issues."

My sister-in-law suffered from a number of maladies including IBS, often opting to stay home to avoid being a party pooper. Laura set things down on my kitchen counter and extended her hand.

"You must be José," she said.

"I am." He took her hand in his. "Nice to meet you."

"Let's cut to the chase," she said and plopped onto a counter stool. "What are your intentions?"

"Laura..."

She held her hand up to cut me off as her gaze remained on José.

"Wow. That really is cutting to the chase." He sat down on another stool close by and looked her straight in the eye. "I have no intentions other than wanting to get to know your brother. I like him a lot already."

Her gaze took him in—head to toes and back. "Well, you're good-looking. I'll give you that." She signaled me to pour her some wine. "I'm protective of my brother, so I'm just letting you know."

"Yeah. She's a real Pinkerton," I said as I handed her a glass. She made a *ha-ha* face and took a sip.

"I understand," José said. "I have an older brother who's the same way with me, even though he lives in LA. He checks in with me all the time. 'Have you met anyone?' 'Are you being safe?' 'Stay away from disease.' All those kinds of comments." He winked at me.

"And?" my sister asked.

"And what?" he said.

She leaned toward him. "Are you disease-free?"

I rolled my eyes. "Sheesh, Laura. Stop it, will you?" I turned to José. "You'll have to forgive her. She suffers from a deplorable lack of decorum." Looking at my sister, I said, "Why don't you ask José a little bit about himself? Don't you think that would be nice?"

"Okay. But I'm not totally dropping that other topic."

She asked José about his family and where he was from. While they chatted, I pulled out some appetizers I'd prepared earlier. The enchiladas for the main course were warming in the oven and the other items were staying warm on the stove. The aroma of my special enchilada sauce caught José's attention.

"Something sure smells good," he said.

Laura puffed up a bit. "My brother is a fabulous cook."

I set the appetizers on the counter. "Yes, I am. But there's little I'm not good at."

"Being modest is one," my sister tossed out.

José smiled. "Hey, if you've got it, flaunt it."

I chuckled, and just as I was about to make a toast, my

phone dinged a neighborhood news alert. I picked up the phone. My eyes widened.

"What is it?" Laura asked.

"Oh shit," I said, looking up at them both. I swallowed hard. "There's been another murder."

●●●

My uncle was always good to me. I learned a lot about being a man from him, about the importance of family. I think I spent as many dinners over at this house as I did at my own while growing up. I worked in his garage with him, woodwork stuff. I even helped him when he rebuilt a motorcycle. A vintage bike from the 1960s—a Harley, of course. Took us over a year working on weekends to get that thing going. It was sweet. I was in my early teens. I couldn't ride myself, but I didn't care. Just hanging out with him, that was good enough. He even taught me how to hold a gun, how to shoot.

[pauses]

A shrink would have a field day with this, right? My uncle being a substitute dad. Probably come up with some Freudian bullshit and determine I suffered from some kind of complex. Wait. I think I know what they call it.

[looks up toward the ceiling, snaps his fingers]

Oh yeah. Father absence theory. Ha! They even call it a theory. But sometimes it's not all that complicated. Sometimes you need someone and a person steps into your life to fill that need. Hell, I know you get that. Look at you.

[pauses]

My uncle's been gone now for a few years. Cancer got him. I wonder what he'd think of me right now. Would he have done what I did?

[pauses]

I bet he would have.

●●●

CHAPTER 10

"**T**URN ON THE TV," Laura said.

I looked at the oven clock. 5:59 p.m. Local news programs were about to start, and I figured this second murder would have to be a lead story. After all, if my neighborhood news app had sent out an alert, wouldn't the Fresno stations be all over this? I strode to the oversize chair and picked up the remote on the end table. Two clicks and we had the news in front of us.

"Yet another murder in Mañana. Just an hour ago, a second body was discovered. As in the case reported several days ago, the victim was a young Latino male. Let's go live to Mañana with Amber Lane."

The image switched to an on-site interview. The same reporter I'd seen several days before appeared on-screen, and next to her was Lieutenant Reed. They were standing outside, a field stretched out behind them. Yellow crime scene tape hung in the distance behind them. She was wearing a different outfit, of course, but I imagined her with those running shoes I'd seen on her feet several days before.

"I'm here with Mañana Police Lieutenant Joseph Reed. What can you tell us about this case?"

She shoved the microphone at him. Reed seemed unfazed as he remained erect and straight-faced.

"I'm not at liberty to give any details at this time, out of respect for the victim's family. All I can say is that this appears to be a homicide."

He sported the ball cap from earlier in the day, and I surmised he must have just finished with Little League practice.

"What would you say was the cause of death?" Amber asked.

"Blunt-force trauma to the head. I really can't say anything more at this time."

Before Amber ended the interview, I clicked the remote to turn off the television, then turned to face José and my sister. "What the hell is going on?"

"I think we know," Laura said. "Fucking hate crimes. Two Latino men? Tell me it's otherwise." She took a hefty swig of her wine.

José's shoulders sagged as he stared at his glass. "I've lived in Madera County most of my life, and this has never happened before. Is someone coming after us?"

I reached for him, resting my hand on his shoulder. Out of the corner of my eye, I spied my sister as she followed my movement.

"We'll see." I lowered my voice, trying to sound reassuring. But my gut churned.

"Okay, okay," Laura said, standing up. She went to the fridge and retrieved the Chardonnay. She poured into each of our glasses. "We're not going to let this news put a damper on this occasion." She set the bottle on the counter and plopped back onto the stool. "So, José...Ready for me to grill you?"

He looked up at her, pulling his shoulders back as he sat up straight. He folded his hands on the kitchen counter, looking like a boy in Catholic school. Laura eyed him, then grinned and winked. That made him smile, and in my heart I knew he'd already made a good first impression.

• • •

LAURA FINISHED HER glass of wine while chatting with José. She rose to take her leave.

"It's been a pleasure," she said.

She stuck out her hand. José clasped both of his around hers.

"The pleasure really has been all mine," he responded. "And the grilling wasn't so bad."

I walked her to the door.

"I like him," she whispered as she turned to hug me good-bye. "But don't do anything stupid."

"Yes, Mom."

I turned the lock as I heard her car start up. Back in the kitchen, José sat there, elbow on the counter and chin resting on his cupped hand.

"Did I pass?" he asked with raised eyebrows.

"Yep. Final grade will come in tomorrow, but at least you move on to the next level."

He stood and took me in his arms and kissed me. "I can't wait to see what the teacher has to offer."

I pulled back a bit and studied his face. I caught a hint of eagerness in his warm brown eyes. I've seen that look before, probably given it off myself. I resisted the temptation, my sister's admonition about me being too quick sometimes pinging in my thoughts.

"I like you a lot, José. I really do. But I don't want to rush things."

He feigned sadness with an exaggerated pout.

"You've already gotten to first base," I said. "You can wait to round to home plate."

He continued pouting.

I held his hands in mine. "Okay. Ready for some dinner?"

"Sure. If you cook as good as my mom, I'm in love."

"Well, hang on to your calzones because these enchiladas will knock them right off of your body."

He chuckled and I served us at the kitchen bar. He delicately lifted a forkful of enchilada into his mouth, savored it, and rolled his eyes as if in ecstasy.

"My mom is going to hate you," he said. "These are better than hers. And you're cuter, too."

He leaned over and kissed me. Once again, I felt a tingle in my body. *Shit. Do not give in. Do not give in.* José may have hit the ball, but I was going to hold him steady on first base. Then, the image of Reed during his television interview popped into my head. Should I call him now? He gave me his cell number. Who was murdered this time? Wait. What am I thinking? This is supposed to be a romantic evening. I brushed the thoughts away.

"By the way, did you ever play baseball when you were younger?" I asked José.

He nodded as he chewed, then swallowed. "In high school. I was the starting pitcher."

I grinned.

• • •

I STAYED TRUE to my word. José and I sunk into the soft leather of my family room sofa and cuddled a little after dinner, but that was it. We promised to talk the next day as we kissed goodbye at his car.

"I had a great time," he said as he held my hands.

"Me too."

One more kiss and he climbed into his car and headed

down the street. I floated back into the house, smiling the whole way. Why does romance make someone feel like a teenager, no matter their age? What is it about the human heart that makes it flutter?

Later, as I crawled into bed, I made a mental note to develop a character based on José. Then I thought, *Oh hell.* Maybe Laura was right and the groundwork for a new novel was stretching out before me. José could figure prominently in that book. Maybe I'd make him the protagonist.

I lay on my back, staring into the darkness, my hands folded across my chest. Now there was a second murder. I wondered who'd found the body and if the victim looked like poor Sergio: buzzard-pecked with a smashed head. And the new dead man was another Latino. Another young male. Blunt-force trauma to the head. I thought about what Sergio's sister had told me, that he was gay. I closed my eyes, but questions flitted in my head like mental gnats.

What about this new victim? What if he had been gay, too? Was there more than just being Latino that connected them? Should I visit with Reed the next day, do a little snooping?

I turned on my side and pulled my knees up slightly, my preferred sleeping position. I tried to drown out my thoughts. I conjured José's kiss goodbye at his car and imagined him in a baseball uniform.

I snuggled into my pillow and let that image carry me into sleep.

CHAPTER 11

I PUT OFF working the next morning and headed downtown to the police station. Just as I pulled up, Reed exited the front door. I pressed the control and the passenger window whirred in descent.

"Hey, Lieutenant," I called out. "How are you this fine Thursday morning?"

Without hesitation, he walked over to my car and leaned into the window with folded arms. Beads of sweat were forming on his forehead. My dashboard clock read 10:00 a.m. and already the temperature was in the low nineties.

"I suppose you heard." His characteristic toothpick twitched on the side of his mouth.

"I watch the news."

"You need something?"

"Well, I was hoping to find out who the victim was. He was another Latino. I'm concerned."

Reed pulled the toothpick from his mouth and spat into the gutter. "Robert Márquez."

My thumbs tapped the steering wheel as I let the name sink in. "Local? From Mañana?"

"Madera."

The lieutenant had just named the next largest city south of us, about twelve miles away.

"But he was found here."

Reed nodded. "Look, Mr. Christian, I respect your concern, but I hope you're not getting any ideas."

I furrowed my brow. "About what?"

"About doing any independent work. You know, *we* are the police. We're doing our job."

"Oh, I know you are." My tone was neutral, but I wondered if the lieutenant thought I was being sarcastic.

He said nothing, merely taking me in with the kind of scrutinizing look he might normally use on suspects. He leaned back and patted the window frame.

"Take care, then." He strode over to his car.

I raised the window and pulled away. A question floated in my head: Was there a connection between Sergio Ramírez and Robert Márquez?

• • •

I PARKED IN front of the Ramírezes' pale yellow house and made my way up the concrete steps to the porch. I knocked. I was happy to see that Julie opened the door. The hinges squeaked as she emerged.

"Will," she said with a bit of surprise surrounding her greeting.

"Hi, Julie. How are you doing?"

She shrugged with slumped shoulders and I read sadness in her espresso-colored eyes. From the house, I once again caught the odor of vanilla candles—a sign that the family continued its shrine to Sergio. Sounds from a television let me know someone was watching *The Price Is Right*.

"Listen," I said, "I'm sorry to disturb you, but I need to ask an important question."

She raised her eyebrows just a bit.

"You heard about the murder yesterday, right?"

She nodded.

"The victim's name was Robert Márquez. Do you know if he and your brother were friends?"

She leaned against the doorjamb. "I don't know that."

I pursed my lips and then launched my next question. "Is there any way you could find out? Maybe look on your brother's phone to see if Robert was in his contacts."

She shook her head. "We can't find his phone. When we went to the police station, his phone wasn't in the bag they handed us."

"What?"

"They'd put his clothes, his wallet, and the gold cross he wore in a plastic bag. But there was no phone."

I pulled my arm across my forehead to wipe away some midmorning sweat as I pondered what Julie had just told me.

"When you say you can't find his phone, I assume you've searched his room."

She nodded. Just then I heard her mother's voice from somewhere in the house call out to her in Spanish.

"*Julieta. ¿Quién es? ¿Qué quieren?*" Her mother wanted to know who I was and what I wanted.

I took that as a cue. "Again, Julie, I'm sorry to disturb you. You still have my phone number?"

"I do."

I turned to leave, and she reached for my arm to stop me.

"I'm going to tell my parents about Sergio." She almost whispered the words and avoided saying out loud what she was referring to. "I want them to hear it from me and not from the news or from the police."

"That's good," I said. "Call me or text me if you need help."

She smiled and then retreated into the house, closing the door softly behind her.

In my car, I let the air-conditioning wash over me as I steered onto the street. Questions piled in my head. How could a twenty-two-year-old not have a phone on him? If it wasn't on his body when they found him, why wasn't it in his car or in his room? Had he lost it? But wouldn't it have turned up if he had? Sure, some people would eagerly keep a smartphone as a valued prize if they found one, but I believed most people were honest and would seek out its owner.

And why was his wallet still on him? I should have asked Julie if there had been money in it, or debit cards, or whatever Sergio might have used to pay for things. If the contents of his wallet were all there, then he hadn't been killed as part of a mugging gone wrong. That would add credence to the idea of a hate crime. But if it was a hate crime, where did the phone go? Did the killer have it?

I was no expert investigator, but I couldn't imagine the perpetrator of a hate crime doing anything other than the dirty deed of head-bashing and then leaving the body as quickly as possible. So why would the killer take the phone? Then, another question shoved its way into my thoughts: Had they found a phone on Robert Márquez's body?

I'd have to find out.

CHAPTER 12

I HEADED HOME and launched a Google search. In less than five minutes, I found Robert Márquez in an online directory along with his address in Madera. I hopped in the car, but before getting on the highway, I pulled into the Save Mart parking lot on a whim. When I entered the grocery store, José stood behind the customer service counter, helping an elderly woman who was clearly irate about something.

"I just don't understand why you don't have a dedicated organic section." She gripped the shopping cart handle so tightly that her arthritic knuckles turned white.

José stood there, hands flat on the counter. "All the organic products are mixed in with the regular products. It's easier for us to stock that way and actually easier for our customers to shop."

"Well, I don't think so," she said. "I have to walk all over the store to find what I want. They should all be together!" She bid him goodbye, turned, and pushed her cart down the snack aisle with a squeak of its wheels. I walked up to the counter. José put on a fake smile.

"May I help you, sir?"

I cleared my throat. "Yes. I'd like to know if any of the employees in this store are organic. You know. Non-GMO and pesticide free?"

He broke into a genuine grin. "Hi."

"Tough shoppers here at Save Mart."

He nodded. "And yes."

"Yes to what?"

He leaned forward and lowered his voice. "Some of us are non-GMO and pesticide free."

I chuckled.

"So, what are you up to?"

"I was on my way to Madera and decided to stop in and say hi," I said.

"Now what do you need in Madera that you can't get here?"

The playfulness in his voice made me chuckle again.

"Well, this morning I found out the name of the second victim and where he lives—er, lived. I thought I'd pay the family a little visit."

José pulled his shoulders back as he scrunched up his face. "Will, are you getting a little too involved?"

"Nonsense," I answered with an exaggerated flap of my hand. "I just need to find a few things out, that's all."

He continued to eye me, so I changed topics.

"Want to have drinks at The Fairway after work?"

"Nice deflection, and you know I'd love to."

"Deflection? That psychology background is showing up."

Just then the overhead speaker called him to the deli section.

"Gotta go," he said. "Who knows what's going on over at the high-priced cheeses and Boar's Head meats."

"Okay. Meet you at five thirty."

As I walked toward my car, I saw a young man sitting in his car with the engine idling. He was busy on this phone, peering at the screen, and then his thumbs flew on the virtual keyboard. I took in the image. As I headed down Highway 99 to Madera, I thought, *Yep, it's highly improbable that Robert*

Márquez did not have a phone with him when he was murdered. I'd soon find out.

• • •

IN TWENTY MINUTES, I was parked in front of the Márquez house. Like Mañana, Madera was divided by the highway into the older section and the newer section. Robert and his family had a home on the newer side in a development populated by stucco houses and manicured lawns. The houses weren't big by any stretch of the imagination, but the neighborhood clearly marked its inhabitants as middle-class—or at least aspiring to be. I strode up the concrete walkway to the front door and knocked. From the backyard, I heard a dog barking, and, after a few seconds ticked off, the door opened. A man about my age answered. I removed my sunglasses.

"I'm very sorry to bother you," I said, "but my name is Will Christian and I'm working on an article regarding the recent murders in Mañana." That was the best lie I could come up with. I was an aspiring writer. I just wasn't working on an article. "I'm so sorry for the loss of Robert Márquez. You are related to him, I assume."

"I'm his father," the man said.

His expression was stoic, like so many men who, in such a terrible time, put on a stiff upper lip for the benefit of their wives and families. The dog continued to bark in the backyard.

"Again, I'm very sorry to intrude at this time of grief. But may I ask you just a few questions?"

A female voice called out to the man to ask him what was going on. He said, "*Nada. No te preocupes,*" telling her not to worry. He stepped out onto the porch, gently closing the door behind him. He folded his arms across his chest and stood with his feet shoulder width apart.

"An article?" he asked.

"Yes, yes. I'm working on a piece for the *Fresno News*." I mentioned the local newspaper, sure that he would not bother to call to see if someone named Will Christian worked there.

He remained expressionless. I almost felt guilty for invading his privacy, but as usual, my curiosity won out over my other instincts.

"What did you want to ask?"

I told him I was taking a personal look at the young men killed and proceeded with a few questions about his son including his age, schooling, work, aspirations, and the like. He answered politely and then said, "You're not writing anything down or recording what we say."

"I don't need to." I tapped the side of my head. "God blessed me with an excellent memory." At least that part of my story was true. "Did Robert have a girlfriend or an active social life?"

The man shook his head. "No. At least he never brought any girls around."

I filed that tidbit away. "How about friends? By any chance, do you know if he knew the other young man who was killed? Sergio Ramírez?"

"I don't know. Robert had lots of friends."

"Well, you might want to look on his phone, then, to see. I'm wondering if the two cases are connected." I eyed him for a reaction.

"We don't have his phone."

I detected sudden puzzlement in his expression. He must have realized that it was odd the police hadn't handed the phone over with Robert's personal effects. But I knew in my heart there had been no phone in his son's possession when the body was found.

I shrugged. "Well, like I said, I was just wondering." I stretched out my hand. "Mr. Márquez, thank you so much, especially at this time. *Otra vez, les doy mi más sincero pésame por su pérdida.*" I used Spanish to let him know once again I was sorry for his loss and to, perhaps, make a connection on a more personal level.

His eyebrows arched. "You speak Spanish?"

I quickly explained my mixed heritage. Just then, the door opened. A woman with red-rimmed eyes appeared.

"*Roberto, ¿qué estás haciendo? ¿Quién es este hombre?*" she asked, wanting to know what her husband was doing and who I was.

He told her to go in the house, that we were finished, and he was coming back in. I nodded at her.

"*Siento mucho la molestia, señora,*" I said, letting her know I was sorry to have disturbed them.

I took my leave, hearing the door close behind me as I sauntered toward my car. I slipped my sunglasses back on as the sun beat down on my head and shoulders. Driving away, I slapped the steering wheel.

"No phone!" I said out loud. "The killer must've taken the damned phones!"

And then I reflected on Mr. Márquez's answers about his son's social life: no girlfriend that they knew of, and that the young man had had lots of friends. I assumed they were all *male* friends. A vague idea was forming in my head when the Bluetooth system in my car signaled an incoming call. I pressed the phone button on my steering wheel.

"Hello."

A familiar voice emanated from the speaker. The tone was flat.

"Mr. Christian. Did you just pay a visit to Roberto Márquez?"

Oh shit. Lieutenant Reed.

"Uh, yes, yes, I did."

"He just called me. Did I not make myself clear this morning? Let us do our job."

My thoughts raced. "Well, you know how I'm a writer? I'm just gathering information. I'm considering an article on what's been going on."

What was a lie to Mr. Márquez sounded like a good cover story for my curiosity getting the better of me. Yeah, I was simply gathering information for something I was contemplating as a new piece. There was a pause before Reed spoke again.

"Okay. I'll buy that for now."

I sighed.

"Oh, and one more thing." His tone shifted. "As you gather information, share anything with me you think is important, will you?"

"Sure. Of course." We hung up.

Share anything important? Like that Sergio was gay? And maybe Robert was too?

My stomach quivered as I sped along.

CHAPTER 13

I WAITED FOR José at an outside table. As was typical for this summer month, the temperature had climbed to the upper nineties—and because of its southern exposure, the best spots on The Fairway's patio were in shaded areas or under umbrellas. Outdoor overhead fans circulated some air.

I drummed the tabletop with my fingers as I looked out on the golf course. My thoughts circled like fall leaves caught up in a dust devil, the question about the victims' phones whirling round and round, waiting to settle but seemingly riding the currents forever.

A lone golfer caught my attention as he practiced his drives. I perked up when I heard the whack of the driver head against the ball. Was that what it sounded like when a heavy swinging object met a skull? My spine prickled, and then I felt sickened as I thought of Sergio and Robert and their last minutes on Earth.

"Hey. Why so serious?"

I looked up to find Mandy peering down at me, hand on hip, tray in the other hand.

"Oh, hi," I said. "I just have a few questions I'm mulling over."

"Trouble in the romance department?"

"Huh?"

"That guy you were with the other day. Your Chardonnay buddy. Everything okay?"

I smiled and waved away her question. "Everything's fine. I'm just, well, I've been thinking about the murders."

She reached over, pulled a chair toward herself, and sat close to me. "There's talk. Latinos are wondering if there's a hate crime spree."

I searched her eyes. "What Latinos? Here?"

She nodded. "You know all of our staff. They've got the heebie-jeebies."

José's voice spoke from behind me. "Who's got the heebie-jeebies?"

Mandy stood up, wiping away her somber tone with a broad smile. "Hi. Nice to see you again." She glanced at both of us. "Chardonnay?"

We answered yes and she was off to the bar. José leaned in and kissed me, then took the seat that Mandy had just vacated.

"What was that all about?"

I gave him the upshot of the conversation. He listened intently, his lips pressed slightly and his gaze focused on mine. Mandy reappeared with our drinks and set them down on cocktail napkins.

"Let me know if you decide on some nibbles later." She disappeared into the restaurant.

José sat up straight, then lifted his glass in a toast. I reciprocated.

"There's something I found out," I said.

"About what?"

"About Sergio. The first victim."

"What was it?"

"He was gay."

I looked at José for a reaction. He seemed to ponder this fact for a moment, his face expressionless.

"How'd you find out?" he finally asked.

"I spoke to his sister."

"I repeat. I think you're too involved."

I sighed. "José, I told you, finding that body the other day did something to me. I can't let this go."

He studied me for a moment. "There's something else, isn't there?"

He kept his gaze on me. He said nothing but I understood the look. He wanted me to talk. I let the whirring sound of a golf cart distract me and watched as a man in his forties sporting sunglasses pulled up behind the restaurant. He hopped down from the seat and jogged up the steps to enter the restaurant. A small dog watched him from the front seat, its ears perked while it wagged its stubby tail in anticipation of his return. When I turned my attention back to José, our eyes met. He'd been watching me the whole time.

I cleared my throat.

"In high school, I lost my best friend. His name was Carlos. We were the same age, fifteen. Both misfits. Both gay. Both too smart for our own good. We did everything together. Bio lab. Drama club. PE class. I was supposed to meet him after school one day, to go get a root beer float at the local Fosters Freeze. It was early April, just before Easter."

I stopped. An image of Carlos floated before me. It was in homeroom. He'd passed me a note, smiling slyly, his handwriting scrawled across a slip of paper. *See you at 3:30.*

"What happened, Will?" José's voice gently nudged me.

I wiped away a tear. "I was late and didn't get to the fence behind the bleachers until four o'clock. That's where we'd leave school, taking the back way out, to cut across the fields and make our way to the main road. When I got there..."

I stopped. My stomach tightened and churned at the same

time, as though twisting in on itself. I sucked in a breath. Then another.

"When I got there, Carlos was sprawled on the grass. His face was bloodied, and his nose was bent at an odd angle. His eyes were fixed on some faraway place, as though he were staring at nothing. His chest didn't move." I brushed away another tear. "I rushed to him, calling his name. I dropped to the ground beside him and reached for his shoulder. I shook him. 'Carlos! Carlos!' I said. He didn't move. I remember gasping, my stomach turning over and over on itself."

I didn't bother wiping away the tear this time. It streamed down my face and fell from my chin. Another one followed.

"I screamed for help. But no one was around. We had no cell phones in those days, so I ran as fast as I could to the main office. They called the police, and the next thing I knew, I was back at the fence. They took my statement as they zipped up his body and slid him into the back of an EMS vehicle."

I gazed out at the golf course. I tried to swallow but my throat was hard and dry. My guts churned. I sucked in several deep breaths.

José reached for my hand and clasped his fingers around mine.

"I cried the rest of the day without stopping." I finally looked at José. "Eventually I had to see his parents. It was so hard. They'd seen him at the morgue, of course, but he'd been cleaned up by then. I couldn't bring myself to tell them what I'd seen. The ME report said he'd died from blunt-force trauma to the head."

"Who did it?"

I shook my head. "We never found out. Could have been bullies at school. Could have been someone random from the area. Someone who didn't like gays, didn't like Latinos. After a year, the case went cold. Carlos never got justice. His parents never got justice. It was as if the cops didn't really care. As if, because of who and what he was, maybe he deserved it."

José squeezed my hand gently. "There's more, isn't there?"

I returned my attention to the golf course, looking out at nothing in particular. Even though I could feel my heart thumping loudly, could feel the blood rushing through me as though my insides all wanted to burst out of my body—I was finally able to swallow. But I remained quiet.

"I think I know." José lowered his voice. "Had you been there on time, you might have saved Carlos—or believe you might have. But you also think that you were lucky because if you'd been there with him, you might have died as well."

I continued staring out at the driving range. "I felt so, so guilty. When I found Sergio's body, it was Carlos all over again. I don't want these murders to go unsolved."

I broke my trance, released the grip I had on José's hand, and grabbed a napkin. I dabbed at my eyes and blew my nose.

I'd never told that story to anyone. My mother had already married my asshole stepfather, and Laura had left the house several years before to be on her own. My family found out only because the police did a follow-up visit the next day. My mom wanted details, but I refused to talk about it. I zombied my way through the rest of the school year, kids pointing, whispering behind my back. With time, the pain and memories of Carlos hid where these things always do—in the dark recesses of our minds. Until they get disturbed. Until they get called back to haunt us.

José pulled his chair closer and wrapped an arm around my shoulder. I leaned into his embrace. He squeezed gently.

"I'm sorry, Will," he said.

"Thank you." My voice was weak.

He kissed me on the head, and after a pause, he said, "How's that Bette Midler song go? 'I'm only here to comfort you.'"

I looked up. "You, you like Bette Midler?"

He pulled his head back. "Like? I *love* Bette Midler." He smiled. "I have every one of her albums."

I offered a faint smile in return. I dabbed at my eyes one last time. "I have all of her movies on DVD."

"I see a popcorn night in our future," he said.

"I'd like that." I picked up my wine and sipped. It started bitter but smoothed as it coursed down my throat.

"Feeling better?"

I nodded. I did feel better, but the memory of Carlos drifted toward the image of Sergio out in the field—and for a few seconds, they lay there, staring at each other.

CHAPTER 14

I EXCUSED MYSELF and headed for the restroom. Bending over the sink, I turned on the faucet and splashed handfuls of water on my face. The coolness was soothing, and I felt my body relax. I examined myself in the mirror, checking for redness and puffiness around my eyes.

"You look okay," I said out loud.

Just then a tall, heavyset man dressed in jeans and a T-shirt barged through the door. He stopped as though startled by my presence. I offered a polite hello and he made his way to the urinal. I grabbed some paper towels and mopped up the water that had landed on the counter. Then I took one last look at myself, smoothed out my shirt, and slapped a smile on my face.

José was waiting for me at the patio table. He'd relaxed into his chair, his legs stretched out in front of him. He'd put on shorts after work and I caught a glimpse of his muscled calves and thighs, with just enough hair to entice someone like me. I wasn't into bears and fur, but I did like the feel of hair on a man's legs. He must have caught me looking.

"You like my legs?" He smiled as he twirled the stem of the wine glass.

"No."

He furrowed his brow.

"I *love* them," I added.

He chuckled.

"I haven't seen you in shorts before."

"Want me to take off my shirt?"

"Maybe later."

"I'll drink to that," he said, taking a sip.

I enjoyed the levity between us and let it buoy me, appreciating how José was working at making sure I was indeed feeling better. I looked up at the cloudless blue sky, the air still, and took in a deep breath. I heard several birds twittering on the roof of the restaurant, a bumble bee buzzing by somewhere. I needed to connect with the here and now and let Carlos slip back into those dark spaces in my mind. I took in another deep breath. I sipped on my wine and then looked at José, letting the intellectual part of me return and take over. I realized I hadn't told him about my jaunt to Madera.

"I did some poking around today. I think the second victim was gay, too."

He tilted his head to one side. "What makes you think that?"

I recounted my discussion with Mr. Márquez, ending with the phone call from Reed.

"So possibly this Robert kid was gay, too, but you haven't shared any of this with the police?" José said, his intonation suggesting he was asking a question rather than making a statement.

I shook my head. "I also found out that their phones are missing."

José shot me a puzzled look.

"Both Sergio's sister and Robert's dad told me their phones were not among their personal effects. Sergio's sister says they haven't found her brother's phone anywhere, either."

José contemplated this, looking up and to the left. "What

twentysomething kid doesn't always have a phone on him, right? Hell, *we* have phones on us."

I leaned forward and lowered my voice. "I think the killer must have taken them."

"If you're right, that means only one thing." He let a beat slip. "There's something on those phones he doesn't want the world to see."

The thought had already occurred to me and was one of the aspects of these crimes that puzzled me the most. Had the two young men been killed and their phones taken? Or were they killed *for* their phones? Phones as motivation for murder didn't make much sense. They were so easily traced through GPS. I was missing something.

"Will?"

"Huh?"

I looked up to find José studying me. "You went away for a moment."

I slumped into my chair. "Sorry."

"Why don't we order some appetizers and talk about something else? I think you need to take your mind off all of this murder business."

He was right. The conversation had gotten too serious. We needed to spend time getting to know each other, talk about ourselves, our lives. We decided to share some appetizers over a second glass of wine. Mandy brought us a plate of potato skins and some stuffed mushroom caps.

"You going to tell me about San Jose?" I asked.

"What do you want to know?" He shoved a potato skin into his mouth, then cleaned his fingers on a napkin.

"Well, you said you'd lived there for a while but, and I quote, 'it didn't work out.' Then you looked down at your glass."

He narrowed his gaze. "Boy. You remember everything."

"Just about."

He cut a mushroom in half with a fork and popped a bite into his mouth. He washed it down with a sip of wine.

"The 'it' was a relationship with some guy. I can summarize what happened very easily."

I leaned forward and rested my chin on my hand. "Okay. Shoot."

"I believed in monogamy. He didn't. And it wasn't an open relationship."

"How long?"

"Two years." He popped the other half of the mushroom into his mouth.

"Were you in love with him?"

"I thought I was."

I sat up and raised my glass. "Here's to you."

José looked at me quizzically.

"I'm with you on monogamy," I said.

We clinked glasses and then I recounted my tribulations with my former partner.

"Ah," José said as I finished my story, "is that why your sister wanted to screen me?"

I fidgeted in my chair. "Yeah. She likes to play the role of wise elder sibling. You know. She thinks I can't make choices for myself or that I make them too quickly. But she was right about John. I stayed in that relationship too long."

"I need to say something." José's voice lowered.

I pulled back, wondering what was coming. He reached out and took my hands in his.

"We've only recently met, and I don't know where we're headed, but I will tell you this. I am loyal and faithful. I could never hurt you that way."

I let the comment sink in as I stared into those chocolate eyes of his. I searched and saw truth and honesty. I saw warmth. I saw passion.

Murder and missing phones seemed so far away.

●●●

You ever watch Criminal Minds? It's the most popular show here. All the guys watch it, especially those marathons on Wednesdays. They run like a dozen shows or so. Ironic, when you think about it. Criminal minds hooked on Criminal Minds.

[chuckles]

The FBI agents on that show were all behavioral analysts. They'd work up a profile and present it to the locals, using words like sociopath *and* malignant narcissist. *I'm not a profile for* Criminal Minds. *I'm no sociopath or malignant narcissist. I mean, really, look at me. Do I show antisocial traits? Paranoia? Am I sick with power? Ha! I'm just able to detach when needed.*

[shakes his head]

Anyway, I never had any inclinations to do anyone harm my entire life. Of course, I would've protected my family if I'd had to. Who wouldn't? So, with that first one, I was surprised to see how easy it was. I didn't think. I didn't reflect. I didn't hesitate. I just went into action. I'm sure some people think I snapped. But I didn't. It was simply something I had to do. It was an obligation.

[pauses]

I just realized how that must have sounded. On the one hand, I talk about not caring, about detaching. On the other, I talk about obligation. How could I feel obliged if part of me was detached and uncaring? Who knows? Maybe I'm wrong. Or maybe I'm lying. Maybe I do *care. Or maybe I am more like those killers on* Criminal Minds *than I admit. What do you think? After all, I didn't stop after the first one.*

●●●

CHAPTER 15

JOSÉ HAD PROMISED to drop in on his parents for dinner, so he left at six thirty. I went home with mixed feelings. I was falling for José—that was obvious to me—and every action, every word from him told me he was falling, too. I thought that once I'd hit middle age, I'd never find love again. And statistically speaking, my chances were slim. So why was I taking my time with him? He clearly wanted to move things along. In all honesty, so did I. Yeah, I wanted him to come home with me after our drinks at The Fairway. I could feel myself being pulled toward more than kisses, that hormonal magnet as old as our species itself.

But instead of spending more time with José, I did some note taking, trying to put my thoughts about the murders in order. I sat with my laptop in front of me at the kitchen counter bar. The house was silent except for the air-conditioning. It kicked in, the blades whirring outside one of the kitchen windows and the air rushing through the ducts to pour out the vents above. After a few minutes, I stopped and stared at the screen. Nothing seemed to jump out at me. I knew that I needed to walk away from the task, somehow let myself get distracted doing something else, and let the grist wheels of my subconscious grind away.

I took a stroll around the neighborhood, The Palms being a gated community of over seven hundred homes with about ten miles of private streets. It was still warm outside, the sun bending to kiss the horizon in about an hour and casting long shadows from the palm trees and cedars that dotted the neighborhood. But at least the temperature wasn't pushing at the upper nineties as it had been in the midafternoon. I checked my phone. Eighty-two degrees.

I passed one of our larger parks and spied two teenage girls sitting at a picnic table. One of the girls lifted her phone and snapped a selfie of the two of them—lips puckered in exaggerated poses—and then her thumbs flew around the keypad. She must have been sending the photo to Snapchat, Instagram, or some other app kids their age used. I smiled and shook my head at young people's self-absorption and obsession with social media. I hadn't traveled more than twenty feet when something José had said earlier reverberated in my head.

There's something on those phones he doesn't want the world to see.

I stopped in mid-stride. Were there photos of the killer on those phones? The victims must have known him—assuming he was the same guy. So, how did they know him? And what kind of photos did they have if they actually had any at all?

I turned and hurried back home. I opened my laptop and began a Google search on the percentage of hate crime victims who know their perpetrators. It took me awhile but on a Justice Department PDF summary I found that 52 percent of the victims of such crimes reported not knowing their assailants. This left 48 percent knowing their attacker prior to the assault.

I reflected on this fact. It wasn't helpful. In the end, there was a 50-50 chance that Sergio and Robert knew their killer—if, indeed, their deaths were the result of hate crimes. As I read on, I found a rather interesting statistic: less than

1 percent of such crimes ended in murder. The vast majority involved some kind of assault or verbal threat and intimidation. What was more, there was a strong correlation between victims' and perpetrators' ages. This meant that, if Sergio's and Robert's murders *were* hate crimes, the perpetrator was likely to be in his twenties.

I looked up and out my kitchen window, staring at nothing, as though the waning sunlight could shed clarity onto what I'd learned. From what I'd read, the chances of Sergio and Robert being victims of hate crimes were exceedingly low. So why were they killed? And then the question I had repeatedly asked myself earlier in the day seemed to float just outside the window, haunting me like a ghost.

Had Robert been gay?

• • •

I BROKE UP the next morning with a trip to the gym, followed by a stop at the Rite Aid, our one and only drug store in Mañana. I picked up some mouthwash and toothpaste, and while I waited to be checked out it occurred to me that no Latinos worked in the front of the store. At least no typical Latinos. Because of my own background, I had to be careful about stereotyping people, but Rite Aid seemed as white a group of employees as I'd seen in this town. That was odd given the 40 percent Latino population of our town. The only Latinos in the store worked behind the pharmacy counter. Silvia was one and Luis was the other.

I made my way back to the pharmacy and found Luis dispensing pills. His head was angled downward as he counted whatever meds were in front of him, his dark hair neatly combed in place. Luis was not the handsomest man, but he had a decent build, was probably in his mid- to late-thirties, and I liked the fact that he was short like me. Shorter guys always get extra points from me no matter their other qualities.

I knocked on the window and he waved. I suspected he was gay by the way he always smiled and greeted me. One thing I'd noticed about small-town living, even in twenty-first-century California, is that gay men loved the term "discreet." No rainbow buttons. No T-shirts from Key West. No use of "fabulous" as an adjective. Instead, they were discreet in manner and speech, blending in as best they could to avoid being labeled. Given there were no gay bars in this town or even nearby, I wondered how men met each other. I'd met José by chance—in the produce section of the grocery store, no less. But neither of us bought into the "discreet way of life." What about others?

Luis came around to the drop-off window. He smiled broadly. "Hi, Will. Dropping off?"

"No. Just saying hi. I have a question."

His eyebrows rose as he tilted his head to the side slightly.

"You know I'm gay, right?" I said.

"I figured."

"Are you gay?"

He lowered his voice. "You want to hook up?"

I grinned and shook my head. "No. I'm actually seeing someone. I just wanted to know."

He hesitated. "Yes. I am."

"Okay. I was just curious." I let a beat slip by before asking him what I really wanted to know. "How do guys in Mañana meet each other?"

He pulled the side of his lip up into a smirk. "How do you think? On DikMe."

DikMe was a gay male dating app, which, in reality, translated into a virtual place to arrange for hookups.

"Oh yeah. That makes sense," I said, not letting on at the connection of ideas firing in my head.

A customer pulled up to the drive-through window and Luis excused himself. As I walked away, thinking about DikMe, I remembered what José had said.

There's something on those phones he doesn't want the world to see.

CHAPTER 16

I MET LAURA for coffee during the afternoon. I needed distraction because my thoughts kept pulling me toward the murders and I needed to get out of the house. We sat at a corner table at Starbucks as the usual din of overhead music, conversation, and steaming milk floated around us.

"I really did like José," she said. She looked at me over her almond-milk latte. "Did you do it?"

I rolled my eyes. "Not that it's really any of your business, Beverly Busybody, but no."

She nodded. "When are you going to see him again?"

"Tonight." I let my gaze drift around the store as I spied people peering at the screens on their phones.

"You're thinking about the murders, aren't you?" My sister's voice brought me back to the table.

"Actually, I am."

"You know, the police are the ones in charge."

I slouched into my chair and thumbed the sides of my coffee cup.

Laura smiled. "Ever since you were little, once you get interested in something, you're like a dog with a bone."

I chuckled. She was right, of course. My unquenchable curiosity would not allow me to let go of these murders. The whole thing was like a novel unfolding before me, and I just couldn't stop wondering how it all would end. Plus, the image of Sergio's body would always be with me. I had never told her about Carlos and what had happened in high school. I decided I should.

"There's something else," I said. As I'd laid it out for José, I told her the story. This time, I didn't cry—even though the image of Carlos's body lying at the edge of the schoolyard could still punch my gut. She listened with narrowed eyes. When I finished, she leaned back in her chair.

"Why didn't you ever tell me this story?"

I shrugged. "Buried it, I guess. Too painful to dredge up. But finding Sergio's body did that without me wanting to remember. And you were already out of the house when it happened."

"Was Carlos your boyfriend?"

I shook my head. "We were just really close. He was the only gay kid I knew in high school. I loved him like a brother."

"Like I love you." She smiled slightly. Then she stood up, came over, and kissed me on the cheek.

"I'm going to the Dollar General. You want to come?"

"Nah," I said. "I don't need any cheap crap right now."

"Don't knock it," she said as she picked up her coffee and walked away. "I'll be doing early Christmas shopping for your present. I hope you can use paper plates."

I blew her an exaggerated kiss and then settled into my chair. I watched the remaining amount of foam in my latte dissipate like spent rain clouds. I sat there, my thoughts tumbling over each other. I needed to find out about Robert. I couldn't shake the feeling that he and Sergio were connected somehow. And their missing phones—what was on them? A familiar voice interrupted my mulling.

"Hey, Will. How're you doing?"

It was Reed's cousin, Tim. His lanky but toned frame towered over me. I smiled.

"Hi, Tim." I offered him a seat.

"Thanks, but I can't. I'm just picking up a coffee." He squinted one eye as he took my expression in. "Why so serious?"

I didn't want to get into it with him. Besides, he was the lieutenant's cousin, and I didn't want the good detective to know the extent of my meddling.

"Just mulling through something I'm working on," I said with as much commitment to the lie as I could muster. "Sometimes I slip away from home to organize my thoughts."

He must have bought it. He tipped the brim of his cowboy hat. "Well, I'll leave you to it, then. Nice seeing you."

I said goodbye and watched him amble to the door and out into the hot afternoon. He was the essence of a modern-day cowboy, in spite of his initial insistence that he wasn't. From boots to hat to the big turquoise belt buckle I'd first seen earlier that week, he was a stereotype. He was attractive, from an objective point of view, with sapphires for eyes and dark hair silvering at the temples. But he was a bit too tall for me and just too guarded. Still, he'd bothered to come over and say hi and it looked like our initial hostile encounter was water under the bridge. I was glad for that because I knew I would need to be on the good side of Lieutenant Reed. I wasn't going to go to him until I'd gotten some answers to my questions, and he'd be pissed off at me for not coming sooner. I didn't need his family members adding fuel to that fire.

I pulled out my phone and texted José, letting him know I was at Starbucks. He showed up five minutes later.

"Hola, handsome," he said as he leaned in and kissed me.

A growling voice emanated from behind him.

"Fucking Mexican faggots."

José spun around, and as I peeked past him, MAGA-hat man stood there with arms folded.

"Excuse me?" José had his back to me, but I could tell from the tone of his voice and his stiffened posture the kind of expression he must have had on his face. I got up and stood beside him.

"Ah, you again," the man said, looking squarely at me. "A bean lover and a faggot. I should have guessed."

As it had last time, the store went quiet save for the overhead music. Several people held up their phones, recording the encounter.

"I think you owe us an apology," José said.

The man remained defiant, arms still folded, feet slightly apart.

"You know," I chimed in, "what you are engaging in is considered a hate crime. I can cite some references for you if you are ignorant of the law. But instead, let me get the police on the phone so they can hear you live." I made no attempt to hide my sarcasm. Then I pulled out my phone, ready to dial.

"You little piece of shit," he said as he balled his fists and took a step toward me.

José leapt into action. He ducked and threw his body weight into the man's midriff while simultaneously grabbing one of his wrists. He then spun around behind him and pulled his arm tight. The move happened so fast that I had to blink and shake my head to make sure I'd seen it. The man grimaced.

"Sir," José said with a calm that belied the situation, "I can easily do one of two things. The least is to dislocate your shoulder. The worst is to snap your arm and break it. I will give you five seconds to apologize to my boyfriend here. If you do not, *I* will decide which of the two moves to make and you will either walk out of here with no more than pain or you will leave in an ambulance for Madera Community Hospital."

As I took in the scene before me, I was flooded with conflicting emotions. On the one hand, I was amazed that José performed the maneuver he had. Where had that come from? It had unfurled like a scene from an action movie. And MAGA-hat man was a good five inches taller than him. On the other hand, I was alarmed at how easily it seemed to come to him—like I should never piss him off. MAGA-hat man was in shock, his eyes bulging, his face red. He clearly had not anticipated this outcome when he'd opened his mouth just a few moments before.

Marta Alonso, the manager, appeared. "I cannot have any violence in my store. I have called the police." She spoke directly to José. "Would you please let him go?"

José looked at me, then back at Marta. Slowly, he released his grip on the man, who quickly began to massage his upper arm. Marta turned to him.

"Sir, this is the second time you have entered this establishment and caused problems." She snapped a photo of him on her phone. "When the police arrive, I will give them your picture. I also have your license plate number. Tomorrow I will file a formal restraining order so that you cannot come within one hundred yards of this store." She stood and stared at MAGA-hat man.

A smattering of applause broke the silence with a few mutterings of "bigot" and "asshole." He looked around, put his head down, and began to leave.

"Just a moment," she said.

He stopped and turned to look at her.

"Don't even think of filing a complaint against this gentleman here." She indicated José with a tilt of her head. "There's a roomful of witnesses and probably several recordings that saw you make a threatening move toward Will. The only aggressor here, sir, is you. Now please leave."

MAGA-hat man turned and pushed on the door, but in one final parting shot, he spun around and gave us the finger. Murmuring surfaced among the dozen or so people present.

"Okay, okay," Marta said. "Everything back to normal. Come on."

Before she could return to work, I reached out and stopped her.

"Thanks. Especially for sticking up for José."

"No fucking asswipe like that is going to ruin my store," she answered. She eyed José up and down and then turned to me. "I like your boyfriend." Then she spun on her heel and headed back to whatever she was doing before.

"You okay?" José asked me, his gaze probing mine.

I nodded vigorously. "You've been watching James Bond movies, haven't you?"

"No," he said as he drew his thumb across his chin. "In addition to playing baseball, I was on the wrestling team. Plus, I had brothers."

I smiled and tilted my head to one side. "Your boyfriend, eh?"

José grinned in return.

"I like the sound of that," I said. "Come on, boyfriend, let me buy you a coffee." I put my arm around his waist and walked him to the counter.

I had come to Starbucks for distraction. Boy, did I get some.

CHAPTER 17

I BUSTLED AROUND the kitchen as I prepared dinner. José was due in half an hour, and I didn't want to be preoccupied with cooking while he sat at the counter watching. I'd planned a nice pasta dish with portobellos, garlic, and olive oil, along with a fresh garden salad tossed with raisins, walnuts, and parmesan. With a bottle of wine and a baguette on the side, it was the perfect easy dish—and because I'd bought fresh linguine, I could cook that up in just two minutes. I'd already chopped and sautéed the garlic, its pungent aroma wafting through the kitchen. I covered the pan to dampen the aroma and shaved some parmesan for the salad. I couldn't help but pick up a piece and pop it in my mouth, the nuttiness of it lingering on my tongue. *Mmm*, I thought, *this is all going to be so good.*

As I picked through the salad greens to make sure none of the pieces were mildewed or brown, the image of angry MAGA-hat man popped into my head. I am not a person inclined toward hate—and certainly not hate toward a type of person or a group of people. Hate gets us nowhere. So it was hard for me to grasp MAGA-hat man's emotion, where it came from, how it led people like him to act. When he took that step toward me at Starbucks, he'd morphed. Whatever inhabited him had bubbled up, distorting the surface into a twisted and red caricature of a human face. Had something like that fueled the two murders that had shattered Mañana's tranquility? Was there a particular kind of hate bubbling below the surface of our town? Was someone like MAGA-hat man involved? Was *he* involved?

My thoughts drifted toward Sergio's and Robert's phones. They were missing. Had the killer taken them? If they were found, would photos of MAGA-hat man be on them?

Before my thoughts could go further, the doorbell chimed. I'd alerted security that José was coming over and that they could just let him drive through the gates without calling me. I liked that aspect of our community—that we had secured entrances and guards. And now that there was murder afoot, I imagined all my neighbors appreciated it even more.

"Hi, handsome," I said to José as I opened the door. We kissed and he presented a bottle of wine.

"We sell this at Save Mart." He made sure I could see the label. "It's a really good Chardonnay from Napa."

I wagged my finger. "Ah, ah. You know you're supposed to support the local economy. How about Crū?" I mentioned the winery that was just six miles south, halfway to Madera.

He pulled the bottle back. "I can keep this if you want."

I yanked it out of his hand. "Nope." I smiled and we kissed again.

At the kitchen counter bar, I poured us each a glass. We toasted to each other, then made our way to the sofa.

"Thanks again for saving me today," I said.

"Hey, no way that asshole was going to get away with that crap." He draped his arm around my shoulder. "And besides, it felt good to call you my boyfriend."

"It's a good thing you passed the sister test," I said. "You know you couldn't be my boyfriend unless she approved."

"Wait until you meet my mom."

I pulled myself into an upright position and looked at him, eyes wide, feigning fright.

"Easy, Will, easy." He pulled me back to be cradled by his arm. "I told her all about you last night. She wants me to take a picture of you."

I relaxed my shoulders. "I'll have to check with my agent."

"*Cabrón*," he said as he leaned in for another kiss. "I think you two will get along great."

We chatted and I toyed with the buttons on his shirt. He told me about his day and that it was largely uneventful.

"Yeah, Save Mart is not a fast-paced environment. I have no interesting stories to tell. Hope you don't mind. You're dating someone boring."

"Oh, come on. There must be some kind of store romance or infighting among employees."

"Nope. Boring, boring, boring." He held his glass up and examined the contents. "Ever notice how Chardonnays can vary so much in color?"

I perked up. "I have an idea. How about we go wine tasting sometime? We could do the Madera Wine Trail."

"Sounds good to me."

We clinked our glasses to seal the deal, and then José asked me about my day. "Other than the Starbucks adventure," he added.

I gave him the rundown, including my interaction with Luis at Rite Aid. José looked at me—his expression a mosaic of surprise and concern.

"What?" I asked.

"One, he probably did think you were hitting on him. Two, you're acting like a private eye regarding these murders. Three, I have a question."

"Before your question, one, I made it absolutely clear that

I was not interested and that I was seeing someone. After all, you are calling me your boyfriend now."

I caught a hint of a grin on José's face.

"Two, I am most definitely invested in these murders, for several reasons, not the least of which is the image of Sergio Ramírez's body invading my thoughts on a daily basis. We've talked about this."

José reached out and took my hand in his. He spoke softly. "I know."

"Till the day I die I will not forget what that poor kid looked like lying out there in the field." I paused as I looked away. "And, of course, there's Carlos." I could feel myself pulled by the memory, my insides churning. Silence hung in the air. After a bit, I shook off the creeping memories. "So, what's your question?"

"What's DikMe got to do with any of this?"

I shrugged. "I don't know. But something is telling me it does. Sergio was gay after all. And I have a hunch Robert was, too."

"Well, then, I think it's obvious," José said.

I cocked my head.

"Maybe they met their killer on DikMe," he added.

I bolted to my feet. "That's it! Yes!"

I paced. "The phones are missing because the killer didn't want anyone to see their DikMe accounts." I turned to face José. "The killer may be using DikMe to stalk young Latino men."

I paced a few more times before I sat down next to him again.

"Have you ever used DikMe?"

He sipped his wine as he avoided eye contact.

"Don't be embarrassed," I said. "I don't care. Well, as long as you aren't now. You're not, right?"

He stood and went to the fridge to pour us some more wine. "I'm not. But I have. Haven't you?"

"Nope." I stood and walked over to him.

"You're kidding."

"Not kidding," I said as I took the glass from him. "I'm a DikMe virgin. Can you show me how it works?"

"Why?"

I pretended to inspect the color of the Chardonnay as he had earlier. "It may be a useful tool."

José set his wine on the counter and enveloped me in his arms. He nibbled on my neck.

"Why do I get the feeling I might have to rescue you again?"

CHAPTER 18

AFTER DINNER, JOSÉ and I sat at the kitchen counter bar and went about the task of developing a DikMe profile on my phone. The app had been around for a while and was billed as a "gay dating site." But the truth was that guys used it for quick hookups or to find friends with benefits.

"First thing we do," he said, "is come up with a name. Lots of guys like to suggest what they're looking for or what they offer in the name they choose."

"Such as?"

"'Hot Bottom 4 Top' or 'Boy Needs Daddy.'"

I rolled my eyes. "It was so much more fun when we just went to bars to pick each other up. You know, checked out the merchandise in the flesh."

"Or maybe grocery stores." José deadpanned but couldn't hold the expression. He broke into a huge grin.

"All right, all right. Back to the name."

"You want the killer to know you're Latino, so that has to be in there somehow to attract him."

"If he really is using DikMe." I thought for a moment. "How about 'Latino Hot For You'?"

José nodded his approval. "You sure you haven't done this before?"

I nudged him with my elbow. He typed in the name, but

the app said it was too long. He retyped it as "LatinoHot4U" and that seemed to work.

"Perfect," he continued. "Now we have to put some information in."

"Okay, but as long as this is fake, I want to make sure I sound great."

"What's that mean?"

"I want to be taller, toned, with a nice butt. I want to be hot."

José just looked at me. "But you are hot."

I air kissed him. "You know what I mean."

We created a five-feet-nine, 160-pound, gym-loving twenty-four-year-old who was into all ages.

"What about position?" José asked.

"What about it?"

"Come on. Are you top, top vers, versatile, bottom vers, or bottom?" He looked at me expectantly.

"Are you sure you're asking for the app?"

He tilted his head and studied me. "Versatile," he said.

"Good choice."

"Especially if it's true."

I toyed with his ear, my finger gently caressing him. "Maybe you'll find out soon."

He twitched at my tickling, so I stopped. We added a few more details about likes and dislikes and José hit the save button. I was now officially DikMe material.

"What about a photo?" I asked. "I'm not twenty-four."

"Most guys don't use face pics, so not a problem—and if you get a hit, you can always say you don't share face pics because you're discreet."

He touched a tab to get to the page marked 'Who's Near.' Twelve profiles filled the screen. Some very close by, others up to six miles away. Only three of them displayed faces. The others were headless body shots, cartoons, photos of outdoor shots, and half of them were blank generic silhouettes of heads. I scanned some of the names. 'Sloppy bj HMU.' 'College boys.' 'Oso.' Some of the names contained symbols such as arrows pointing up or down, eyes looking to the left, peaches, eggplants. I pointed to one.

"What's 'HMU'?"

"Hit me up."

"And the peach?"

"That stands for butt or ass."

I pointed to a silhouette with the profile name 'DL Top.' "What's DL mean?"

"That stands for 'down low.'"

I nodded. "Oh. Of course." I scanned the twelve images and names. "I didn't know I'd have to learn a whole new language."

"I think guys like this code because it saves time and space. Inserting an arrow pointing up takes less space than typing, 'I'm a top'. You'll learn fast."

"I can always google what I don't understand."

José explained how the app worked, including the message center and what "nudging" was.

"If a guy just wants to break the ice to see if maybe you're interested, he'll nudge you and it will show up here." He clicked on the icon where messages and nudges appeared. Then he handed me the phone. "You're all set."

He looked at me but I couldn't read his expression. "What?"

His gaze lingered on me for few beats. "Are you sure you want to do this? *Should* you be doing this?"

Ahhh. I understood the look. It was the same he'd offered

the day before. We'd been going out for less than a week and he'd already stepped in to ward off a perceived attacker and had called me his boyfriend in public. He was watching out for me. Part of me melted. A good-looking, former-baseball-playing, sweet man had found his way into my life. Was it too good to be true?

"Why are you staring at me?" he asked.

"Oh, sorry. I was just thinking." I smiled. "Yes, I want to do this. One thing you should know about me is that I'm the curious type, the type who can't let go of a nagging question."

He opened the fridge and retrieved some wine. "You should probably let the police know what you're doing," he said while pouring.

I shrugged. "Maybe. What are you worried about?"

He straddled the stool and pulled it closer to the counter bar. "I don't want anything to happen to you."

His eyes probed mine, as though he were trying to read where my thoughts were headed.

"Will, you're trying to bait a killer here. This is not some game."

"Oh, I'll be okay. If and when I get something, I'll let the police know. Besides," I added as I leaned in, "I've got you to protect me."

I kissed him deeply, letting my tongue explore his mouth. He pressed into me. After a moment, he pulled back. I saw expectation in those eyes, small round disks of chocolate-colored anticipation.

"Do you keep a toothbrush in your car?" I asked.

He shot me a puzzled look.

"You know. In case you need it."

"No," he said. "I keep one in my locker at work. Why?"

"Because you'll need one in the morning." I kept my focus on him as comprehension spread across his face.

"Oh." He grinned.

I snapped my fingers. "Wait. I have extra toothbrushes in my guest bath."

He was leaning in to kiss me again when an odd chirp emanated from my phone. I'd never heard it before.

"That's an alert from DikMe," he said. "Someone's interested in you."

Was I going to let my new app spoil the moment? I felt the strong tug of curiosity, the magnet that had lured me to this time and place, starting with Sergio's body. Was it the killer, already zeroing in on me? I glanced over at the phone. I could see the little red dot that signaled a message or a nudge. It beckoned me. And then I felt José's hand slide up my thigh. My attention remained on the phone until I felt his hand on my crotch. *Oh shit.*

I turned to José. His lips met mine, and then his mouth engulfed me, sending a firestorm of sensation throughout my body.

I reached over and hit the button to silence the phone. If it was the killer, he'd have to wait until the morning.

● ● ●

I have a confession. I did what I had to do but there was a part of me that liked doing it.

[pauses, eyes me]

Don't get me wrong. I didn't pop a boner or experience any of those sexual thrills that some guys do. That's some freaky shit, if you ask me. Seriously, getting off on strangling someone? That would be malignant narcissism for sure. What I mean is that I didn't mind doing it. It was like any chore, you know? Like mowing the yard or washing your car. You get a certain satisfaction once the job is done—especially if you do it well. No one praises you, like my uncle used to do when I worked with him in his garage. Always told me what a fine job I did, saying something like, "Look at you, Slick. You're becoming a real shop worker."

[pauses, stares at nothing]

But we're not kids. We have to take pride in the work ourselves, right?

[stops staring]

Like I said, I never considered harming anyone before in my life. And what I learned was that after you've done it once, it's easier the next time.

[pauses]

I've never said any of this to anyone. Not to my lawyer. Not to the psych evaluators. That would have been stupid with a trial pending. But I don't mind telling you. Nothing much they can do to me now anyway. I'm put away for life. No possibility of parole. I wonder if Criminal Minds will still be in reruns in ten or twenty years.

[smiles]

But what I was thinking was this: If you hadn't stopped me, would I have kept on going?

[pauses]

Possibly.

[smiles]

Probably.

• • •

.

CHAPTER 19

J OSÉ SPENT THE night, and the next morning he left early
to go home and change. I kissed him goodbye, turned, and
pressed my back up against the door. It was odd. Forty-nine
years old and I felt light, like a teenager experiencing love for
the first time. Over the years I'd learned to distinguish
between actually liking someone and thinking I liked someone because I felt desperate, alone, or even bored. Yes, I had
dated out of boredom. I think most people have, if they'd
only admit it.

But with José there was a real connection. He had all the
qualities I'd hoped to find in someone. He was smart and
kind. He was fit. And he had a certain sense of humor, a quick
wit, that meshed with mine. He was also in the right age
range and seemed to share my liberal values.

I floated into the kitchen to prepare some coffee. As my
Nespresso machine produced a vanilla-flavored brew for my
latte, I dialed my sister.

"It's early," she said. "What's up?"

"José spent the night."

"Okay. First question. Did you use protection? And don't
roll your eyes. I can tell over the phone when you roll your
eyes."

I told her everything had been safe and that José and I had
talked about those issues. We also talked about monogamy
and getting tested regularly.

"Second question," she said. "How do you feel?"

"Well, to be honest, I've fallen for him. With these murders occupying my thoughts, it's nice to have someone to turn to."

"That's what family's for."

"You know what I mean."

She slurped on some coffee. "You're not moving too fast, are you?"

Of course, I'd already thought about that. I probably was, but at my age, how many chances would I have for love?

"Let's talk about that later."

We said our *love yous* and hung up. As I sipped my coffee, I remembered the DikMe chime from the night before. I'd turned off the sound on my phone so that José and I would not be disturbed, and since then I had forgotten all about the app. I opened it and touched on the message center. There was a text from a guy named "LatinoLover." My heartbeat quickened as I tapped on it.

I like what I read

I returned to the guy's profile. No pic and little info. All it said was, "Mature man seeking younger bottom guys, Latinos +++." I took the plus signs to mean that being Latino added extra points to your profile. *Hmmm.* Why was he afraid to put his information out there? I noticed the green dot next to the profile indicating he was online. I replied.

No face pic?

Within seconds I got a "photo received" message and clicked on it. I found myself looking at his penis. I laughed at the audacity and texted back.

Thanks but I need a face
pic

Almost instantly I received his reply.

I'm on the dl

No kidding! I thumbed again.

You can trust me

I waited. Nothing. I sighed and set my phone down as I went to prepare a second coffee. Just as I pulled a Nespresso pod from a kitchen drawer, I heard another chime—a signal that he must have responded. Another "photo received." I chuckled.

"What? Another photo of your dick?" I said out loud.

I tapped on it. My eyes widened.

"Holy shit!"

Without hesitation, I dialed José. He'd just made it to his house in Madera.

"What's up, sweetie?" he said. I loved that he called me *sweetie*. "Miss me already?"

"I missed you the minute you walked out the door. But guess what?" I waited a few beats to add dramatic pause to my announcement. "I just opened up the message from last night and texted that guy."

"And?"

"You'll never guess who it is." Another dramatic pause.

"Well, who is it?"

"I hope you're sitting down. It's MAGA-hat man."

CHAPTER 20

JOSÉ PLEADED WITH me not to do anything without him being around.

"That guy's the violent type," he said.

"I told you already. I won't do anything stupid." I cooed the words, hoping to assuage José's concern.

I texted MAGA-hat man, asking what he was looking for and if he wanted to meet sometime. He informed me he was a top and liked getting blow jobs—especially from young Latino men.

> Can you host?

His question was asking me if I could have him over to my house. As per my promise to José—and my own sense of caution—I texted "no" and let the mean streak in me suggest something else.

> Meet in public space first.
> Starbucks?

I chuckled at my own inside joke. His reply was swift.

> No. How about the
> Fairway parking lot?

Oh Jesus. A parking lot? Then I thought, *Why not?* I suggested the end of the day, when I knew José would be off work. We agreed on five thirty. I set my phone down to finish preparing my coffee and thought about MAGA-hat man. *What a sick fuck, using DikMe to lure young men to their deaths. And bashing their heads! Did he get some thrill out of the moment?* I shivered.

My attention was diverted when a ping signaled a non-DikMe text. I didn't recognize the number.

> This is Julie. I talked to my
> parents.
> Not good. Can you talk?

Oh shit. Sergio's sister. I thumbed a response.

> What do you need?

She asked me to meet her at Starbucks before lunch. *Poor kid*, I thought. And the image of her brother's buzzard-pecked body made me want to vomit all over again.

• • •

WHEN I ARRIVED at Starbucks, the whoosh of the fly blaster greeted me as I walked through the door, along with the familiar smells of coffee and the sounds of espresso machines. As usual, the staff shouted out, "Hi, Will!" Julie was already seated at a corner table. I slid onto a chair facing her as I said hi. I took in the drawn expression on her face.

"What happened?"

"My parents got angry. At first, they accused me of making it up and said I was defiling the memory of my brother." She brushed away a tear with the back of her hand. "When I told them I'd known he was gay for a few years and that Sergio was afraid to tell them because of their Catholic beliefs, my dad flew into a rage. He almost punched a wall. My mom had to stop him."

She avoided eye contact and stiffened at times. She told me that her dad had said if it were true, then Sergio had to have been seduced, that he had always been a good boy.

"He said he'd kill the man who had turned his son into a *puto*."

I bristled slightly at hearing the Spanish word for *fag*.

"My mother cried and cried. I probably shouldn't have said what I did."

I was confused. "You mean telling them he was gay?"

"No." She finally looked at me. "I loved my brother, but he wasn't as good as they think. He used older men. Let them buy him things. Give him money."

I tried to suppress my surprise, but my jaw dropped slightly. Finally, I asked a question. "How do you know this?"

She picked at a piece of skin next to her thumbnail as she looked down. The sunlight poured in from behind her, casting her dark hair with a glow of reds and light browns.

"I noticed some of the new things he had. I knew he couldn't afford them. When I pushed, he confessed some man had bought him those things and that the man gave him fifty dollars each time they met." She looked up at me. "My brother was a prostitute!" The tears began.

I reached for her hands and held on to them tight. "Julie, listen to me. Your brother was no such thing. These older men were preying on him. They do it all the time. Some younger guys mistake it for love. They think that when an older man buys them things and gives them money, it means more than it does."

She looked up, eyes red and tears cascading. I looked

around to see who was watching or listening. There weren't many other people seated inside, none of them close to us.

"I...I ruined the image of my brother for my parents," she said between sobs.

A heaviness settled on me as I watched the pain in her face. I gently patted her hand.

"No, no, you didn't. You just told the truth, that's all. They'll need time to digest it. They're grieving over his death. And you're right to have done it. How would your parents feel hearing it from the police or whispered from neighbors?"

Just then, Bobby came from around the corner with fresh garbage bags to clean up the condiment station and remove the trash. He stopped when he saw us. Julie's head was bent forward, but it was clear from the shaking of her shoulders she was crying. His gaze went from her to our interlocked hands and then to my face.

"Is she okay?" He mouthed the words. I nodded. He took one last look and then went about his business, pretending he hadn't seen anything.

After a minute of sitting there in silence, Julie regained some composure. She withdrew her hands and wiped her eyes with a napkin.

"Thank you for listening."

I told her I'd be there for her if she needed anything else. She got up and hugged me, and as she departed, I thought about Sergio and the new information I'd just learned. Now I felt even more urgency to meet up with MAGA-hat man later in the day. If he was the killer, I doubted he was Sergio's sugar daddy. But then, you never know what a murderer is capable of.

Especially if that murderer is a racist.

CHAPTER 21

I HAD AGREED to meet MAGA-hat man in the last row of parking at The Fairway, far from the front door. He would park next to a center island containing a large crape myrtle and some low-lying shrubs. I checked the time. Five fifteen. When I looked up, José had just stepped out of his car in a parking spot at the end of the row. I hurried over to him.

"I'm glad you're here," I said.

His eyebrows drew together as he looked at me squarely. "I'd never let you do this alone. He's an asshole. And vicious."

"I know, I know." I rubbed his upper arms and looked at him. "And thank you for caring so much." I gave him a slight peck on the cheek and then we proceeded with our plan.

José stood off to the side of his car, out of the line of site where MAGA-hat man would be. There was only a smattering of cars in the lot, so I hid behind someone else's vehicle just a row closer to The Fairway's front door. Even there, we were a good three hundred feet from the entrance. Heat rose from the asphalt and I could feel my mouth going dry. Dampness spread in my armpits and sweat trickled down my back.

At 5:25, a silver Hyundai pulled in and parked at the center island. MAGA-hat man exited and leaned against the driver's door. I cast a glance over to where José was. He nodded to indicate he was ready. I sucked in two deep breaths and then strode over. I stopped about three feet from my target and crossed my arms over my chest.

"Well, look who's here," I said.

"What the fuck are you doing here?"

His face was red, but whether this was from sunburn or anger I couldn't tell. His red cap was conspicuously absent. I was surprised to see a full head of hair, given most men wore ball caps to cover their baldness.

"I might ask you the same thing," I replied. "Parked a little far from the door, aren't you?"

"Where I park is none of your business."

"But it is. You see, the jig is up. I know your secret."

His lip quivered. "What, what secret?"

I saw José inching around his car, coming from behind—a baseball bat slung over his shoulder. I continued.

"You like to lure Latino men to meet you. Tell me, what do you do to them?"

"I...I don't know what you're talking about."

"Does the screen name 'LatinoLover' mean anything to you?"

His eyes widened. "You piece of shit! Are you baiting me? What is this? Blackmail?"

I cocked my head. "Blackmail?"

"You want money? Is that it?"

José continued to creep around from behind.

"No, I don't want money. I want justice."

"Justice for what? What do you care if I get a blow job or not?"

I stared. "Blow job? I'm talking about killing people."

His face twisted as he furrowed his brow. Then suddenly, his eyes widened as they had earlier.

"You think I'm killing people? You think I'm involved in those murders?"

"I've seen you spew your hate in public."

Before he could respond, a familiar voice called out from behind me.

"Will, what's going on here?"

I turned to see Lanny, from the gym, his massive six-feet-two frame lumbering toward us. He gestured toward José. "And what's he doing?"

MAGA-hat man spun around to find José and his baseball bat. He turned his attention back to me. "Just what the fuck is going on here?"

I spoke to Lanny. "We've caught the killer."

"What?"

I pointed. "Him. He murdered Sergio Ramírez and Robert Márquez."

MAGA-hat man took a step toward us. Lanny puffed himself up, knotted his hands into fists. José gripped his baseball bat. I stood my ground, my hands planted firmly on my hips.

MAGA-hat man put his hands up and retreated. "I haven't killed anyone. I'm not a murderer."

I let my gaze bore into him. "You find young Latino men online, lure them out, and then bash their heads in."

Lanny pulled out a cell phone. "I'm calling the cops."

"No! Please don't!" MAGA-hat man looked at the three of us, his expression one big plea. Then his head sagged, and he looked down at his feet. He shifted as he stood there. "Shit. This is going to ruin me."

I tossed a glance to José, who stood there, studying the man, still gripping the bat firmly. Lanny held off on the phone call.

"I'm married," MAGA-hat man said, finally facing us again. "But I occasionally hook up with men. I...I like car play."

"Bullshit," I said. "You hate Latinos. You called us Mexican faggots the other day and were ready to punch me."

He looked up at me. "Yes, yes, I did. I, well, I..."

Silence punctuated the scene, save for several goose honks from the flock that populated the golf course behind The Fairway. I waited, sweat continuing its trail down my back. I could hear José let out a long breath next to me. Lanny simply stood there, his arms hanging at his sides as he studied the man in front of us.

"It's complicated," MAGA-hat man said. "I don't really mean the things I say."

"What? It's all an act?"

He shrugged. I threw my hands up, then turned around in my spot.

"Wait, wait. You mean you only pretend to hate Latinos? Hate gay people?"

He looked at me with pleading eyes.

I turned to the others. "I'm finding this hard to swallow. He wears a fucking MAGA hat!"

The man slumped. "That's just cover. I didn't vote for him." He looked at me. "I swear."

José lowered his bat. "I'm sensing some truth here, Will."

I searched José's eyes to see if maybe he was just trying to avoid an escalation. I didn't see that. I glanced over at Lanny.

"This is not my wheelhouse," Lanny said. "I'm just a retired firefighter. And I'm not gay or bi or whatever you call it, you know, with all those letters."

I resisted the temptation to fill in those letters for him and turned my attention back to MAGA-hat man. I studied his face, his posture. He looked like a limp flower, with hunched shoulders and arms wilted at his sides. His eyes seemed vacant, far from those that might radiate defiance or anger.

"I'm...I'm sorry," he said, almost sheepishly. "I really don't want my wife to find out." He stuck out his hand. "The name is Sam. Sam Allison."

I stared at the gesture. I could not get myself to reciprocate. José stepped forward and grasped the man's hand.

"José Torres."

He let go and Lanny stepped forward and introduced himself. There was an awkward pause while MAGA-hat man waited for me.

"Oh, fuck." I offered my hand. "Will Christian."

The four of us stood there, the sun beating down, none of us knowing what to say. Finally, Lanny broke the silence.

"Well, this is weird."

"I think we should all sit down and talk about this," José said.

Lanny pointed over his shoulder with his thumb. "They have drinks in there."

"I don't know," Allison replied. He gestured toward Lanny. "He's right. It is kind of weird. I'm not really comfortable talking about any of this."

"Tell you what." José slung the baseball bat over his shoulder. "We either sit down and talk or Lanny here calls the cops."

Allison quickly glanced around, taking us all in. Inwardly, I smiled at the cleverness of my boyfriend. In a sense, MAGA-hat man was getting blackmailed.

"Okay," he finally replied.

José dashed to his car and threw the baseball bat in the back seat. He joined us as we headed for the front door of The Fairway and put his arm around my shoulder, pulling me in.

"Bet you didn't think this would happen."

"No, I didn't," I said. "Do you really believe him?"

José kissed me on the cheek. "One way to find out."

Yep, I thought, *one way to find out.*

CHAPTER 22

A S WE ENTERED The Fairway, Lanny spotted some friends who he'd planned to meet earlier, so he excused himself and said he'd see me at the gym soon.

"Sure will," I answered.

He leaned in and slid into his characteristic sotto voce from the gym. "I think he's telling the truth. I know a few like him." He winked and walked away, swallowed up by the country music filling the bar.

"What was that about?" José asked.

"Not sure. I'll tell you later. Let's head for the patio."

We made our way through the restaurant and out the back door to find a nice shaded table. A few birds sang out from the edge of the overhang while the large fronds on the palm trees dotting the edge of the golf course waved and rustled. Mandy was out within a minute and took our orders, with José and me doing our usual Chardonnays and Sam asking for a scotch and soda. We sat in awkward silence until José spoke.

"So, you want to tell us what's up?"

Sam fidgeted in his seat. He looked around, then cleared his throat. "I'm a married man." He spoke in low tones. "Been with my wife for twenty-five years. No children, though." He paused when Mandy showed up with our drinks.

"Any eats for you gentlemen?" she asked.

We declined and she said she'd check back in a few minutes. Once she was out of earshot, Sam hoisted his glass to us and took a long sip.

"Ahhh!" he said. "If I'm going to talk, I need lubrication." He paused, looked around one more time to see if anyone was near. "I'm on the down low, I guess you'd call it."

José and I exchanged glances.

"I love my wife. Can't imagine being without her. But, well, shit." He took another swig. "I've always had a certain attraction to men. Not to fuck. And not to be fucked, either. I don't get into that." He looked at his glass as he toyed with its sides, slick with condensation.

There was a certain derision in the way he made his last statement. I wanted to say something, but José gently put his hand on my arm. I remained quiet. Sam looked up at us both.

"I don't consider myself gay. Certainly not like you guys. Maybe I'm bi. Hell, I don't know. All I know is I like a good blow job from a man now and then."

"Specifically Latino men?" José asked.

Sam nodded. "Especially the young ones. But I'd go older, too."

I was about to say, "Well, hands off my boyfriend, fucker," but instead I asked a question.

"Are blow jobs really all you want out of them?"

"What do you mean?"

I shrugged. "Well, are you always on the receiving end? Ever do a little giving?"

"No, I told you I'm not gay."

"Bisexuals give blow jobs," I said as calmly as I could.

He fidgeted in his chair once again. "Okay. I guess, maybe, a couple of times I have done that."

A few beats slipped by before José asked the question that waited behind my lips.

"Tell us about this hate thing. Is that really an act?"

Just then Mandy reappeared. José and I were barely halfway through our wines, but Sam had already downed his scotch and soda. He ordered another, waiting until Mandy had returned and served him before he answered José's question.

"I was bullied by my dad growing up. Used to beat the hell out of me. He said he wanted to make sure I turned out to be a real man. A tough man. I guess it didn't take."

He rattled the ice around in his glass, the cubes knocking into each other, jostling for space as though trying their damnedest not to melt. I studied him, taking in his body language. Gone was the fighting MAGA-hat man I'd encountered twice before. He seemed smaller, less sure of himself. The breeze that moved among the palm fronds pushed at the graying hair that hugged his forehead. In the background, I heard the familiar crack of a driver's head meeting a ball. I cringed and pushed away the image of Sergio's bashed head, refocusing my attention on Sam.

He let out a long sigh, then looked at me. "I don't really act that way around Latinos or gay people. I mean, like I did in front of you."

"Did something recently trigger you?" José asked.

"Trigger?"

"Yes. Did something happen to you that set you off?"

"You're a smart dude," he said, studying José. "Two weeks ago, I hooked up with this young guy who demanded money and called me a closet case. Said he'd expose me if I didn't give him a hundred bucks. I gave in and told him that if he ever contacted me again, I'd have his ass thrown in jail for prostitution and extortion."

He downed the rest of his drink. "Since then, I've been

on edge. Pissed off. Wondering what the fuck I'd been doing. How I was a failure to my dad. How I was a fraud. I guess I lashed out because I was scared. Scared I'd be found out. Mad at that young kid for what he'd said."

"But you answered my profile," I said.

"Fuck," he said. "What can I say? The urge is stronger than the will." He looked at his watch. "I should head home. Told my wife I was meeting a few guys for a drink, so at least now I'm not lying to her."

"But you are lying to her," José said gently. "Sam, you need to get some help. Work through this. Otherwise, you're going to wind up in the same position you were two weeks ago."

"Yeah, you're right." He stood, then pointed to the drinks at the table. "I'll take care of the bill on my way out. Thanks for listening." He turned but then stopped. "This won't go further than the three of us, right?"

Both José and I said "Yes."

"What about your friend who showed up? Lanny?"

"Oh," I said. "He won't say a word. And I'll talk to him anyway."

Sam mulled on that and nodded. Then he was through the door that led back inside.

I turned to José. "Well?"

He pursed his lips. "Seems on the up-and-up to me."

Before I could respond, Lanny lumbered toward us, drink in hand. "Just saw your friend leave. How was your chat?"

"It was good," I said. "I think I understand a few things better now. And I promised him you wouldn't mention this to anyone."

Lanny patted me on the back. "Told you, Will. I know a few like that. You're not the only gay person I know." He winked once more, said goodbye to us both, and then left.

"What the hell?" José said.

I looked at him and smiled, happy he was at my side. "Let's get out of here."

CHAPTER 23

J OSÉ CAME OVER to my house after The Fairway for some alone time together, even though he didn't spend the night. As he examined the painting of *The Girl Who Loves Coyotes* over the fireplace, he brought up what had just happened.

"Sam is pretty fucked up. But I've seen his type before."

I stared. "What do you mean?"

He turned and smiled. "I did complete one year of my master's, you know. I had an internship as part of the second semester. I sat in on some sessions with a counselor who was working with a closeted married man."

"And?"

"I'd never seen such self-hate. And the behaviors he engaged in to deflect from what he was—everything from name-calling to picking a fight with a guy at a pizza parlor once. He confessed to being beaten by his father, too. Maybe Sam's dad sensed something, something to suspect his son might turn out gay. It's an old story, Will."

I slumped onto the sofa. "I guess I jumped the gun. Hearing Sam talk made me realize how fortunate I am that I never went through that."

José came and sat next to me. "And think about all the teens who commit suicide because they can't accept themselves or are trapped in households that won't accept them. Maybe their fathers are beating them as we speak."

"And not just fathers," I added, thinking of that day I found Carlos out in the field behind the bleachers.

José nodded, then put his arm around me. We snuggled for a while, letting the conversation drift to this and that. After he'd left, I thought about Laura's comment and how quickly our relationship was moving. But I couldn't get myself to think it was a bad thing. Maybe it was meant to be. He'd turned up at the right time in my life, so maybe the hand of fate was involved.

As to be expected, such thoughts evaporated as Sergio's image floated in to occupy the front spaces of my consciousness. I needed to know what had happened to him. Julie had said he was getting gifts and money. Had he fallen in love with an older man? And was that the man who murdered him?

What a waste. It pissed me off.

• • •

THE NEXT MORNING, I hopped on my bike for an early ride to beat the heat, showered, and then worked for several hours. When 11:00 a.m. rolled around, I decided to take a little trip to Madera. The other day I'd found out from Robert's father that he'd worked at the Walmart in Madera. I had a hunch I might learn something from some coworkers, but first I stopped at Starbucks to grab a coffee for the ride. On my way out, I ran into Lieutenant Reed.

"Mr. Christian."

"Lieutenant. How is your day going?"

"Fine." He looked up at the bright expanse of blue through his sunglasses, and then back at me. "It's going to be another scorcher. Oh, well, that's life in the Central Valley."

"Yep."

We stood in silence. Then Reed removed his sunglasses.

"Is there anything you'd like to tell me, Mr. Christian?"

The moment of truth. Should I tell him about the phones? About what I'd found out about Sergio? About Robert? That I was on my way to Madera to do a little snooping?

"No, Lieutenant."

He turned to survey the parking lot. After a pause he looked at me again and said, "If you learn anything, you should tell me."

I nodded. "Understood."

He eyed me. I remained calm, but inwardly I squirmed. He must have suspected I was holding back. I was about to bid him good day when he spoke.

"Well, then, I'm going to get my coffee now. Have a good day."

"You too."

He slipped inside. I sighed, then slid into my BMW and headed for the highway. If I stepped on it, I could be in Madera in fifteen minutes.

• • •

ONE THING ABOUT chain stores, they all look alike. This Walmart was the spitting image of every other one I'd ever been in. And like every other Walmart, the lot was full of cars. I parked a good distance from the door, and once inside, the din of shoppers and digital registers filled my ears. I made my way to customer service where a plump Latina in the characteristic blue vest greeted me. I gave her my story about being a writer and that I was working on a piece about the recent murders.

"I was wondering who might know if Robert had any close friends here in the store, so that I could ask them a few questions."

I smiled as I spoke, and the charm worked. Her eyes glowed, and I detected a sense of eagerness to talk.

"Oh, a terrible, terrible thing when we heard about Robert," she said. "I knew him a little, but not well. He worked over in electronics. You might check there."

I thanked her and made my way back to where computers, tablets, and other gadgets were on display. A young man, probably in his early twenties, was ringing up a sale for a customer. I took in the workspace, amazed at how free of fingerprints the glass counter seemed to be, how neat and organized it all was. It certainly didn't look like other sections of the store where towels were tossed back unfolded onto shelves, shopping carts were left abandoned in the middle of aisles, or T-shirts hung at odd angles on the rack because customers were too lazy to put them back properly. When he finished, I approached and greeted him with a smile. I read the name on his tag: David.

"Hi. My name is Will Christian. I'm a writer working on a story about the two recent murders."

As soon as I said this, his eyes narrowed and his face flushed.

"David, I was hoping to speak to some friends of his, to get a personal side to his story." I used the young man's name to establish some kind of bond and watched as he relaxed just a bit. "Did you know Robert very well?"

"I...I did." His voice cracked. He gulped, then cleared his throat. "We, uh, we went to high school together."

"Did you hang out much?"

"We went out sometimes, yes, after work or on the weekends."

He shifted, looked around, and then he turned his attention back to me. He placed his hands on the counter and I could see the stubby nails, the red cuticles. A chewer. Maybe a little OCD, which explained why his workspace was so clean.

"I hope this is not too painful to talk about," I said. "I'm very sorry for the loss of your friend."

"It's been, well, it's been hard."

"I'm sure." I let a beat slip by. "Did Robert have a girlfriend? I was hoping to find someone he was really close to."

He looked away. "I really shouldn't be talking. I mean, well, I just shouldn't."

"It's okay." I dropped my voice. "Anything we talk about is confidential."

He looked at me, studied me.

"I promise," I said. I offered him another smile. "So, did he have a girlfriend?"

After a pause, the young man shook his head. "No. Robert was..." But he pulled back, his posture drooping, as though he didn't want to finish.

"I think I know what you were going to say." I leaned in and lowered my voice. "You can tell me."

He quickly looked around once more. "He liked guys."

"Did he have a boyfriend?"

"No."

His face flushed once again, and I concluded David probably had some unrequited feelings for Robert. I dove in.

"Did you and he ever date?"

"Oh, no!" He almost blurted out the response. He regained composure and lowered his voice. "We were just friends."

I raised my eyebrows and nodded to encourage him to continue.

"Robert actually liked older guys."

An *Aha!* feeling gripped me but I suppressed it from spreading across my face and steadied my voice. "Did you know any of the men he'd seen?"

David shook his head. "We talked, but he didn't always give me details. I never pushed him, either."

Yeah, because you didn't really want to know who your competition was. "How did he meet guys?"

"The way everybody does. On DikMe."

I was about to ask another question when David looked over my shoulder. I turned to see a customer in need of assistance.

"Sorry," he said, "I have to get back to work."

"No problem—and thank you."

"Are you going to use all that information in your article?"

I offered a faint smile. "No. Some things are not meant to be public. And no one will know I talked to you."

I handed him a card with my name and phone number, and then stuck out my hand. As we shook, he thanked me and then made his way to the customer.

As I walked out to my car, the synapses in my brain started their rapid fire. Now I knew for sure that both Sergio and Robert had been gay, that Robert had been on DikMe, and that both had liked older men. Just as I settled into my car, Lieutenant Reed's words echoed among my thoughts.

If you learn anything, you should tell me.

But of course, I wouldn't. Not yet, anyway. First, I'd have to change my strategy on DikMe.

CHAPTER 24

MY STOMACH RUMBLED on the drive home, so I called Laura and told her to meet me for lunch. But when I neared the exit to Avenue 21, traffic slowed to a crawl.

"Shit."

I pulled up the traffic screen on my dashboard console and a thick red line revealed a jam about a mile ahead. I texted my sister to tell her I might be delayed. Cars inched along, and I considered what I'd learned from David. Robert was into older men, just like Sergio. More and more I believed there had to be a connection. I just couldn't put my finger on it. I considered the possibility that maybe they'd both been seeing the same guy. That would be one big-ass coincidence, but maybe not. There wasn't a huge gay or bi population in this part of the Central Valley, either open or on the down low. An incoming phone call interrupted my thoughts. I recognized the number on the screen and pressed the phone button on my steering wheel that engaged Bluetooth.

"Hey, Beth."

Beth was a friend from Chicago. We hadn't spoken in a while.

"Hi, Will. How are you?"

I avoided saying, "Oh, steeped in murder here in small-town California. You?" Instead I used the standard social convention. "I'm good. Trying to get work done, but it's a slow go. What's up?"

"Jeremy died."

Beth was not one to beat around the bush, her bluntness being a trademark of her character that we all knew too well back in Chi Town. The running joke was: "I wonder what Beth thinks." "Don't worry. She'll tell you."

My heart sank, no matter how she just delivered the news. Jeremy was a neighbor who'd lived in our high-rise. He'd been a good ten years older than us and lived alone. We'd spend Sunday mornings in his junior penthouse drinking coffee, eating bagels, and reading the *Tribune*, a ritual I missed in Mañana.

"How?" I asked.

"He had a heart attack. The cleaning lady found him slumped over the kitchen counter."

Poor Jeremy. I imagined him, those last minutes alone, maybe realizing what was happening. I didn't want to die like that.

"Is there a service?" I asked.

"No." Beth paused.

I pictured her sitting in her unit, a cup of coffee in front of her. She worked remotely from home and might still be in her pajamas even if it was two o'clock in the afternoon there.

"He didn't want one and his family has already come and made arrangements for the cremation. I just called to let you know."

"Text me info about where to send flowers or a letter."

"Of course."

"How are you doing?" I asked.

There was another pause and then a sigh. "I'm all right. I cried, of course. Mostly because with you gone and now Jeremy, I, well...life changes so much, doesn't it?"

With that comment, I realized exactly how long it had

been since we'd spoken. I needed to tell her about José, perhaps about the murders and what I was up to, but this just
didn't seem to be the right time.

"You know I love you," I said.

"Me too."

"Why don't you come out and visit soon?" I asked. "You
know I have a big house and lots of room. You can work
remotely from here. I have a library upstairs with a desk. You
can use that as a work area."

"I'd like that," she answered. "Tell you what. Let me look
at the calendar and then check on some flights. Maybe in a
couple of weeks?"

"Whenever you want, sweetheart."

We said our goodbyes and hung up. Just then I
approached the reason for the traffic jam. Two cars lay crumpled on the side of the highway, one upside down. Both wind-
shields were spiderweb fractured, and I saw blood smeared
across one. An EMS team was loading a covered body into
the back of its vehicle. Given the team seemed to be in no
hurry, I surmised that someone had not made it. Indeed, even
the face on the victim was covered.

I sighed. Another fatality on Highway 99 would be
reported on the news. Jeremy had just succumbed to a heart
attack. Sergio murdered. Robert murdered. *So much death*, I
thought. *So much death.*

• • •

WHEN I PULLED into Mañana, I headed downtown to
Bonita's, a little Mexican eatery—one of those that from the
outside didn't look like much and with an inside to match.
The dark red vinyl booths were cracked and lumpy, the

linoleum flooring was yellowed, posters hung on the walls as art, and half of the menu on the wall was handwritten on whiteboard. But the food was the best in our small town, except for mine, of course. And the people who worked there were delightful. Laura was waiting for me at a table when I walked in.

"No Amanda?" I asked.

She sucked on a straw protruding from a can of Diet Pepsi. "No. She's home paying bills. She wants me to bring her some enchiladas afterward."

I slid onto the seat across from her, my ass barely comfortable on the banquette, and almost immediately Adela showed up to take our order.

"*¿Quieren lo de siempre?*" she asked, wanting to know if we were going to order our usual.

We answered "*Sí*" and she proceeded to the kitchen to tell the cook to prepare chicken tacos for my sister and chicken enchiladas for me.

"What happened on the highway?" Laura asked.

"An accident. I think someone died."

We sat in silence for a few seconds.

Laura cleared her throat. "So, you and José are hot and heavy now."

She played with the straw and rubbed it against the can opening to make that obnoxious squeal when plastic meets aluminum.

"I guess so. Who'd-a thunk, right?"

"Why don't you invite him over to play cards and drink wine with us?"

I was surprised by the invitation. Laura and Amanda were not the most social people, preferring to stay home, and only occasionally coming to my house for dinner.

"Sure," I said. "Maybe next week."

Adela arrived with chips and salsa. Laura dug in immediately. I refrained—my constant internal checking of calories kept me from overindulging. Between crunches, Laura asked me if I knew anything more about the murders. I kept my prowling on DikMe and the incident with Sam Allison to myself, not wanting to hear a lecture on needing to be careful. I told her about my interactions with the two families.

"And I just got back from Madera where I spoke to a friend of the second victim."

"What'd you find out?" Crunch, crunch.

I quickly summarized for her. When I'd finished, she said the predictable. "Brother. I love you. Be careful. Don't get too involved."

Just then, Adela returned with our food and the conversation shifted. But in the back of my mind, her admonition echoed along with José's. Was I too involved? Was I headed for trouble? I'd almost made a mess with Sam Allison. I wondered what Lieutenant Reed would do if he found out what I knew and what had happened in The Fairway parking lot.

But I was damned if I was going to let go of any of it.

CHAPTER 25

A T HOME, I set myself to the task of working on my DikMe account. I knew, now, that both Sergio and Robert were into older men. I opened the app and edited my profile, changing my name to "Latino Wants Daddy." If that name didn't attract the right kind of guy, nothing would. An alert let me know a regular text was coming through. I smiled when I saw it was from José.

> Hola, handsome. What's
> for dinner tonight?

I grinned and put my thumbs to work.

> Me. Oh wait, that's dessert.
> Let me think on it.

> Cute. I'll bring some wine.
> 5:30?

> Perfect. I'll be waiting with
> just an apron on.

> Mmmm.

Well, as my sister said, I guessed José and I were hot and heavy. I hoped that what we had wasn't fleeting, that instead it was the start of something long-lasting. It had been some time since I'd felt this kind of attraction, this kind of passion. And during this time of murder and how Sergio's body had dredged up memories of Carlos, it sustained me. After the phone call from Beth, I felt even more of a need to have someone like José around. A chirp from DikMe let me know a message had arrived. I pressed on the tab. It was Sam Allison.

> Just want you to know no
> hard feelings.
> Thanks in advance for
> keeping everything to
> yourself.

I stared at the text. A week prior I would never have anticipated such a message from anyone. I debated replying and then I thumbed:

> Secret is safe. Just stop
> spewing your hateful
> words and ditch the hat.

I waited. I did not see the familiar rolling dots that DikMe used to indicate someone was responding. I set my phone down and made myself a cup of coffee. Just as I was pouring in the milk, the app chirped.

> Ha ha.

What the hell was going on? One day this guy was telling Bobby to get the fuck out of this country and next he was telling me he was giving up on his ways. Leopards don't change their spots, as the saying goes. How much could I believe? But as I pondered his text, it occurred to me that I—and several others—knew he was closeted. That had to count for something. He was probably scared shitless in case it all came out.

I was going to type a reply when I got a text from Beth

about where to send something to Jeremy's family. I wasn't sure if flowers were the right gesture or not, but I went ahead and got online and found a nice wreath to send. On the gift card I expressed my condolences and said to let me know if there was a charity or fund to send a contribution in his honor. As I completed the purchase, I remembered my thought from earlier in the day.

So much death.

• • •

AFTER DINNER, JOSÉ and I snuggled on the sofa while we watched *For the Boys*. It turned out it was not only my favorite Bette Midler movie but José's as well. My head rested on his lap. I was content lying there, not just enjoying the movie, but feeling the rhythmic breathing of José, taking in the faint smell of cologne that he must've put on at the start of the day. A DikMe chirp interrupted the peace of it all. José arched an eyebrow. I reached for the remote and paused the movie.

"I see your fishing expedition is getting nibbles," he said.

"Stop using straight metaphors."

"Gay people fish. Look at St. Peter."

I rolled my eyes, retrieved my phone from the end table, and looked to see who had messaged me.

"False alarm," I said. "Some twink is saying hi. By the way, I changed my screen name."

"To?"

"'Latino Wants Daddy.' If I'm going to fish, I need better bait."

"Stop using straight metaphors." He deadpanned his words. "And why didn't you tell me earlier you'd done that?"

"We were busy earlier. I just told you now."

He shook his head. "Will, think about everything you're doing. Don't forget what happened yesterday. And you are engaging in fraudulent activity."

"Huh?"

"You've created a fake identity on a dating app to lure someone in. That's got to be a crime."

I folded my arms on my chest. "They do it all the time on those predator shows. No jury would convict me."

He rubbed my shoulder. "Go to Lieutenant Reed and tell him what you know. Let him take it from there."

I stood up. "I can't. I need to follow this through." I began to pace.

José followed my movements, letting a few seconds tick off before he responded. "Tell me what you're thinking."

I stopped. "When I was a little kid, they noticed I had tremendous curiosity. My teachers told my parents to encourage it. Give me puzzles to solve. I was driven by learning things. I taught myself chemistry in the third grade."

José stared.

"Yes, I did. I even made a poison bomb for the bullies that tormented me."

"You what?"

"It was a chloramine balloon bomb. You put a bleach-filled balloon inside a balloon filled with ammonia. When you toss it, the balloons burst, and the liquids mix together to form chloramine vapor."

José's mouth fell open.

"You can't kill anyone with it. It is pretty irritating, though. It can incapacitate you for a while."

"And you thought of that on your own in the third grade?" he asked.

I nodded. "Those bullies were relentless. I hated recess

because they would hunt me down, pick on me for being a sissy, a short Latino half-breed. The gringo kids called me 'queer bait' and the Latino kids called me '*maricón*.'"

José stood up, put his hands on my shoulders, and looked at me squarely. "I think you're still trying to fight the bullies. And not just the ones in grade school."

"What do you mean?"

"You're also fighting the ones who killed Carlos."

I stood there, unable to respond. I had been driven by curiosity my whole life. That was true. I'd forged a career as a major researcher in my field before I left academia. I had always felt compelled to prove myself, prove those bullies wrong, that I was worth something. I understood that. But was José right about Carlos? For so many years I had suppressed my memories of him. Maybe I was substituting one case for another, an attempt to rectify a crime from long ago that, in reality, had no rectification.

I sighed. "Well, that's possible. Regardless, I just can't turn this over to the police without doing something."

José pulled me in and hugged me. Not hard, but gently, as you might a child. I appreciated the gesture and I melted into his arms.

"Honey," I said, my hands clasped around his back, "I already told you I'd be careful. I wouldn't do anything by myself."

He pulled back. "What did you say?"

"I said that I wouldn't do anything by myself."

"No. Not that." A small smile played about his lips. "What did you call me?"

"Oh." I shrugged. "It just slipped out."

His gaze firmly fixed on me once again, he said, "That's the first time you've said anything other than my name. I liked it."

I moved in and kissed him with a passion that geysered up from inside. Little did I know I'd wake up the next day to find out another murder had been committed.

And that I already knew the victim.

• • •

You ever date anyone younger? I mean significantly younger. What do you think it is about men over forty that they like to chase younger tail? Gay or straight, it seems to make no difference. I mean, look at Woody Allen. Dumps Mia Farrow for her twenty-one-year-old adopted daughter. The fucker was fifty-six! Oh, and better than that, Hugh Hefner was eighty-six when he married what's her name. She was only twenty-six.

[pauses]

I've had time to think about that, you know. Not much else to do around here. So it's occurred to me that as men get older, they get more and more attracted to younger people because they're afraid of aging. Something like a fear of death. You hit the mid mark in life and you realize there's less time left than what you've already used up. You think a young guy or gal will somehow keep you from shriveling up and dying, keep you from getting cancer or Alzheimer's. Yeah, that's why men do what they do. It's a fear of death. Has to be.

[pauses]

But the real question is why the younger ones want someone older. What's in it for them?

• • •

CHAPTER 26

ANOTHER TEXT ALERT from our neighborhood group buzzed at around eight in the morning. José had already left to go home and change, and I was in the kitchen making a second coffee. I reached for my phone. The posting was from a woman who lived on the other side of The Palms. I tended to ignore her because she ranted about the home-owners' board and the lousy job it and the management did. This time, I froze as I read.

> What is going on in our town? Just found out there's been another murder. That makes three. In less than a week! Do we need to arm ourselves now? I didn't move from the Bay Area to be around this!

I grabbed my coffee and hurried to my office. I pulled up a news feed from Fresno on my computer. Sure enough, as reported an hour before, another body had been found in Mañana. The victim had already been identified. Luis Pérez. I sank into my chair and closed my eyes.

Luis. From Rite Aid. I'd seen him several days before. He'd given me the DikMe lead.

"No, no, no!" I ran my hands through my hair. I picked up my phone and hit Laura's number.

"What's up, little brother? It's so early."

"You know the guy who works at the pharmacy in Rite Aid? Luis?"

"Yeah. What about him?"

"He's dead. Murdered."

"Oh, no..."

I heard my sister-in-law in the background ask what the matter was. Laura quickly explained then turned her attention back to me.

"How'd you find out?"

"Neighborhood group text. Then I searched online."

I told her I needed to get going on my day and we'd talk later. As I finished my coffee, I pondered this latest tragedy. Silvia and the others at the drug store had to be devastated, assuming they'd heard. It was still early in the morning, so it was possible the news hadn't reached them yet. Poor Luis.

It occurred to me that although he was Latino, Luis wasn't in his twenties like Sergio and Robert. But maybe he shared their penchant for dating older guys. I remembered the way he'd looked at me several days prior, when I asked him if he was gay. He'd replied, "You want to hook up?" I detected a slight glimmer in his eye, a willingness—if that had indeed been my inclination. And, of course, I knew he had been on DikMe.

I groaned. The killer had to be using the site to find and lure Latino men into his trap. But why DikMe? If the killer wasn't gay, why that app? Why not just stalk Latinos, pick out a victim, and then go from there? I was missing something in this puzzle. Maybe the killer was gay. I just didn't want to believe that. Gay people have had enough on their plates socially and politically to also have to answer for a serial killer. But why were *gay* Latino men the targets? In the midst of these thoughts, my phone chirped a DikMe message. I hit the message button. It was from Sam Allison.

> Just heard the news.
> Another murder. I swear
> it's not me! I'm glad we
> talked the other night. I
> need to get help. I know
> that now. I'm just so afraid.

I thumbed a quick reply.

> I believe you. I'm glad
> you're getting help. Look
> what fear has done to you.

The other night, José had admonished him, told him to seek professional help. I hoped he was following through and not just texting words he thought would appease me. I made a mental note to check in with him at a later date. My thoughts drifted back to Luis and I knew I'd have to speak to Lieutenant Reed. By 10:00, I was showered, dressed, and on my way to downtown Mañana.

I pulled up to the police station and rushed inside. The receptionist with heavy eye makeup greeted me.

"I'm here to see Lieutenant Reed," I said.

"He's out on a call."

"Do you know when he'll return?"

She said no, so I left my name and phone number and told her it was urgent. On my way back to the car, I pulled out my phone and dialed his cell number. He didn't pick up. I left a message.

"Lieutenant. This is Will Christian. I just stopped by the station. I heard the news this morning about Luis Pérez. I was hoping to speak to you. Thanks."

Because downtown Mañana was so small, I was only two blocks from Rite Aid. I hopped in my car and was there in less than three minutes. I passed through the sliding glass doors and made a beeline for the pharmacy. I stopped short at the aisle containing analgesics and ducked into where the baby products were lined up. Reed was at the pharmacy window talking to Silvia. Although I wanted to talk to him, I didn't want him to see me in the store. He would know I'd come by there to do my own snooping. I strained to hear the conversation, but nothing reached my ears. I could make out he was taking his leave, so I slid down the aisle and disappeared around the corner to avoid being seen as he walked by. When I thought it was clear, I sucked in a breath and gingerly made my way to the pharmacy. If I'd still been religious, I would have made the sign of the cross. Silvia came up to the drop-off window.

"Hi, Will. Are you dropping off?"

"No. I just came to say I heard about Luis and how awful you must all feel. I'm so sorry."

Her eyes moistened. "I can't believe it. He was such a nice guy. A great coworker." A full tear emerged from one eye and began its descent. She brushed it away.

"Well, I won't bother you, then. I was hoping to ask you a few questions about Luis. But that can wait."

She nodded and then signaled that someone was behind me. I once again said how sorry I was and left the counter. I hurried out of the store, contemplating how I might get some information on Luis. As I stepped out into the bright sunlight, I stopped dead. Lieutenant Reed was leaning against my car with arms folded. He saw me, of course, so I made my way toward him.

"Good morning, Lieutenant."

A toothpick twitched in his mouth. He looked at my empty hands and then back at me. "Couldn't find what you came in for?"

I had to think quickly. "Actually, I was ordering a prescription refill."

He pulled the gnawed toothpick from between his lips, looked at its frayed end, and tossed it to the ground. "Got your voicemail. So, you know about the other murder."

I nodded.

"And you knew the victim, Luis Pérez."

"I did."

"And you came here to drop off a script and not to do some snooping?"

I cleared my throat. "I did need a refill. But, yes, I would like to talk to someone here, you know, for the piece I'm working on."

He studied me for a minute. Then he straightened himself and said, "Remember, Mr. Christian. If you learn anything or know anything..."

"Well, I kind of do now."

He folded his arms across his chest once more. "I'm listening."

"Sergio was gay. So was Luis. I think Robert was, too." He tilted his head. "Yes, they were all Latino, but it's odd to me they were gay Latino."

"That is odd," he said. "Anything else?"

Of course, I was going to lie—José's warning about my fraudulent activity echoed in my head.

"No. Just that."

He unfolded his arms and fished in his pocket for the keys to his vehicle. "I appreciate the information." He told me to have a good day and then walked over to his car, a beep-beep signaling his door was unlocking. I watched as he drove away. Then I did what I knew I had to do.

I hurried back inside Rite Aid.

CHAPTER 27

I STRODE TO the pharmacy and looked for Silvia. Another clerk was helping a customer at the counter and so I waited. At the drive-through, a woman shouted into the exterior mic, not understanding that the attending clerk could hear her just fine—and everyone else for that matter.

"Will this really take care of my yeast infection?" she shouted.

I winced. After a few seconds, Silvia appeared from behind a wall of medications and I waved to get her attention. She signaled for me to go over to the checkout area. No one was there, and I was glad for the privacy.

"I'm sorry to bother you again," I said, "but I'm working on a piece about the recent murders, and I need to get some information on Luis."

"Oh, yes," she said with a faint smile. "I remember. You're a writer."

"That's right, yes." I shifted where I stood. "I thought maybe you could tell me who his family was and how I might contact them."

She nodded. "He lives—lived—in Merced. I have his brother's phone number, if you'd like it."

"That would be wonderful."

She fished a cell phone out of the pocket of her pharmacy jacket and searched. Merced was about sixteen miles north of Mañana.

"Here it is," she said. "Would you like for me to write it down?"

"Would you mind?"

She pulled off a small piece of register tape and jotted the number for me.

"Thank you so much. And again, I can only imagine what you all must be feeling." I reached over the counter and patted the back of her hand.

Again, she offered a faint smile. "Thank you."

I said goodbye and hurried out of the store. Back in my car, I started the engine and cranked the AC. Sun glinted off the hood. Like so many parking lots in Mañana, there were few shade trees and the interior of my BMW felt like a kiln that was heating up, just waiting for the clay. As the cool air curled about my face, I looked at the information Silvia had given me. Luis's brother was Jesús Pérez. I dialed his number. He picked up after three rings.

"Hello."

"Hi. Is this Jesús Pérez?"

"Yes. Who is this?"

I tried to contain my eagerness and sucked in a breath. "My name is Will Christian. I'm a writer and I'm working on a piece regarding the recent murders in Mañana. I know this is a terrible time. You and your family have my heartfelt condolences."

"Thank you, Mr. Christian."

His tone was flat, and I wondered if maybe it was not a good thing to call so soon. But my curiosity compelled me to continue.

"If you have time and are willing, would you mind answering a few questions for me?"

"I don't mind, but the police have already spoken with my family. Are your questions any different?"

"They are. You see, I'm interested in the personal side of things."

"I'm sorry, but I don't really know you..."

I understood the hesitation. I should have driven up to Merced and done this in person, as I had with Sergio's and Robert's families. I was being too eager, but still, I pushed on.

"Mr. Pérez, I understand your skepticism. I assure you I'm on the up-and-up. I've already interviewed the other two families and it was Silvia at Rite Aid who gave me your number. She can vouch for me if you want to call the store and ask her."

There was a pause. "That's okay. What do you want to know?"

I asked him some of the same questions I had asked Robert Márquez's father, not really caring about the answers because I already knew the main thing about Luis that was relevant: he was gay. Jesús kept his answers brief and he confirmed that Luis was thirty-six. When I'd finished with the question about Luis's schooling and how he'd gotten into pharmacy work, I paused and went for the information I really wanted.

"By any chance, do you know if Luis's phone was returned to the family?"

"Now that you ask, no," he said. "I was the one who collected everything from the police. They gave me his clothes, wallet, and all that stuff. But there was no phone. Why do you ask?"

I had my excuse ready to go. "Oh, well, sometimes there are good photos on a cell phone that could be used in the kind of article I'm writing. Looking at his photos gives a writer like me a sense of who he was as a person."

"If you need a photo, I could send you one or two."

I hadn't anticipated that. "Well, sure. You can send it to this number when you get a chance. I would appreciate it."

I thanked him for his time and once again expressed my regret. I immediately headed for the Save Mart. Marisela, one of the checkers, was at the second register waiting for a customer to begin transferring his items from the cart to the moving belt. She smiled at me as I approached.

"Hola," I said. "Is José around?"

"I think he's helping stock milk."

"Great, thanks."

I gave her a wink and hurried to the back of the store where the refrigerated section of dairy products lined the wall. This section of the store was next to the open shelves of eggs, yogurt, and cheese, and the ambient temperature plummeted. I rubbed my arms from the chill. I saw movement behind the glass doors. I peeked between cartons of almond milk, and there was my boyfriend. I waved. He waved back and then turned and walked away. I headed for the double doors to the right of the dairy section, knowing that's where José would exit the small warehouse area. He pushed though the swinging doors and greeted me with a smile.

"What's up, sweetie?" He took his gloves off and kissed me with lips chilled from the refrigeration he'd been working in.

"Did you know there was another murder?"

The cheer on his face vanished as he nodded. "I just heard from someone here. I was going to text you, but knowing you, I figured you already knew."

"It's different this time," I said. "I knew the victim."

His eyes widened. "You did?"

"Yes. I'll tell you everything later. Do you want to meet for lunch?"

He frowned. "Can't. I'm going to work through lunch today because we're short on staff. But after work sounds good."

We made a date for him to come over to my house after five. He would pick up a few things for dinner and we'd cook after he arrived. In the meantime, I dashed home and opened up my laptop and dove into the notes about the murders. Sitting in the kitchen, I typed a few lines and then examined what I had on the screen.

Sergio Ramírez, 22, Latino, gay, liked older guys, no phone on body

Robert Márquez, 23, Latino, gay, liked older guys, no phone on body, DikMe

Luis Pérez, 36, Latino, gay, no phone on body, DikMe

Looking at the information, I decided to pencil something in for Sergio and adjusted my notes.

Sergio Ramírez, 22, Latino, gay, no phone on body, probably DikMe

Given Luis's question about whether I wanted to hook up the other day, I amended his profile.

Luis Pérez, 36, Latino, gay, maybe liked older guys, no phone on body, DikMe

The pattern was in place except for one thing: age. The first two victims were in their early twenties, the third victim in his midthirties. Otherwise, everything else made for a neat set of connections among them. I stared at my computer screen, and after a few minutes, I typed my questions.

Why no phones? Did it have something to do with DikMe?

Were these hate crimes? If so, against Latinos or gays or both?

• • •

WAS THE KILLER stepping out of his preferred age group? Did he have an age group?

I sat, transfixed on these questions. Then, something clicked. Maybe there was something else the three dead men had in common. I typed another set of questions and sat back in my chair, chin resting on tented fingers. I wondered if there was a way to do a search on DikMe to find answers. I could probably find out on the internet how to do that. Or, I could just ask José later. He would know. Could I force myself to get back to work and not let my curiosity draw me away from the editing deadline I had? I sat and stared at the questions.

What sex preferences did they have? Were they tops or bottoms?

I asked myself why I thought it mattered. And then I set about trying to get my answers.

CHAPTER 28

I LAUNCHED A browser window and asked how to do a search on DikMe. I clicked on one suggestion and, sure enough, all I had to do was tap on the question mark in the upper right-hand corner of the main screen. I grabbed my phone, opened the app, and touched my finger to the icon. Something called "filters" showed up.

I studied the list. There were tabs for age, weight, height, tribes, body type, and—*aha!*—position. I clicked on it. Choices appeared ranging from top to bottom with in-between categories such as versatile and vers bottom. As I looked at these options, I wondered what I would really find out. Oh, well, nothing ventured, nothing gained.

I clicked on versatile, bottom, and bottom vers only. I hit "save" and a number of profiles disappeared on my main screen. I scrolled to see if I could find twenty-two- and twenty-three-year-olds within a fifteen-mile radius. Two twenty-two-year-olds and one twenty-three-year-old popped up. Luckily, the twenty-three-year-old had a photo. I tapped it and looked at the distance: fourteen miles. That was about how far Robert's house was from mine. I stared at the photo, having no idea what Robert had looked like.

I switched to my computer and googled his name. Luck was on my side. I found a news article about the murders in the *Fresno Bee*—and both his and Sergio's photos were there. I held my phone up to the computer screen and compared the two pictures. God bless technology! It was Robert. I scrolled down his profile in DikMe.

> DL Latino looking. 40+. Bottom here, so need top. Average or toned, no fat guys. Will trade pics.

Farther down, he only listed one tribe: daddy. *Daddy* was the gay term for guys aged forty and up. Yep, David at Wal-mart had been right; Robert liked them older. Now, if only I could do the same for Sergio. I had his photo from the news article in front of me, but neither of the twenty-two-year-olds I'd just found had face pics, only the default generic silhou-ettes that DikMe provided. Then I noticed that one had his distance at twelve miles while the other was at four miles. Sergio's house was about four miles from mine. I tapped and studied the profile.

> Bottom looking for tops. Must be clean and ddf. Into older guys so 40+ HMU.

After I'd determined that "ddf" meant "drug and disease free," I checked out what was listed for tribes. There was the magic word: daddy. That had to be Sergio's profile. Okay, so both he and Robert were bottoms.

I did a final romp through the rest of the profiles and didn't see one that looked like Luis. Then I remembered he'd lived in Merced, which was about eighteen miles north of Mañana. As I scrolled, I found the name "Vers 36." Thirty-six was Luis's age. Again, there was no photo, but at least the dis-tance seemed right: nineteen miles. I tapped and studied the profile.

> Discreet Latino. Into good hot times. NSA. Any age is fine. I'm vers but prefer bottoming.

I had to look up "NSA": no strings attached. Sheesh, these guys and their acronyms! I focused on the additional information, and under tribes he listed "clean cut," "daddy," "discreet," and "twink." The inclusion of "daddy" and "twink" corroborated that age didn't matter, given that twinks were generally eighteen- to twenty-three-year-olds.

I sat back. Was this Luis? The information sure fit. Damn! If only he'd included a photo. But it had to be him. Who else at nineteen miles from me could it be at age thirty-six? I went ahead with the working assumption that I had found all three profiles and adjusted the notes on my laptop screen.

Sergio Ramírez, 22, Latino, gay, no phone on body, DikMe, bottom, older guys

Robert Márquez, 23, Latino, gay, no phone on body, DikMe, bottom, older guys

Luis Pérez, 36, Latino, gay, no phone on body, DikMe, preferred bottoming, older guys

The pattern was clearly there. Some guy had plucked these three men out of the crowd, and although I didn't know who he was, he had to be advertising himself as a top and probably also as a daddy.

I rubbed my hands together and redid the filter to include only those with the two characteristics I'd just uncovered: "top" and "daddy." My main screen changed. Of course, there was Sam Allison. Because he was discreet, there was no photo, but I recognized his screen name: "LatinoLover." I shook my head.

"Sam, Sam, Sam."

As I looked at all the profiles, I realized I had no idea whether the killer was local or not. His distance could be two miles, five miles, twenty miles, or even more. How would I sort through these?

I glanced at the clock. 2:25. I needed to walk away from this. I couldn't turn to work, not at that point. My mind was too clogged with thoughts of what I'd pieced together. I stood and stretched. My body told me it was time for the gym. A good workout would distract me. By the time I came home and showered, it would be close to four thirty. Then José would be over soon after that.

I hoped he would be ready for me to pick his brain.

• • •

José arrived at five fifteen, sporting a polo shirt and shorts and carrying a grocery bag.

"I see you managed to change," I said as we kissed at the front door.

"Well, you like my legs so much, I thought, 'Give him a treat.'"

I took the bag from his grasp and peeked inside. "What'd you bring?"

"I thought instead of cooking we could eat from the deli. Their rotisserie chicken is great. I also grabbed some bean salad. And, of course, some wine and a baguette."

"Sounds perfect," I said, taking in the aroma of the chicken as it wafted up from inside the bag. "You really are getting to know me, aren't you?"

He leaned in for another kiss, put his hands around my waist, and then dropped them to my ass. He squeezed.

"And I like what I know."

"Awww. You make me blush."

I pulled him by the hand into the kitchen. I put the

chicken in the oven on a very low setting so it could stay warm and put the bean salad in the fridge. In the meantime, José poured us some wine.

"So, you going to tell me about the victim?" he asked, throwing his leg over a stool.

"He worked at the pharmacy at Rite Aid."

I told him the little bit I knew about Luis and then about what I'd found out today in my conversation with his brother. "And you won't believe what else I've been up to," I added.

"I can only imagine."

"Look."

I pulled my laptop over in front of us and opened it up. I slipped onto the stool next to him and I described my romp through DikMe today as I showed him my notes.

"So, what do you think?"

I must have beamed my excitement because José seemed to pick up on something in my expression.

"You would make one helluva private eye," he said.

"Except for one thing."

"What?"

I explained about not knowing where the killer was from, how close or how far. José looked at my notes again, then back at me.

"Weren't the bodies all found in Mañana?" he asked.

"'Tis true, my love."

"Well," he said, taking a long sip of his wine, "seems to me that the killer is probably local."

I scrunched up my face. Could that be right?

"If shows like *SVU* and *Criminal Minds* are accurate," he added, "don't killers have a comfort zone, and that's normally close to where they live?" He tilted his head with a slight smile.

Of course! I looked at him, grabbed his face, and planted a huge kiss on his lips. "God, I wish I'd known you years ago!"

He pulled back a bit. "Same here. But you know the expression: better late than never."

"Mmmmm..." I leaned in and kissed him again. As I did, my phone chirped a DikMe alert. I picked it up and hit the tab.

"False alarm," I said. "Some nineteen-year-old from Merced offering to give blow jobs." I sighed. I held up the phone for José to see.

"I feel for these kids," he said, peering at the profile. "I wonder how many are closeted and this is their only outlet."

"I know," I said. "I just hope they all play it safe. He could be a target."

"Probably not. He listed his ethnicity as white."

As he said this, it struck me. Was I being irresponsible by not going to Lieutenant Reed and telling him what I believed about how the killer was hunting his victims? Was there some way I could prevent another death? But if I went public with the information and we alerted DikMe, it was possible we would never find the killer. He'd go underground like a frightened ground squirrel. Maybe DikMe would research the victims' accounts. I doubted it. They'd probably claim privacy rights and would only yield under a subpoena. And what about José's admonition that I was engaging in fraudulent activity? I could feel uncertainty creeping into my thoughts.

"Hey," José said, pulling me back into the moment, "it's all going to be okay. You'll see."

I looked into his eyes. "I hope you're right."

•••

You probably want to know details about the murders. Everyone wants the details. Of course, I got asked after my arrest. I said what needed to be said. No more. But around here, I'm hounded about the details. Every single guy wants to know what I did, how I did it, if my eyes were open, if they were closed, if I got a hard on, if the victims cried, moaned, or pled. How much I'd planned, how I chose my weapon, and on and on and on. Inquisitive fuckers.

[pauses]

You know what one guy asked me? He wanted to know if I whistled. Whistled! Like I was in a fucking Disney movie or something. Wait. How does that song go? "Just whistle while you work."

[whistles a tune]

Stupid. Anyway, when I told him no, that I didn't whistle, he seemed disappointed. He looked at me and said, "Too bad." Later, I found him whistling while doing his chores. There he was, mopping the common room, whistling as loud as could be. Turns out he killed his wife and her lover. Claims he whistled while he wrapped their bodies up in shower curtains and tossed them into the San Luis Reservoir. He was probably hoping to find a kindred spirit in me. Yeah, like whistling would make us best buds.

[pauses]

I don't normally whistle. Not one of my things. I guess you might say I just get in there and do the job. And if you want details, forget it. I won't give any. You already know everything there is to know. For everything else, I don't care if you make it up. Use your imagination.

•••

CHAPTER 29

THE NEXT DAY was Sunday and I was glad that José didn't have to get up early and go to work. I always thought Sundays were useless days wedged in between Saturdays and Mondays. I wasn't a churchgoer—and as it turned out, neither was José, much to my relief—so I just didn't have the feel for Sundays that many families had. Mostly, I'd treat it like any other day with work, sometimes the gym, and some reading.

Over morning coffee José suggested we go wine tasting, do some of the Madera Wine Trail. The suggestion delighted me, so I pulled up the info on my laptop. We mapped out an itinerary, hitting up five wineries and ending at Dulce Vineyards, down off of Avenue 7. Dulce specialized in ports and it seemed fitting to end the tour with a thick and sweeter after-dinner wine.

I prepared a big Mexican breakfast with eggs, chorizo, beans, and tortillas. I loved the smell of chorizo cooking, even though I knew it was nothing but cholesterol on a plate. The sweet, spicy aroma it gave off just made Sundays seem a little less dull. José loved it.

"I could really get used to your cooking," he said, shoving a piece of tortilla laden with breakfast food into his mouth.

"And I could get used to cooking for you."

We kissed.

"Why don't we go in my car?" José said. "We can stop at my house so I can change. And you can see where I live."

"I like that idea."

The time we'd spent together so far had been in Mañana, largely because José worked there and Save Mart was just over a mile down the road from me. It would be nice to see how José lived, what his taste was like. I was intrigued.

• • •

IT TURNED OUT José lived not too far from where Robert Márquez's family lived. His house was a one-story with a manicured lawn and well-tended white rosebushes, daylilies, and a large redbud tree. We entered through the garage and into the kitchen area.

"Boy," I said, "you must be OCD or have one hell of a cleaning person. This place is immaculate."

I took in how the kitchen counters were clear of clutter, how the stainless-steel stove top shined in the low light, and how neatly laid out the family room furniture was: one small leather sofa and two easy chairs. A wine refrigerator hugged one wall and framed art dotted the others.

"My house is no gallery like yours," he said, watching me survey the surroundings. "But it's comfy. And it's what I can afford."

"Don't be humble," I said, "this house has both charm and elegance."

He kissed me on the cheek. "I'm going to go change. You can come see the rest of the house if you'd like."

I followed him down the hallway, passing the formal area, the front door with its small foyer, a guest room, a den, and finally the master bedroom.

"What is this?" I asked. "About two thousand square feet?"

He nodded as he kicked off his shoes and put them away. "Just about."

The bedroom itself was large and could easily accommodate a king-size bed, although José's was a queen. As in the case of the rest of the house, this room was decorated with taste: dark, masculine woods; a quilted duvet flaunting desert colors; and several pieces of art that looked to be giclées of originals.

José emerged from his walk-in closet sporting fresh shorts and a polo shirt. "Ready to hit the trail?"

"Just one thing," I said. I maneuvered him over to the bed, gently forced him into a seated position, and then cupped his face in my hands. I leaned in and kissed him. "There. That's all."

He smiled. "Is that all you want here in my bedroom?"

"All I want for now." I grabbed his hands and pulled him into an upright position. "Now, how about that wine tasting?"

• • •

BY ONE THIRTY, we had made it through three wineries and headed for the fourth, La Viña, on Avenue 9. We pulled into the gravel parking area and crunch walked our way to the front door. It had a spacious inside area, with a soaring ceiling, art for sale on the walls, sofas and chairs as well as tables, and, of course, the tasting area. Just after entering, I stopped when I saw Lieutenant Reed at the wine bar. He was with a woman who resembled the one I saw in the photograph on his desk. Chatting with him was his cousin, Tim Shakely, and a woman I presumed was his wife.

José leaned in and almost whispered. "What is it?"

"That's Lieutenant Reed. He hasn't seen us. We could turn around now."

José put his hand against my back. "What? You're bothered? We're already here. Let's enjoy it. Just act cool."

We strode up to the bar, and on our approach, Reed spotted us. He lifted his glass to signal us. His three companions turned around, and when Tim saw me, he offered a slight smile and lifted his glass. I sucked in a breath and made my way toward them.

"Hello, Lieutenant. Tim," I said.

We all shook hands. The two men introduced their wives and I introduced José.

"Doing the wine trail?" I asked.

"No," Reed said. "We're members here and they are sampling a new Tempranillo."

"We're big fans of reds," his wife chimed in. "How about you?"

José spoke before I could answer. "Will and I are partial to whites, especially good Chardonnays."

"I didn't take you for a wine drinker," I said to Reed.

"Cops do more than patrol and drink beer, Mr. Christian."

José gave me a slight nudge behind my back.

"Well," I said, "it was nice seeing you. We'll leave you to your tasting."

José and I positioned ourselves at the end of the serving bar. The windows opened up to a beautiful terrace with a parklike setting surrounded by rows of grapevines on undulating low terrain. La Viña was known for outside events such as weddings and parties, but on a hot day in late June,

I just couldn't imagine sitting out there. A few brave souls were parked at high-tops under the immense overhang of the patio, sipping on wine and munching on whatever food they'd brought. Outdoor fans circulated air from above, but I couldn't imagine they offered much cooling.

José informed the server we only wanted to sample whites, and so he began pouring, starting with a Marsanne as a prelude to their Viognier blend—to be followed by a Chenin Blanc. We were on the second wine when I heard Reed's voice from behind.

"Mr. Christian. May I speak with you?"

I swiveled on my stool to face him. "Lieutenant, what is it?" I glanced around. The rest of his party must have already exited.

"I appreciated the information you gave me yesterday. I was wondering if you wouldn't mind stopping by the station tomorrow. I'd like to review something with you." He paused, those steel-colored eyes boring into me. Then he looked at José with no expression, and then at me again. "In private."

"Sure," I said, suppressing a gulp. "How about late morning? Around eleven?"

"That would be perfect." He reached into his shirt pocket, retrieved a toothpick, and inserted the end between his teeth. He nodded then left.

I turned to José. "That was odd."

"What do you think he wants?"

I pressed my lips together and shook my head. "I don't know. Did he sound upset to you?"

"No. He sounded genuine when he said he appreciated the information. When did you see him?"

I quickly recounted how I'd run into Reed in the parking lot at Rite Aid the day before.

"So now he knows all the victims were gay," José said.

"Yep."

"Maybe he's reconsidering what kind of crimes these murders are."

I settled back onto my stool and turned my attention toward the door where Reed had exited.

"Maybe," I said.

CHAPTER 30

AFTER AN EARLY-MORNING bike ride, I settled into work. I'd had several DikMe hits on my phone, but they were all from young guys looking for friends with benefits. I ignored them, of course, and was happy to slip into my routine. Sure, the murders floated among my thoughts, but I was able to focus and not let anything distract me. Maybe it had to do with José. Even though we'd known each other a short time, his presence in my life was calming. I looked forward to seeing him every day, and perhaps that was tempering my compulsion to solve these murders. When 10:45 rolled around, I stopped working, hopped in my car, and headed for downtown Mañana.

I entered the police station to find Lieutenant Reed behind the glass window checking on something with the receptionist. When he spotted me, he waved and held up a finger to signal that he'd be with me soon. I sat on one of the hard plastic chairs. I caught a whiff of cleaning solution and concluded that someone had recently mopped the floors and wiped down the seats. *God this place is depressing*, I thought as I looked at the lack of color and the grayness surrounding me. Were all police stations as sad as this one? As I studied the directory of names next to the reception window, my phone buzzed a text. It was from Sergio's sister, Julie.

My brother's memorial
service is this afternoon.
Here's the info if you want
to come.

The service was set for 2:00 p.m. at the local Catholic church, only three blocks from the police station. I replied, thanking her for the information and telling her that I would be there. I texted José to let him know I was going to the service and would see him at the end of the day. Just as I hit the send button, Reed emerged from the office.

"Mr. Christian, thank you for stopping by. Would you come with me, please?"

I followed him, and once inside, he offered me a seat. His office looked exactly as it had the week prior, the piles of cases on his desk not seeming to have moved at all. However, a half-eaten protein bar and coffee mug printed with "World's Greatest Dad" sat to one side. Behind his desk and against the wall were the cardboard boxes I'd seen before. I wondered how many cases sat in those cardboard homes waiting to find their way into a filing cabinet or a shredder.

"You said you wanted to review something with me?" I asked.

"Yes," he said, settling into his own chair. "I wanted to follow up on the information you gave me the other day."

"About the victims being gay."

He nodded. "Our leads haven't gotten us anywhere, and I'm wondering just how you came by this information."

I shifted in my seat. "Oh, well, you know, just talking to people."

"Just talking to people."

"Yes. Just talking to people." *Oh, what the hell*, I thought. "You see, I'm not police. Plus, I'm gay and half-Latino. And

I speak Spanish. People may be more comfortable telling me private things."

"Private things."

"Exactly. Like if they're gay or not. I mean, this is Mañana. It's not San Francisco."

He mulled on that. "So how'd you find out Sergio Ramírez was gay?"

"His sister told me."

"You know his sister?"

"I do now." I kept my gaze on him, wondering where he was going with this conversation.

"How do you know her?"

"I met her when I went to pay my respects to the family. She's reached out to me."

His eyes were locked on mine, like he was studying me. I felt a bit of dampness in my armpits.

"Lieutenant, why am I here? What exactly do you want?"

He leaned forward and clasped his hands, resting them on the desk. "I'm stymied, Mr. Christian. I've interviewed family members and coworkers, and the issue of the victims being gay never came up."

"Sergio's parents didn't know he was gay, so that wasn't information you would have learned from them. Probably the same for the others."

He shook his head. "You see, that concerns me."

"How so?"

"I can't do my job if I can't get all the facts. That's where you come in."

"I don't follow."

He leaned back into his chair. "Earlier it concerned me that you were snooping around. Now I'm going to encourage it."

I couldn't hide my surprise. He put his hand up.

"But, with the stipulation that you keep me apprised of things you find out. Quite frankly, Mr. Christian, you're an asset to me and to this case."

As he said this, thoughts tumbled over each other in my head. Should I tell him about Sam Allison? About DikMe? About my profiles of the three victims? About the possibility the killer is an older man? About anything? In the end, I decided to hold my cards close to my chest. After all, I was committing fraud on DikMe by creating a fake persona.

"Thank you, Lieutenant. I'm going to the memorial services for Sergio this afternoon."

He raised an eyebrow.

"His sister contacted me a while ago," I said. "I'll talk to her some more after the ceremony. I'll let you know if I find anything else out." I stood to leave.

"One more thing," he said. "How'd you find out that Robert Márquez was gay?"

I shrugged. "I talked to his friends."

He pulled one side of his lip up into a smile and shook his head. "Of course you did. And you already had found out about Sergio, so you must've asked the right questions."

"I guess so." I grabbed the door handle but stopped and turned. "One question for you, Lieutenant."

He arched his brow and tilted his head slightly.

"That day at Starbucks I told you Sergio's death might be a hate crime."

"I remember."

"Now there are three murders. All Latino. All gay. What are your thoughts on that matter?"

He sighed. "It's a troubling pattern."

Okay, he wanted to hold his cards close to his chest, too. "Yes. It is troubling," I said. "Well, have a good day."

He nodded in return and I left.

As I headed home, my phone chirped an alert. At the red stoplight by Starbucks, I picked it up and looked. Ah, progress. It was from "DaddyWantsBoys."

CHAPTER 31

I HAD A healthy fear of texting and driving, so I waited until I got home to see what "DaddyWantsBoys" was up to. I walked into the kitchen. As usual, my house was quiet except for the hum of the refrigerator and the occasional honk of geese as they landed in the pond behind. The blinds above the sink let filtered light slip in. I perched on a stool at the counter bar and tapped on his profile. There was no photo, just a blank silhouette. He was fifty, white, top, and said he was looking for younger guys, eighteen to twenty-five. Latino was a plus. He certainly fit the profile. I texted.

> What r u looking for?

I waited, but not long.

> NSA. Younger guys.

Of course. No strings attached. I asked for a face pic. His reply was swift.

> DL. Don't do face pics
> here.

I pinched my lips. What was with these down-low guys? I wondered if he was married. I thumbed a reply.

> Meet first? Starbucks?

A few seconds ticked off. I heard the signal from DikMe that he had typed a response.

Sure. Which one?

Mañana.

Oh. I thought you were
closer. I'm in Modesto.
Sorry.

I looked at the distance on his profile. Sure enough. Fifty-seven miles.

"Shit!"

I should have looked from the beginning. I replied "okay" and then set my phone down. If José was right about the comfort zone, this guy was way too far away. Plus, he was too quick to agree to meet in a place like a Starbucks. The killer had to be highly secretive and unwilling to be seen in public with his victims.

Damn! A dead end on this one!

My stomach felt empty, so I glanced at the oven clock. It was just past noon. I decided to make a sandwich and watch some TV. Later I would get ready and head to the memorial service for Sergio. Perhaps new information would turn up there. But then, I wasn't going to an afternoon tea party to gossip. I was going to pay my respects to the family and honor a young man cut down before his life had barely begun.

• • •

I ARRIVED AT the church fifteen minutes before the ceremony started. From the looks of the parking lot and street, not a lot of people were there. When I entered, Julie greeted me in the vestibule.

"Thank you for coming," she said. She hugged me. "I was hoping you could talk to my parents, you know, about what we talked about at Starbucks."

"Julie, I'm not sure this is the time and place for that."

She bit her lower lip and nodded. "You're probably right. At least they can meet you and then maybe you can come over sometime."

She escorted me inside and I saw about thirty people seated. The lighting was low, somber almost, and a soft din of voices filled the air. It was a simple church, with white painted bricks and not much else. Votive candles flickered on either side of the church to highlight the stations of the cross. Up on the dais, to the left of the altar, was a large framed icon of the Virgin of Guadalupe, and above the altar hung a crucified Jesus. Flowers decorated the area, and I caught the scent of roses and carnations. An easel held a poster- size photo of Sergio. His smile beamed out at the audience and I was glad for the image. I wanted to remember him like that and not the way I'd found him the previous week.

Julie walked me up to the front pew where her parents sat along with the little boy I'd seen at their house before, Julie's younger brother. Their faces were drawn, and her father's hand was clasped around her mother's.

"Mamá. Papá. This is Will. I invited him. He's...he's, well, he's a friend."

"I remember him," her mother said. She leaned over and whispered into her husband's ear.

He immediately stood up. "You're the one who found our boy." He reached out for my hand, enveloping it with both of his.

"I'm so, so sorry for your loss," I said.

"Thank you."

I turned and gestured toward the photo. "He looks so happy in that picture. He was handsome."

"Yes, yes, he was," Mrs. Ramírez said with one of those forced smiles people use to mask their grief.

An awkward silence hung between us as we all looked at each other, no one talking.

"Well, I'll go find a seat now," I finally said.

Mr. Ramírez pointed. "Oh, please sit with us."

"I couldn't. This is for family. I'll be fine back there."

I took my leave and walked to the first empty pew and sat near the nave. Julie sat next to her parents. She leaned in and whispered something to them. Her father turned to look at me, his eyes narrowing. He turned back to his wife and said something. She shook her head. He stood and she reached for him, pulling on his arm to restrain him, but he shook her off. He pulled on his jacket and marched red-faced down the nave to where I was seated.

"You are not welcome here," he said.

"Excuse me?"

"My daughter told me what you are. Are you the man who turned our son into a *puto*?"

I stood. "Sir, I never knew Sergio."

He leaned toward me and glared.

"Look," I said, "I am here to pay my respects. I found your son out in that field and I will never forget that for the rest of my life. I feel connected."

"No!" His face reddened. "It was some man like you who seduced my son. Made him something he wasn't!"

Julie appeared at his side and gently slid her hands around his upper arm.

"Papá. It's okay. He's a really good man. A very decent man. And no one turned Sergio into anything. Sergio was just who he was. And he loved you, Papá. He loved you very much. I think Will can help you understand."

"Señor," I said, "I know you're grieving. And I know you're angry. But listen to your daughter. Remember your son as the loving human being I'm sure he was."

Mr. Ramírez's lip quivered. "I wish, I wish he would have told me. I loved him, too. Now, now it's too late!" He covered his face with his hands. "*Ay, Dios! ¡Lo extraño tanto!*"

"I'm sure you do miss him." I reached for his shoulder. He looked up, red-eyed, his cheeks slick with tears.

"I, I should have known. Been a better father."

I held his gaze. "You were a wonderful father. Just like you're a wonderful father to Julie."

He pulled his jacket sleeve across his eyes to wipe away tears. "He, he had his whole life ahead of him. Who would do this to my boy?"

I spoke in Spanish. "*No sé, pero le juro que lo voy a averiguar.*" I don't know. But I swear to you I will find out.

Julie wrapped her arms around her dad and the three of us stood there. Amid the sobs of Mr. Ramírez, I let my focus shift to the smiling Sergio in the photo.

That's how I want to remember you.

And yes, I will find out who killed you.

CHAPTER 32

JOSÉ AND I had decided to meet at The Fairway for drinks, and when he found me on the patio, I already had a Chardonnay in front of me. I sat, slumped in my chair, staring out at the golf course. It was relatively quiet, hardly a breeze as the palm trees stood tall and still. Even the handful of geese that liked to flock on the driving green were quiet, most of them lying down with tucked heads. The only sound was the occasional whack of a golf ball, each one causing me to cringe as the vision of Sergio's smashed head appeared before me.

"Couldn't wait for me, eh?" José said as he approached.

I turned to face him. "Sorry, it's been one of those days."

He leaned in and kissed me. Mandy appeared with another glass of wine.

"I saw you round the corner. Here you go, handsome." She placed the drink on a cocktail napkin and asked her usual question about eats.

"Not right now," I answered. "Maybe next round."

She left and José said, "So why such a long face? Didn't it go well with the lieutenant this morning?"

"That's not it. I mean, well, it went fine with him." I summarized our conversation.

"So he wants your help?"

"That's basically what he said. Actually, he said, and I quote, 'Quite frankly, Mr. Christian, you are an asset to me and this case.'"

José chuckled. "You have a memory like an elephant. I'm going to have to be careful what I do and say around you. It may come back to haunt me."

That comment forced a smile from me. "Too late."

I then told him about what was really bugging me: the memorial service, my encounter with Sergio's dad, the promise that I'd made.

"You should have seen him, José. He was devastated. He fell apart in front of me."

"Sweetie, you're putting too much on yourself."

I looked at him with moistened eyes. "And the photo of Sergio. Young, handsome, and, oh, that smile! So much life ahead of him." I shook my head. "I can't let this go."

I didn't have to say anything else, didn't have to mention memories of Carlos.

José reached for my hands and grasped them gently. "I'm here to help."

I nodded. "Thanks." I wiped away a tear.

"Let's talk about something else," he said. "I know."

"What?" I said, reaching for my glass.

"When this is all over, how about we take a little trip? Maybe to the coast. You like Carmel?"

"Of course I do," I said, brushing away another tear.

He smiled broadly. "Okay. It's a deal."

He lifted his glass and we toasted to a future getaway. A warm sensation coursed through me, sweeping away my earlier thoughts. If one thing good was coming of all this murder business, it was my relationship with José.

• • •

I WOKE UP the next day as José planted a soft kiss on my lips.

My eyes fluttered open and soft light peeked through the slats of the blinds. I rubbed my eyes and smiled.

"You know," I said, "this is ridiculous, always having to go home in the morning."

"What are you saying?" He stroked the hair around my forehead.

I propped myself up on an elbow. "Well, sometimes I could stay at your place. But because you work just down the street, maybe you can keep some things here. That way, you don't have to rush in the morning when you stay."

His finger traced the outline of my mouth. I pretended to nip. He tapped my nose.

"I think that's a great idea," he said. "When?"

"Well, bring some things tonight if you want."

"We'll see. I have to go to Modesto today for a sales manager thing."

He kissed me again and then got out of bed. He dressed and I threw on a robe. Once downstairs, I made us some coffee and toast.

"It just occurred to me," he said. "It's been one week since you discovered Sergio's body."

I stared at my coffee. I hadn't thought of that. Had it only been one week? With three murders and a new relationship, it seemed so much longer.

"And you know what else?" José asked.

I looked up. "What?"

He walked over to me and slipped his arms around me. "It's been almost one week since we met."

"Oh yeah." I draped my arms around his neck. "I'd rather think about that than the other thing."

He pressed his forehead to mine. "Happy week-iversary."

"Happy week-iversary."

He pulled away. "Let's celebrate tonight. I'll pick up some champagne."

He grabbed his car keys on the counter and started for the front door. I followed.

"I'll think of something special for dinner."

We kissed goodbye and I closed the door behind him. So, now he was going to move some things into my house. I could only imagine what my sister would say. I shrugged.

"It's just some clothes," I said out loud. "And besides, you're not getting any younger, Will."

As I headed back to the kitchen, my phone chirped a DikMe alert. I hit the message tab, but it was a nudge and not a text. It came from someone named "TastyDaddy." I looked at the profile. Skimpy and no photo, just that he was a top and was discreet. I looked at the distance marker. No information. I checked my own settings and discovered there was a tab to hide my location. Shit. I closed the app and buried my head in my hands.

I stood and headed for my bedroom. I donned my cycling outfit, made my way to the garage, and checked my bike tires for air. I needed to clear my head, get some adrenaline pumping. Maybe I'd go ahead and do a full twenty miles.

Off of Avenue 28, I slowed down by the field where I'd discovered Sergio's body the week before. I stopped and got off my bike. I approached the area where the buzzards had been feasting. It now looked like the rest of the field, packed dirt with patches of scrub brush and parched grasses dotting the ground. A few tumbleweeds had gathered, like they had come to wither and turn to dust where Sergio had lain. The only indication that something extraordinary had happened was the tattered police tape hanging impotently from the makeshift posts the forensics crew had put up. I closed my eyes and the image of Sergio's vulture-pecked body appeared. My stomach churned. I opened my eyes and shook my head. I took several deep breaths and was trudging back to my bike when something caught my eye. I squatted to get a closer look.

It was a freshly gnawed toothpick.

Lieutenant Reed must have been there before me. Why? What could he have been interested in a week after the murder? A chirp from my phone interrupted these thoughts. I pulled it out from my riding pack. TastyDaddy had left me a message.

Hi. Whatcha into?

I stared at the text. What was I into? That was a good question. I turned to take one last look at where I'd found Sergio. I sighed and then made my way to my bike. I hopped on and pedaled down Avenue 28, trying to clear my head and enjoy the ride. But TastyDaddy's seemingly simple question was at the forefront of my thoughts.

Whatcha into?

No, I thought, *What are you into?*

● ● ●

I've been asked a number of times if I feel remorse. Psych eval-uators. Lawyers. The judge. Do you know what remorse is? Of course you do. Here's the thing. You have to believe you did some-thing wrong to feel remorse, to feel regret. Does the lioness bring-ing down the zebra feel regret? Does the hunter scoping the deer feel regret? Does the soldier taking out the enemy feel regret? Like I said before, I did what I did out of obligation. Why would I feel remorse?

[pauses]

The families of those guys were at my trial. I could feel their eyes on me the whole time. Once, when I stood up to be taken out for a recess, I glanced at the father of that first kid. He was easy to recog-nize. He looked at me as they turned me around to put the hand-cuffs back on. His face was drawn, expressionless. Like he wasn't sure how to feel toward me. I did what I thought I should do at the time. I smiled at him. His expression changed as he narrowed his eyes. Then he called out to me. I don't speak Spanish, so I asked one of the guards what he'd said.

"He said, 'I loved my son.'"

As they hauled me out of the courtroom, I wondered why he'd said that. Was that supposed to make me feel something? Finally feel that remorse that so many people asked me about?

[pauses]

It didn't.

● ● ●

CHAPTER 33

A FTER MY BIKE ride, I cleaned up and settled in to work. I had one editing deadline and it didn't take long. After two hours I stood, stretched, and decided to head to Starbucks for a midmorning coffee.

I texted Laura, but she couldn't meet me, so I went alone. When I entered, the place was filled with post-breakfast coffee drinkers, so the din of voices was greater than usual. Gigi, one of the baristas, was working the counter.

"You getting your usual?" she asked.

"Never change." I looked around. "Is Bobby here today?"

"He was supposed to do an eight-to-four but didn't come in today," she said, punching info into the screen in front of her.

"I hope he's okay."

"We're kind of worried. You know, with everything going on."

I wrinkled my brow. "What do you mean?"

"He didn't call or anything. He just didn't show up."

My stomach tightened. I looked at my phone. 10:30. "Has he ever done that before?"

"Not that I know of. That's $3.89."

"I'm assuming you called his family." I scanned my phone app to pay.

"He lives with a roommate in Madera. His parents moved back to Los Banos. Marta called them."

"And?"

"They don't know where he is. He hasn't spoken to them for almost a week."

"And his roommate?"

She shrugged.

I trudged over to the pickup counter, resting my butt against the side of the condiment bar. I swallowed hard as my imagination took over. Could Bobby be victim number four? I didn't know if he was gay or not, although I had my hunch. He was Latino, that was sure. All of a sudden, I lost my taste for coffee. I called out to Gigi.

"Put a hold on my latte. I'll be back later."

I dashed outside and dialed Reed. He picked up after two rings.

"Reed here."

"Lieutenant, I'm concerned about a missing person. Somebody didn't show up for work today at Starbucks." I quickly recounted what I knew.

"Unless he was abducted in the parking lot at Starbucks, Mr. Christian, it's not my jurisdiction. He lives in Madera."

"Well, don't you know anyone down there?" My tone was probably sharper than it should have been. All I could think of was whether or not Bobby was in trouble. Or worse, dead. I ran my hand through my hair. "Can't you call and have them check?"

A few seconds slid by before Reed answered. "I do know the guys down there. I can call, but I can't guarantee anything."

I bit my lip. Of course he couldn't guarantee anything. Still, trying something was better than nothing.

"Thank you, Lieutenant."

I hung up and plopped onto an outside chair. I buried

my face in my hands. The door swung open and someone approached.

"Will, are you okay?" Gigi asked. "You ran out like you'd gotten bad news or something."

I looked up and eked out a smile. "I'm okay. Sorry. I just remembered I needed to call someone."

"Do you still want your coffee?"

I stood. "No. I'll get it next time."

She nodded, her eyebrows slightly drawn together. I could tell I hadn't convinced her nothing was wrong. Then she turned and went back inside. I hurried to my car.

Where was Bobby?

• • •

AT HOME I couldn't concentrate. Bobby was missing and if he was gay, he fit the profile of a potential new victim. I paced in my kitchen, unsure of what to do. I remembered when I'd first met him at Starbucks. He told me he was working his way through college and that he felt like his life was backward.

"What do you mean?" I'd asked.

"I'm working almost full time and going to school part time. It should be the other way around. At this rate, I'll be thirty when I graduate."

That made me laugh, and I took an immediate liking to him. In the end, he did finish college at the age of twenty-three, just the year prior. He was contemplating what to do next and took the assistant manager position at Starbucks in the interim.

What could I do? Nothing but sit and wait. But that was not my forte. Plopping down at my computer and throwing myself into work was out of the question. I needed something physical to do. It wasn't even noon. I looked around my kitchen.

"Why not?" I said to no one. "When the going gets tough, the tough get cleaning."

I fetched my Swiffer, a bucket, some cleaning towels, and my bottle of Fabuloso. I retrieved the rubber gloves from under the sink.

"Okay, floor. You're it."

CHAPTER 34

S WIFFERING THE TILES and then getting on my hands and knees to clean like my grandmother was just the tonic I needed. To help, I put on a playlist of my favorite disco music and let the bump, bump, bump of each song pulse through my body. I went over the floor twice. With each wipe, with each wringing of the towel, the tension of waiting to find out about Bobby lessened. When I finished, my back ached from the position I'd been in. My knees were in worse shape. Nothing like physical labor and the pains it causes to take your mind off other things—that and Donna Summer along with Gloria Gaynor, Cheryl Lynn, and a cast of late-1970s divas.

For lunch I threw together a tuna fish sandwich, my go-to on busy days. And on warm days like this, I limited stove-top cooking to once a day. I perched on a stool and between bites checked my phone to see if I'd missed any new messages from TastyDaddy. Nada. I sighed, then stood and took my plate to the sink to rinse it. As I placed it in the dishwasher, my phone rang. I hurried over to the counter.

"Hello."

"Reed here."

I grabbed for a stool and lowered myself onto it. "Hi, Lieutenant. Any news?"

"Yep."

I swallowed hard as my body tensed.

"Your friend is fine. They just picked him up in Kings Canyon. He'd gone hiking the day before with his roommate."

I sighed with relief. Bobby was alive.

Reed continued. "It was a whim. They'd gotten up in the morning and decided to head for the mountains. Both kids lost their phones while trying to take selfies at an overlook. That's why no one heard from them. Not that cell coverage is particularly good up there. On top of that, by the time they got back to their car, it was dark. Then, the damned thing wouldn't start. They spent the night in the vehicle and didn't wake up until this morning. Then it was an hour hike down to the station where the park ranger called for road assistance for them."

"How'd you find all this out?"

"Madera police have a dispatch connect with the county sheriff who has a connect with the park."

In the background, I could hear someone knock on his door. He asked me to hold on. After a few seconds, he returned.

"Sorry. I had to sign some paperwork."

"Of course. Do you know if his parents have been notified? His work?"

"Madera took care of that."

"That's great. I know his coworkers were worried. Lieutenant, I appreciate the call."

There was a pause before Reed spoke. "Is this Bobby kid special to you?"

"Not sure what you mean."

"I mean, well, do the two of you have history?"

I bristled, and had Reed been present he would have seen

my eyes narrow and my lips purse. He would also have seen that I was giving him the middle finger.

"Lieutenant, I prefer men my own age. I'm not the daddy type and I don't go picking up twentysomethings. I just know him from his work, and he's a good kid."

Again, one of those pauses. "All right, then. If you don't need anything else, I need to go."

He hung up, and although I had been awash with relief, Reed's last question turned me sour. What the hell did he think guys my age did? Run around and look for younger men? Then, I thought of Sergio and Robert.

Yes, some older guys did do that. Like those I'd been investigating on DikMe. With the hubbub about Bobby, I'd put that stuff out of my thoughts. I grabbed my phone, reread TastyDaddy's message, and examined his profile.

DL top looking for 21-30.
No fems, masc only.
Latino+++

Of course, there was no photo. Well, not of his face, anyway. Just an image of a baseball cap. I'd noticed that lots of guys on DikMe used objects such as cars, mugs of beer, weight benches—just about anything instead of a face or body photo. One profile from a twenty-one-year-old displayed an image of Mickey Mouse. When I saw that, I laughed.

"Disney-loving twink," I'd muttered. Turning my attention back to TastyDaddy, I thumbed a message.

Send pic

The green dot on the screen indicated he was online at the time, and sure enough, a response came back fast.

DL so no face pics. You?

I replied as fast as I could.

Same

Almost in an instant, I got a photo alert from him. I tapped. There was his penis, of course. I sighed. Okay, yeah, it was impressive but not what I was interested in. I texted a response.

Nice. But would still like
face pic

Later

The green dot went blank, meaning he'd gone offline. I tossed my phone onto the counter and ran my hand through my hair.

Well, at least no one had gotten Bobby.

CHAPTER 35

I HEARD THE motor of the ice maker in my freezer kick in, dumping a load of cubes into the internal bucket. I stood, grabbed a glass from a cupboard, and dispensed some ice. I added water and took a sip. Bobby was okay, and that was great news. I'd see him soon at Starbucks again, and that made me smile.

"See, Will? You worried for nothing," I said out loud.

Relief was replaced by a mixture of irritation and impatience as I thought about TastyDaddy's elusive nature. He was probably married, like Sam Allison. Why else would he need to hide? But if he was the killer, he'd have other reasons to hide, wouldn't he? I placed my drink on the counter and picked up my phone to look at TastyDaddy's message one more time. This guy was the exact profile I was expecting, but I didn't know if he was local or not. As José had said, most murderers work within a comfort zone—close to home. I did a filtered search on DikMe, looking for DL tops. A whole page showed up, but none seemed to be local and many had turned off their distance indicators. I inhaled a deep breath then released it. I'd just have to wait to see how I might get more information out of TastyDaddy.

A regular text alert pulled me back to my phone. It was José.

Gonna be a few minutes
late today.

Oh shit. I'd forgotten I was going to make something special for dinner. I texted a reply.

No problem. See you when
you get here. Kiss.

Kiss to you

I plopped myself onto a stool.

"Okay," I said out loud, "what's on the menu for tonight?"

As I sketched out a meal, Bobby, DikMe, and everything else from the morning receded into the background.

• • •

José greeted me with flowers, champagne, and a big kiss. He also pulled a small carry-on behind him.

"I know what's in there," I said, grabbing the handle and pulling the little suitcase over to the side.

"Just a few things." He winked. Then he turned and took in a lungful of air. "Mmm. Smells good. But I can't put my finger on that aroma."

"It's saffron." I led him by the hand into the kitchen. "I'm making a chicken paella."

"Ooooh." He hurried over to the stove to get a closer whiff. "It really does smell delicious."

"Thanks. It'll be ready in about thirty minutes."

I handed him the champagne to uncork along with two flutes while I fetched a vase and arranged the flowers in some water. I bent over and took in the sweet smell of yellow roses. I set them on the middle of the kitchen table, which I'd already fixed up with a tablecloth, place settings, and glasses for wine. We stood at the kitchen counter and toasted.

"I'd like to say something," he said.

"Okay."

"I've never fallen so quickly for someone. I know it's been a pretty short time but, Will, you have won my heart. I can't imagine being with anyone but you."

His eyes searched mine for a reaction. I smiled.

"I feel the same way. I've had an emptiness inside me for some time now. I didn't expect at this stage in my life to ever have it filled. But you have."

We kissed and I felt the heat rise in me. "Let's not get carried away before dinner. After all, I don't want to ruin your appetite."

I winked and went to check on the paella. I rotated the flat pan so that the heat would distribute as evenly as possible.

José sat on one of the stools. "Any developments?"

I laughed. "Just wait." I recounted the episode with Bobby.

"At least that turned out okay," José said.

"It did. And then, this guy named TastyDaddy has been in touch. Sounds like a candidate."

José tilted his head down as he looked at me, and I imagined him peering over reading glasses, like a scolding teacher.

"Sweetie, he's not running for president. He's a potential murderer."

"I know, I know," I said as I walked over and draped my arms around his shoulders. "As I promised, I'm not doing anything without you." I kissed him on the forehead. "Okay. How about some light nibbles to go with our champagne? Mediterranean-style because of the paella."

I reached into the fridge and produced an array of Manzanilla and kalamata olives I had prepared earlier.

"My favorite!" José almost squealed as he popped a purple olive into his mouth. "Mmm. Mmm. Mmm."

I also retrieved baguette slices from the toaster oven. I had lightly browned them with olive oil, a dash of salt, and a hint of freshly crushed garlic. José eagerly reached for one of those, then washed it down with a sip of champagne.

"I'm going to have to marry you just for your cooking," he said.

I moved in close to him and purred. "Well, when this murder business is all over, I'll be ready for a proposal."

We kissed again and I caught the hint of garlic on his tongue and lips.

"You taste good." I pulled away and walked over to the stove. I turned the pan several times again. "So how was your training day?"

"You know, nothing exciting. We tossed around some new ideas for the region. Oh, and we're forming intramural softball teams for Mañana and Madera. We start practice tomorrow."

"Right up your alley."

"You should come watch," José added. "It'll be after work, around five fifteen at the Little League baseball park here in town."

"Sounds like fun." I sidled up next to him. "I get to see you in action, swinging your bat. And this time it won't be in a parking lot behind Sam Allison."

"Ha-ha." He popped another olive into his mouth. "Hey, have you heard from Sam?

I sipped on my champagne and shook my head. "I did see his profile online, though. He hasn't deleted it."

"My guess is he will, eventually." Another olive flew into José's mouth. "So, what else do you know about this Tasty-Daddy guy?"

"Only that he's a top and fifty years old." I reached for an olive and grimaced as I bit into it. "Oooh. Part of a pit." I spit it into a paper napkin. "He won't share a face pic, though."

José pulled one side of his lip up in a smirk. "That's DL for you."

I kissed him. "Thank you for being so understanding about all of this."

"Hey," he said, pinching an olive and then bringing it to his lips, "that's what boyfriends are for."

And for a split second I thought about Sergio and whether or not he'd ever had a boyfriend. If he had been into older guys, had it all been just about sex? Or had he yearned for something romantic, something permanent? Maybe he'd fallen for some older guy he'd hooked up with, just like I'd said to Julie. If he had been desperate enough, he would have mistaken the guy's actions for something they weren't. I pushed away the thoughts and went to the stove to turn off the heat under the paella to let it rest for ten minutes. I turned to look at José.

I had certainly fallen for someone quickly. Had I found something permanent?

CHAPTER 36

T HE NEXT MORNING José left for work and I sat at my computer as usual. I slipped in a trip to the gym. The place was filled with the noise of grunts and dropping barbells, each thud reverberating in my head. I couldn't help but think of what it must be like to receive a massive blow to the head. Would you hear a crack? Would the world spin, lights flash in front of you? And then I thought of the pain. I closed my eyes for a moment, hearing the overhead fans whir in place as they pushed the rank smell of sweat throughout the facility. When I opened my eyes, Lanny was looking at me.

He let go of a cable, sending the weights to their resting position with a loud clank. I tensed. He mopped his brow with the back of his hand and jutted his chin at me.

"You don't look very happy."

"It's going to take a long time for me not to think about the body I discovered." I told him about attending the memorial service.

"Well," he said, "that was nice of you to show up. You're a good guy."

"Thanks." I forced a smile.

"Any more news?"

I knew what his question really was: whether I had found any other suspects in my little side investigation.

"None to relate."

We fist-bumped and I went over to the stacks of cubicles

by the water fountain to put my stuff away and start my work-out.

Later, at home, I sat at my desk staring at my notes about the victims. My thoughts drifted toward TastyDaddy. I had hoped to hear from him again, but I hadn't. I tried to conjure an image, what he might look like, act like. Was he tall? Good looking? Piercing eyes? Or was he overweight and grayed to the point of almost having white hair—his eyes a washed-out blue, maybe bloodshot from too much drinking? Killers came in all types and sizes, right? But I couldn't imagine the smiling Sergio I'd seen in his memorial photo hooking up with someone who looked like a diabetic grandpa.

My phone rang. It was my sister. I didn't feel like talking to anyone right then, so I let it go to voicemail. I'd call her later. Instead, I opened up DikMe and shot a text to TastyDaddy, even though he wasn't online.

You disappeared. Hope you come back.

• • •

I HAD AGREED to meet José at the Little League park after five, where a number of the employees from Save Mart would gather for their first softball practice. The park was across from the city hall and sported three playing fields for the different divisions of Little League. Surrounded by high chain-link fencing and gates that remained locked when the fields weren't in use, it almost resembled a prison exercise yard. Like a lot of public spaces in our town, it suffered from drought and lack of care, with the grass being half weeds and the base-lines rutted and in need of repair. Rust nibbled at the fencing, and the black lettering on signs stating the park rules had been sun bleached to dull gray.

When I arrived, José and his group were already gathered at the gate waiting for a Little League group to exit. I spied Lieutenant Reed and his cousin Tim gathering up equipment. I sauntered over to José.

"Did you see who's here?" I asked.

He nodded and then leaned in for a kiss. "I got here ten minutes ago and saw him and his cousin batting flies to the outfield and grounders to the infield. Looks like a good coach."

Kenny, a lanky late-twenties colleague from Save Mart, whistled to him. "Come on, Loverboy. Time to take the field."

I accompanied my boyfriend to the gate. Reed and his cousin stopped to shake his hand.

"José, right?" Reed said.

"Yes. Good memory."

"Hope you brought lots of ice water," Tim said, carrying a sack of baseball bats. "It's hot as hell on the field." He pointed to the group of youngsters who were eagerly gulping Gatorade and sucking on popsicles that the two coaches must have brought for them.

José grinned. "Yep. Well, if you'll excuse me." He pushed through the gate and jogged onto the field.

Reed turned to me. "Nice to see you again, Mr. Christian. Are you playing with them?"

I shook my head. "No. I'm the dutiful partner. You know, the behind-the-scenes support who bakes cookies, makes lemonade, and comes out to cheer them on." I smiled like a Stepford Wife.

We all turned when we heard José call out to everyone.

"Okay! Let's hustle! I'm going to hit some flies out there!"

He stood at home plate, tossed a ball in the air, and with a solid wallop sent it deep into center field.

"Your boyfriend has a good swing," Reed said. "Better not get him angry. Imagine what that bat would do to you."

"José's not the violent type."

Reed rubbed his chin. "How long have you known him?"

"Long enough."

He shot a glance at Tim and then looked back at me. "Well, then, I guess you know him." He started to leave but stopped. "And I'm glad your friend from Starbucks is okay."

They headed for Tim's truck, tossed the equipment in the back, climbed inside the cab, and drove off. I stood there, watching them fade into the distance, the lieutenant's question echoing in my head.

How long have you known him?

As the kids wandered off to either walk home or wait on the sidewalk for their parents, I turned and took a seat under the shade of some tall trees. José sent out shouts like "Heads up!" and "Here it comes, left field!" Each time, he tossed, swung, and drove the ball exactly where he wanted it.

But with each swing and the whack of metal bat meeting softball, I flinched, thinking of Sergio. I remembered José had accompanied me on my outing to confront Sam Allison the week prior. He'd grabbed a baseball bat from inside his car and snuck around behind Sam. Why would he keep a baseball bat in his car? He hadn't been on any team prior to forming this one with Save Mart, had he? At least, I didn't think so. Did he carry it around for protection? Some people slept with bats by their beds, just in case. Maybe he kept one in his car. Still, that seemed odd to me.

Imagine what that bat would do to you.

"Okay! Let's practice some grounders!"

José began hitting the ball so it would go low and roll between bases. Players rotated positions so all could get practice with different kinds of hits. After about forty minutes, José called for a water break and rest. Dripped in sweat, people scrambled for the Igloo chest that Kenny had brought, rubbing icy-cold water bottles against their heads and necks before chugging down a few good gulps. José walked over to me, swigging on a bottle of water.

"You have a nice spot in the shade." He furrowed his brow. "Why the serious look?"

"I have a serious look?"

He tilted his head and pulled the side of his mouth up into a smirk, the baseball bat resting on his shoulder.

"I was just thinking about Sergio," I said.

"What about him?"

I shook my head. "Let's talk about it later." I stood. "How about I go home, make sure some nice wine is chilled, think about dinner, and just wait for you."

He faked a frown. "Ahhh. You're bored."

"No, honey, I'm not. Honestly."

That was the truth. I wasn't bored. But I didn't want to say that I was trying desperately not to stare at the bat he was carrying.

"The memorial service the other day got to me, that's all. I've been thinking about his dad and how he broke down."

My first lie to my boyfriend.

"Okay, sweetie. I'll see you later."

He jogged back to the ice chest and clapped his hands together, telling everyone it was time to do a little more work.

"Another forty-five minutes and it'll be time for you all to head home to those nice cold beers," he said.

The group chuckled and trudged back onto the field. He turned and blew a kiss. I blew one back. As I walked to my car, the image of him sneaking up behind Sam Allison with a baseball bat haunted my thoughts. What would he have done to Sam if he'd had the chance?

"Damn!" I said out loud. "You can't be thinking these things. And damn you, Lieutenant Reed, for putting these thoughts in my head!"

A loud caw caught my attention and I looked up. A crow sat perched on the aging fence, its striated talons gripping the wired mesh. It twisted its black head toward me, tilting slightly to signal curiosity. Or was it trying to tell me something? Then it cawed once more before taking flight with a flap of its wings. From behind me, the whack of bat against ball made me shudder, and suddenly a vision of buzzards pecking on Sergio's body hung before me.

Man, I needed a drink.

CHAPTER 37

WHEN JOSÉ ARRIVED, a sweaty T-shirt clung to his chest and back. His face was equally slick with perspiration, and his clothes looked like he'd slid into home plate. He took off dust-covered tennis shoes and placed them neatly next to the door.

"I need a shower," he said after he kissed me.

"You sure do!" I pinched my nose in pretense.

He guffawed and hustled up the stairs. At the landing he turned and said, "I'll be quick. Have the wine ready!"

Within seconds I heard the glass door open and close, then the small storm of shower water. I entered the kitchen and poured myself a glass of wine, mulling over my suspicious thoughts from earlier. How could I have so easily gone from marveling about our relationship to wondering if José would yield a bat to injure someone—or worse, kill them? Had Reed planted that seed in my head on purpose? But why would he have done that?

Then I remembered what José had said about his former boyfriend in San Jose. Was infidelity the only issue in that relationship? Was there something that José hadn't told me? I heard the hair dryer upstairs, and within minutes he bounded down the stairs and into the kitchen.

"You sure have a big house for one small guy," he said, smiling. "I wonder how many steps you get a day going from one room to another."

"Plenty. Why do you think my ass looks so good?"

I had to make light of the situation, had to get my mind out of the place where it had wandered. Silence settled on us, save for the sound of air pouring forth from the AC vents and the soft whir of the overhead fan as it merry-go-rounded its way above the family room sofa. I had a glass ready for José on the counter and he retrieved the wine from the fridge and poured. He looked at my half-empty glass.

"Top off?"

I nodded and he added a splash. He pulled a stool up next to me.

"So, what's for dinner? I'm starved," he said.

"I bet. All that running around at work, and then some softball afterward. I wonder how many steps *you* got in today."

He leaned in and kissed me on the cheek.

"By the way," I added, reaching into the fridge for a plate of sliced cheeses I'd prepared as nibbles, "you looked pretty good on the field. Why didn't you pursue baseball after high school?"

"I did." He slid a piece of cheese into his mouth. "I had a baseball scholarship for college. But I didn't really want a professional career, so I just used it for the degree. Remember? I told you I did a year of grad school in psychology after that. Why'd you ask?"

"Just wondering. You seemed pretty comfortable with a bat in your hands today."

"Muscle memory." He took a healthy sip of wine. "Change of topic. It's hot and I don't want you to have to cook. Let's order a pizza from The Fairway. I'll run over and pick it up. We can have a salad with it."

"You are one smart guy. What do you want on it?"

We decided on The Works minus the pepperoni and

sausage. Ham was about the only four-legged meat product I could endure, having given up beef years before, and I didn't need all the fat from the sausage and pepperoni. The cheese was enough. I reached for my phone and punched the listing for The Fairway. After two rings, someone picked up.

"It's a great day at The Fairway. This is Mandy." Country music blared in the background.

"Hi, Mandy. It's Will Christian."

"Well, hi, sweetie. What can I do for you?"

"Tonight we're picking up a pizza." I gave her the order, said thanks, and hung up. I turned to José.

"You know brick ovens. Ten minutes."

"I'd better put some shoes on."

He tossed back another sip of wine then went looking for his sandals.

"Anything you need while I'm out?" he asked.

I shook my head and he disappeared out the front door. I gathered items to make the salad. As I rinsed the greens, I thought back to when José first spent the night and realized it was after Robert Márquez had been found. So for at least the first two murders, I had no idea where he had been. He was with me the night before Luis was found. But what did that mean, really? I needed to talk to Lieutenant Reed about estimated times of death. Once I did, I could put together a timeline, make sure José was with me when they suspected Luis had been killed. Only then could I bury these thoughts forever. Or so I hoped.

"Shit!" I said out loud. "Why are you going down this path?"

I grabbed an avocado and as I cut into its wrinkled skin, the knife slipped and bit through my finger.

"Son of a bitch!"

I turned to the sink and ran cold water over the wound. I leaned in to examine it. Just a nick. I pulled out a Band-Aid from a drawer and taped it over the wound.

"See, Reed? You've got me all fucked up now."

I returned to the avocado and sliced it up. I added some walnuts and raisins and then grated some Parmesan cheese into the salad, its nutty and pungent aroma stirring my appetite. I mixed together some balsamic vinegar, olive oil, and a dash of salt. While I was tossing everything together, I started a mantra in my head.

José is not a killer.

José is not a killer.

José is not a killer.

But snaking around this chant was Reed's question, dripping venom around the words.

How long have you known him?

I looked at the oven clock. José would be back soon. I grabbed my phone and reached for Reed's card in a drawer. I punched in his number. He picked up after the third ring.

"Joseph Reed."

"Lieutenant Reed. Will Christian here."

"Mr. Christian. Didn't I just see you a few hours ago?"

"Yes, yes, you did. I have a question for you." I heard a car door slam. I bit my lip. "Will you be in your office tomorrow morning?"

"Unless I get called out, yes."

"Okay. Great. I'll come by as early as I can. Thanks."

I hung up as the front door opened.

"Lucy! I'm home!"

I forced a smile as my boyfriend sauntered into the kitchen with a pizza box grasped between two hands. The aroma of brick-oven dough and a dozen sizzling ingredients immediately filled the air. I should have felt elated, happy at my new-found romance, happy at the large brown eyes that twinkled when they saw me. But as I glanced down at his hands, I didn't see them holding our dinner. I saw them gripping a baseball bat.

I had a restless night while José slept soundly, the slightest of snores accompanying the rhythmic movement of his chest.

One thing I've been asked—and I bet you've wondered, too—is why three murders so quick and then a hiatus. I mean, boom, boom, boom, and then nada. Maybe you think I got worried or decided three was enough. What's that saying? "Bad things come in threes."

[pauses]

That's a myth, you know. I read about that in college. Things don't happen in threes. The human mind likes to project that. I don't remember the word for it but it's a bias we impose as we look for patterns that aren't really there. Some psychologists think it might have to do with religion, you know, the Holy Trinity and the Three Wise Men. Or because threes exist in other areas like the three-act play, and stories like "The Three Little Pigs," "Goldilocks and the Three Bears." Weren't there three witches in Macbeth? *Then there's the superstition about three on a match. Ha! And there were Three Stooges, not two, not four. Who knows? We make up all kinds of things in our minds. Rub-a-dub-dub, three men in a tub. Three, three, three.*

[pauses]

To be honest, I did consider quitting after the third one. Wouldn't it have been great to stop and have three unsolved murders? Let people wonder if it was all over. Did you notice, by the way, there was no outcry from the public? I knew the Latino community was on edge, but they said nothing. If this were a big city like San Jose or Los Angeles they would have picketed the police, community leaders would have had press conferences, with cries about what the police were doing to find the killer. There would have been signs like "Latino Lives Matter!" But this is Mañana. Small-town people don't protest. They don't get up in arms. Instead, they whisper among themselves. You can see them—at the grocery store, at Starbucks, at the Shell station. "I have no idea what's happening in this town." "When you do think they'll catch him?" "Only Mexicans, it looks like." They part ways, telling each other to take care, all the while keeping their eye on the news for any developments. Yep, small towns don't engage in uproar.

[pauses]

So, I did think about stopping and leaving behind a legacy of the "unsolved Mañana murders." Then opportunity knocked again. I thought, why not? Just one more.

• • •

CHAPTER 38

IN THE MORNING, I huffed and puffed my way through a twenty-mile bike routine, showered, and then headed for the police station. It was only nine, and as I pulled into a parking spot across the street, Lieutenant Reed came from around the side of the building where employees kept their vehicles. He waved when he spotted me. I hustled to the front door where he lingered.

"Bright and early," he said.

"Well, I have lots of things on my agenda today, and I wanted to see you as soon as I could." I wiped at the back of my neck, the sweat forming from the intensity of the morning sun.

He pocketed his car keys, took off his sunglasses, and eyed me. "Something wrong?"

"No, no. Shall we go in?"

He greeted the receptionist behind the glass window as we entered, and I followed him down the drab corridor to his office. I had been there several times already, so I stopped taking in the surroundings and concentrated on the piles of folders on his desk. They didn't seem to have grown but they hadn't gotten smaller, either. Some files looked fresh, like he'd barely cracked them open. Others had worn corners and tabs, victims of fingers repeatedly assaulting them in search of whatever information was inside. Or maybe they'd simply been reused. I wondered what was in all those files. Just how much crime was there in Mañana? I pointed to one of the stacks.

"Haven't gone digital yet, eh?"

"I always start with paper. Old school." He tapped the top of one of the stacks with his index finger. "These will get entered into the system as I work on them. Have a seat." He plopped onto his swivel chair and looked at me. "So, what can I do for you, Mr. Christian?"

I leaned forward. "I was hoping you could tell me about the estimated times of death for the three victims."

He narrowed his eyes. "Why would you want to know that?"

"Just curious. Don't forget, I'm writing a piece on these murders."

I searched his expression to see if he was buying my story. Reed must have been one hell of a poker player. I couldn't read anything on his face. He drummed his fingers on the arm of his chair. I found the sound disconcerting, if not irritating.

"The killer is pretty consistent," he finally said. "Each death is estimated between 10:00 p.m. and midnight."

Inwardly, I sighed with relief. José had been with me when Luis was killed.

"Why don't you tell me what you're really after?" Reed said.

I felt heat rise within me. Was I turning red? "I told you. Pure curiosity. You know me. I've been snooping around these murders since I found Sergio's body."

Again, he studied me, saying nothing for a few seconds. Then he said, "There's something else."

I didn't yield. I sat there and looked at him, poker face to poker face. "No, there's not."

He leaned forward. "Mr. Christian, I can't possibly fathom

how knowing the estimated times of death is relevant to anything you write. Care to try again?"

I held his gaze but knew in the end he would win. "Okay," I said as I shifted in my seat. "You unnerved me yesterday when you commented on José's swing."

Reed said nothing as he continued to look at me, those blue-gray eyes like small reflectors, keeping me from seeing what was inside. *Christ! Was he like this with his family?*

"Well," I continued, "it made me realize that in reality I don't know him all that well. We've only been dating for over a week."

He pulled one side of his lip up into a sly smile. "I see. And now you wonder where he was at the probable times of the murders."

"Sort of. Well, yes."

I looked past his shoulder to the certificates on his wall, was going to make a comment about them to distract from the discomfort I felt. Guilt had crept in for even having suspicions about José. I looked back at Reed.

He leaned back into his chair, pulled a toothpick from his pocket, and inserted it into his teeth. He began gnawing. "To be honest, Mr. Christian, the thought has crossed my mind about both of you."

I stared.

"I couldn't quite understand why you were so obsessed with these murders. And after all, you did find the first body out in a field that most people would have passed by unaware."

My jaw dropped. "You suspected me?"

Again, that sly smile. "Never rule out anybody in a murder case." He picked up a rubber band and stretched it repeatedly with his fingers. "You see, some killers like to insert themselves into the investigation. Makes them feel even sneakier than they already are. Gives them an extra jolly, as if killing someone wasn't enough. They think they're being clever, cleverer than the police."

"And what do you think now?"

"Oh, clearly you aren't involved. I've studied you. Spoken with you. You just aren't the type."

"And José?"

He shook his head. "Nope. My joke at the ball field yesterday was simply that. A joke. Just trying to make light. But, just in case, don't ever piss him off." He smiled and winked.

I ignored the jest and narrowed my gaze, pausing. "Wait. You didn't just discard us as suspects based on your observations, did you?"

He arched his brow.

"You had us under surveillance. Probably had patrols parked outside The Palms' gated entrance to see if we came and went in the middle of the night. Let me guess, between ten at night and two in the morning." I paused, as it was my turn to eye him. "And let me guess. You've run background checks on us."

Again, he smiled. "You'd make a good detective."

I was unsure how to feel about that. I had no record to speak of. Just a traffic ticket ten years before in Chicago. I guessed José didn't, either. Should I bother to tell my boyfriend later what I'd just found out from Reed? *Hmm.*

The lieutenant stood and tugged on his belt to hoist his pants, giving me the cue our time was up. "As I said, never rule out anybody in a murder case. But you can rest easily knowing that your boyfriend is not on our list."

I stood. "Well, that's a relief." I tried not to sound irritated, but I couldn't help letting my feelings float among the words. I turned to leave and then stopped.

"I don't know about being a good detective, Lieutenant, but I have figured out several things."

"Yes."

"You were a smoker, weren't you?"

"What makes you say that?"

"The toothpicks. You need to satisfy an oral craving. And you fidgeted with the rubber band just now. Your fingers miss holding a cigarette. Telltale signs of an ex-smoker. I've known a number of them."

He grinned broadly. "Very good, Mr. Christian."

"I also know you are deeply troubled by these cases." I leaned forward and placed my hands on his desk as I locked on his gaze. "The other day you went to the site where I found Sergio's body. My guess is you stood there and contemplated the scene, wondering when you would break this case, hoping to get some inspiration."

"And how do you know that?"

I pointed to the toothpick in his mouth. "Be careful where you drop those. You're like Hansel and Gretel leaving crumbs behind." It was my turn to smile. I bid him good day and left.

I stepped out into the bright sunshine of a rapidly heating Central California summer day. I slipped on my sunglasses and bounded toward my car, a wide grin spreading on my face. I was happy at what I'd learned and was eager to see José.

On the way home, I pulled into the Starbucks on an impulse. I dashed in, and sure enough, Bobby was back at the counter.

"You gave some of us a scare yesterday," I said.

Bobby grinned. "Yeah. Stupid me. It would all have been okay if I hadn't dropped my cell phone. It's at the bottom of a mountain somewhere. Got a new one yesterday afternoon." He held it up.

"I'm just glad you're okay."

"You want your usual?"

I shook my head. "No. I just wanted to stop in and say hi to you."

He pushed his eyeglasses up on the bridge of his nose. "That's very nice of you."

"And do me a favor," I said as I started to walk away. "Don't do anything stupid."

He furrowed his brow.

"Beware of strangers." I exited, half-chuckling for sounding like my mother.

And I realized that both Sergio and Robert must have heard that a million times from their own parents.

CHAPTER 39

JUST AS I reached my car, a chirp announced an alert from
DikMe. I slid into the driver's seat, started the engine, and
let the cool air of the AC rush over me. I pulled out my phone
and tapped the message center. TastyDaddy had texted.

I'm back. So whatcha into?

Hmmm. I wanted some information first.

You really 50?

The typing signal appeared. Then, chirp!

Yes. Too old?

Not at all. You married?

Make a difference?

Just curious why you're DL.

Yes, I'm married.

Aha! Now we were getting somewhere. My thumbs flew
across the keyboard.

Where do you live?

Gotta go. Later.

Damn! The green dot disappeared and he was offline. He

must have been at work and someone walked in. Or he was at home and his wife had entered the room. Or maybe he didn't want to reveal his location. These DL guys and their secret lives! Why was he being so cagey? Why the little nibbles on DikMe, just to vanish almost as soon as he signed on? Or was I just an impatient amateur who didn't really know what I was doing? I looked at his last message.

> Gotta go. Later.

"Where are you, you stupid fuck?"

I threw my phone onto the passenger's seat and dropped my head to rest on the steering wheel. After a few seconds, I sat up, sighed, and shifted the gear into drive.

I didn't feel like going home. So I headed down Avenue 28 past The Palms and out into the farmland that surrounded Mañana. Soon I was flanked by thousands of acres of almond trees anchored in the dry and dusty terrain of this part of the Central Valley. As I drove I mulled over my strategy, asking myself how I was going to find out where TastyDaddy lived. In my gut I knew he was local, knew that he was fishy, but gut instinct wasn't enough. I needed to bait him somehow, find some way to reveal more about himself. Maybe, instead, I just needed to bite the bullet and set up a face-to-face.

Shit.

I rode the rough asphalt of the country road as I passed a small resevoir on my left, the only interruption in the miles of almond orchards around here. The gates were chained, and I saw a sign saying the reservoir was closed for the season. Huh? A reservoir closed in the summer? But then, it wasn't a hot spot for tourists and boaters, being an equalization site for water needed by farmers. Typical of this part of California.

Soon I approached the intersection of Avenue 28 and Santa Fe Drive, a crisscross of two-laned roads, each of which led to more farmland, more orchards. I looked up toward the east, the Sierras masked by the dust and smog of the valley. I chuckled as I considered the irony. TastyDaddy was masking himself behind his profile, tucked behind the limited information he put out on the app. My phone signaled a message from DikMe. I grabbed for it but was disappointed to find just another nineteen-year-old looking to give blow jobs.

"Go away, little twink."

I sat at the intersection, pondering what to do, where to head. Then it occurred to me that if I turned right, Santa Fe would turn into Road 22. That route led to Valley State Prison. It was an all-male facility, having been converted from a female-only prison back in 2012.

Why was I considering a drive to the prison area? Why did that seem like something to do right then and there? I tapped the steering wheel with my thumbs. Then, without further thought, I turned right and headed south. The road was potholed and felt more like a bumpy amusement park ride than a paved surface for cars. But soon it smoothed out where railroad tracks severed the asphalt, and in just two minutes I was at Avenue 24. The prison was on my right. I turned and made my way to the entrance.

A set of large brick and cut stone signs flanked a driveway wide enough for a semitruck to make a U-turn, and a guard shack and security gate regulated visitors and employees where the driveway funneled into a one-lane passage. I pulled off to the side and looked out over the expanse of buildings. Trees blocked some of the view, but I could make out the tall fence topped with barbed wire and the prisoner barracks that dotted the massive compound like giant Legos. A multistory security turret dominated the grounds, and I knew armed sentries must be perched inside keeping a vigilant eye over the six hundred acres of inmates, guards, and workers.

Behind the fortified fence was a hothouse of convicted drug dealers, rapists, and murderers. I'd read somewhere that Charles Andrew Williams was doing his time at Valley State—fifty years for a school shooting in which he'd killed two classmates and had wounded eleven others. So was Andrew Luster, a great-grandson of Max Factor, the cosmetics king. Luster had been convicted of multiple sexual assaults using a date-rape drug. He, too, was there for a fifty-year sentence.

I snapped a photo of the entrance. I'd post it as the wallpaper on my computer, a reminder of what I wanted for Sergio: justice. I threw my phone on the seat next to me and took one last look at the central turret while I pressed my lips together and squinted my eyes. Just then a shadow crossed the hood of my car. I craned my neck and looked up through the windshield. A buzzard was floating low on the updraft of the rising heat. I sat back and pulled the gearshift into drive.

"Hang on, Charles and Andrew," I said out loud as I pulled away. "I'm going to send you a new friend soon."

CHAPTER 40

JOSÉ WHISTLED AS he sauntered through the front door. I emerged from the kitchen wearing a chef's apron and holding a glass of Chardonnay.

"Someone's in a good mood," I said.

He kissed me and then took in the aroma wafting from the kitchen. "And someone's cooking another great meal. I smell enchilada sauce."

I handed him the wine. "Something like that. It's chicken in my famous five-chile mole. Go change into something comfortable. I have a few things to take care of."

Back in the kitchen, I stirred my sauce, the pungent smell of chiles, garlic, and other spices drifting up from the pan. I pulled the chicken tenders out of the fridge and dusted them with my usual onion powder, salt, and just a dash of cumin. I'd let them get to room temperature and then pan sear them later before adding them to the sauce. José appeared in a fresh polo shirt and shorts.

"I love coming home to you," he said.

"Of course you do," I said with an exaggerated tone. "I'm the bomb."

"Yes, you are," he said as he encircled my waist with his arms.

I turned off the sauce and moved over to the fridge to pour us more wine.

"To my favorite cook," he said, holding up his glass.

"And to my favorite store manager," I said. "Let's go sit outside."

I slid open the patio door and we slipped into the shaded part of the backyard. It was warm, but the overhang was big enough that we were protected from the sun, making the temperature tolerable. I switched on the overhead fan to add a light breeze.

I didn't have much of a yard, given that the rear of my house faced a pond. But I did have a two-part covered patio, large enough that on one side a dining table for six sat with wide armchairs. On the other side was a gas grill, a chaise lounge, and enough space to install an aboveground hot tub for eight people. I loathed such things, believing they were just bubbling cauldrons of people's germs and dead skin cells. So, the area was largely empty save for the Central Valley dust that accumulated everywhere.

José spun an armchair around to face the open water, checked for spiders, and plopped onto the thick cushions. I pulled another chair in front of him.

"Here, honey. Put your feet up."

"Awww. You spoil me."

I sat in a chair next to him. Sunlight bounced off tiny ripples of water, like diamonds pulled upward into the sky. A pair of Canadian geese paddled and honked their way in front of us, their slender necks forming delicate black question marks against the sparkling green-blue of the water.

"You know," José said, reaching for my hand, "geese mate for life." He squeezed gently and then interwove his fingers with mine.

"So do swans. I prefer swans to geese. Much more elegant."

He let his head loll back as he turned to look at me. "Right. Tchaikovsky didn't compose *Geese Lake*."

I chuckled. "I saw Lieutenant Reed today."

"And?"

"Turns out he had us under surveillance, well, probably me more than you. He was suspicious because I'd found the first body." I withheld the information about having our backgrounds checked.

José's face morphed into a scrunch. "Why would that cause him to be suspicious?"

"Well, as he put it, quote, 'Never rule out anybody in a murder case.'"

José sipped on his wine and looked back out on the water. "Guess that makes sense. I suppose you're in the clear now."

I nodded. There was a pause in the conversation as we both watched the geese plunge their heads into the water, tails up. After a few seconds, they righted themselves, shook their heads, and honked.

"Why'd you see Reed today?" José asked.

I hesitated. If I told him I had been interested in estimated times of death, he'd want to know why, and that would take me down a path I didn't want to go down. I couldn't ever tell him that I had questioned whether he was capable of the murders that haunted Mañana.

"Oh," I said, "on my bike ride I stopped by where I found Sergio's body. You know, just to reflect a bit. I found a freshly gnawed toothpick on the ground."

José looked at me, eyebrows arched.

"Reed has a habit of chewing them. Remember how he stuck one in his mouth at the winery when he left?"

"Oh yeah."

"I knew that chewed-up toothpick was his. I was curious as to why he was out there, why he was surveying the scene." God, I felt terrible for lying. Why had I even brought this up?

"What did he say?"

"He said he sometimes does that. Revisits crime scenes to get inspiration, to think."

José nodded and I was glad he accepted my explanation. Yet, something compelled me to ask a question. It was my curiosity that always kept me asking questions and looking for answers—and sometimes got me into trouble.

"Hon, why do you keep a baseball bat in your car?"

He turned to me, swatting at a fly that buzzed near his face. "Huh?"

"That day we went to meet Sam Allison in the parking lot. You had a baseball bat in your car."

"Will, I don't keep one in my car. I took it out of my garage and put it there after you told me to meet you in the parking lot."

He studied me for a minute. "You thought I carried it around for protection?"

I shrugged. "Some people do. I'd prefer that to a gun in your glove compartment."

He removed his feet from the chair and leaned forward as he turned more of this body toward me. "Is there something you want to tell me?"

I stiffened. "No. Why?"

"Are you sure?"

"Yeah. I'm sure."

I took a sip of my wine to let my gaze drift. I looked for the geese, but they must have paddled to some other spot on the lake. When I turned to look at José, he was staring.

"What?" I asked.

After a beat, he settled back into his chair and put his feet back up. "Did Reed say something to you about me?"

"No, of course not."

"So," he said, swirling what was left in his glass, "he didn't mention my criminal record?"

My mouth dropped. "Huh? What record?"

"I was arrested in my late teens. Robbery."

"You, you, what?"

He turned to look me squarely in the eyes, stone-faced. "I was waiting to tell you. A friend and I robbed a liquor store. It's not something I'm proud of."

Something caught in my throat. Why hadn't Reed told me about that if he'd had us checked out? I tried to form a question, but nothing came out. Then José broke into a huge grin.

"Got ya!"

My eyes opened wide. "You shit!" I slapped him playfully on the shoulder.

"Hey!" he said. "Careful. That's my pitching arm."

"Serves you right!" I stood. "I need to go finish dinner."

José reached for my hand to stop me. "Sweetie, I told you before. I would never hurt you. Not in any way." His gaze probed my eyes for understanding.

I smiled, bent forward, and kissed him. "I know that."

"And I would only hurt someone else if they tried to hurt you."

"Yeah. I saw that at Starbucks."

I squeezed his hand and headed for the patio door. I knew his gaze was following me as I entered the kitchen.

And it dawned on me: I could never hide anything from this man.

CHAPTER 41

I HAD JUST seared the chicken and placed the pieces in my sauce when my phone rang. I recognized the number.

"Lieutenant Reed. What can I do for you?"

José had been setting out plates and stopped. He arched one brow.

"Sorry to bother you," Reed said. "I just got called in to the station. My men arrested a man who...well, he's here for lewd behavior, but I think there's more to it."

"And what does this have to do with me?"

"He knows you and wants you to come down and bail him out. I recognized him the minute I saw him. His name is Sam Allison."

Reed had been called out that day at Starbucks when I'd first confronted Sam while he was still MAGA-hat man. Of course he'd recognize him.

"Sam Allison?" My voice rose in pitch.

José pulled his head back and scrunched up his face. He mouthed "Sam Allison?" I nodded and held up a finger for him to hold on.

"He's been arrested and he wants me to come down to the station?" I asked Reed.

José's eyes widened.

"That's right," the lieutenant answered. "I'd call his family but he's insistent about having you come down."

"Well, sure, I guess. Did you say he was arrested for lewd behavior?"

"I can't say any more, Mr. Christian. How soon can you get here?"

"Ten minutes."

I hung up and looked at José. "Did you catch all that?"

He nodded. "I'm going with you."

I turned off the stove burners and moved the pans off of the heat.

"Damn!" I said. "What has that guy gotten himself into?"

And as I grabbed my key fob and headed out the door, I questioned why Sam had asked for me and why we were even going.

• • •

WE HURRIED INTO the police station at just about 6:15. José took one look at the lobby and whistled.

"Boy, is this place depressing," he said with a lowered voice.

"Tell me about it."

"I can only imagine what the holding cells look like."

Reed appeared at the bulletproof reception window.

"Thank you, Mr. Christian." He turned to José. "Nice to see you again, Mr. Torres."

José smiled in return and nodded.

"So what happened?" I asked.

"Well, seems like your friend had his pants down around his ankles and some young man was going to town on him. Normally, we look the other way or just tell them to go home and keep things private. But this happened in a restaurant parking lot and he was seen by a man, a woman, and their ten-year-old son."

I sighed. "Oh, Christ."

"She dialed 911 and, well, Mr. Allison got arrested for committing a lewd act."

"What about the other guy?" José asked.

"Oh, he managed to slip out and hightail it just as my men got there. Your friend couldn't give him up because, according to him, it was an anonymous hookup."

I suppressed a swallow. "Where's Sam?" I asked. "Could I see him?"

A toothpick twitched between Reed's lips. "Only if you're here to bail him out. He's already been booked, fingerprinted, the whole nine yards." He pulled out the toothpick and tossed it into a waste bin.

"Has he called an attorney?"

"Negative. The only person he mentioned was you." He leaned on the counter. "Odd, though. He didn't have your phone number. Lucky for him, I did."

José touched my arm. "Let's talk in private."

Reed gestured toward the seats in the lobby and then retreated to a chair behind a desk in the reception. José pulled me over and sat me down.

"Will, this is really serious." He spoke in hushed tones.

"I know."

"This guy is not your friend. You just met him last week. You want to go out on a limb for him?"

"I don't. But don't you think the least we can do is get him in touch with an attorney? Explain the delicate nature of the situation."

I searched José's eyes to see if what I said resonated with him. I couldn't tell.

"You know," he continued, "last week you wanted to bash the guy. Now you feel sorry for him?"

I shrugged. "The guy's been caught in the worst way. His whole life is about to change, and not for the better. Hey, you were sympathetic last week, remember? How did that script get flipped?"

José twisted his lip and looked down. "Yeah, you're right." He looked at me again. "Do you know any attorneys?"

"Actually, I do."

I pulled out my phone and punched the call button for a friend.

"Jake? Hi, it's Will. I'm at the police station. Somebody I know has been arrested and I think he needs your help. Can you come down here?"

I quickly described the situation and Jake said he could be there in thirty minutes, if not sooner. I hung up.

"Done," I said.

I went to stand but José stopped me.

"Sweetie, don't forget how you know Sam."

"What do you mean?"

"I don't think you want to tell Reed what you've been up to on DikMe."

"Oh shit." I spun in a circle. I'd forgotten that I was engaging in fraudulent activity.

"And another thing. Why was Reed called in for this kind of arrest? Why didn't the officers on duty call you? There's something else, I'm sure."

I mulled for a few seconds. "Okay. I'll be careful."

We stood and approached the reception window. Reed was on the phone. When he saw us, he told whomever he was talking to he needed to go and then he hung up. He sauntered to the window.

"So, what's the verdict?"

"I have an attorney coming to assist," I said. "His name is Jake Williams. He should be here soon."

Reed looked at me then at José. "Sounds like the right thing to do. Take a seat, gentlemen, and let me know when he gets here."

We returned to the hard plastic chairs and plopped down. José put his arm around my shoulder.

"How do you know this Jake guy?"

"He lives in The Palms. I met him at a homeowners' meeting."

"And he does criminal law?"

"Yep. Mostly white-collar stuff, but he should be able to handle this."

As we sat there, I mulled over the situation. I hoped Sam had kept his mouth shut or maybe *I* would need the services of Jake Williams as well.

CHAPTER 42

INTRODUCED JAKE to José as soon as he entered the door. Jake was in his midforties, good-looking with piercing blue eyes, sandy-blond hair, and a square jaw. He kept fit but he wasn't a gym addict, and at six feet he was the perfect specimen of someone you'd want to defend you in front of a judge or jury. He was dressed in khakis and a polo shirt.

"Thanks for coming," I said to him. "I hope this isn't interrupting your dinner."

Just then, José's stomach rumbled.

"Sorry," he said as he put his hand over his midriff.

Jake just smiled. "I should be able to get us out of here within an hour. I already called for bail."

He told us to wait while he went to the reception window. José and I sat down once again and watched as he interacted with Reed. Then the side door opened and an officer ushered Jake inside. We sat in silence for a minute or so until the door opened again and Reed appeared. He approached us and sat next to me.

"Mr. Christian, you almost had an altercation with Mr. Allison last week. How is it that he's now asking for you?"

I cleared my throat. "It's a long story, but the short version is we ran into each other again, and let's just say we had a little chat. It turns out that he's not what he appears to be."

"Are you sure?"

"What do you mean?"

Reed turned in his chair so he could better face me. "I wouldn't normally come down to the station on my off hours for something as routine as some guy getting a blow job."

He paused as he simply looked at me, steely eyed and expressionless as usual. Then it hit me.

"You think he might be involved in the murders?"

José closed his eyes, shook his head, and muttered, "Holy shit."

"What do you think?" Reed continued to study me.

"I'm not sure what my opinion is worth, Lieutenant. But I don't think Sam is the murdering type. He's just a hothead—and a little mixed up about his identity."

Just then an officer opened the door and called to Reed.

He stood. "Excuse me." Then he turned and followed the officer.

I spun in my chair to face José. "What the hell was that?"

José shrugged with his face. "I don't know."

"But we know Sam's not involved, right?"

Nodding, José said, "That's what we concluded."

I sat there, thinking. Sam couldn't be involved. I understood he had problems with his sexuality, but after José and I had chatted with him, I really did believe he wasn't the killer. Just some screwed-up closeted married guy. My thoughts were interrupted when the door opened and Jake appeared.

"All done. Sam will be out in a minute. Given this is a first offense, bail was easy. I'm pretty sure I can get him a minimal fine and community service. No jail time. Judges are more worried about rapists and killers than they are closeted men who get serviced in a parking lot."

I shook Jake's hand. "Thank you. I'm sure Sam appreciates it."

The door opened and Sam appeared. His face was drawn, his eyes empty of expression. He trudged over to us.

"Thank you, Will. Thank you so much."

Jake took care of something at the reception window and then turned to us.

"If you'll excuse me, I have a wife, kids, and dinner waiting for me." He looked at his watch. "Only 7:15. Not too bad." He turned his attention to Sam. "Remember what I told you in there. Do not talk about this to anyone. Do not answer any questions from anyone. You have my card. We'll talk tomorrow."

The two men shook hands and then Jake left. Sam looked at the two of us.

"I really could use a drink."

"Where's your car?" José asked.

"At Farucci's."

Sam had just named a restaurant off the highway that also had a bar. I thought it was a dive, full of farmers and truck drivers who pulled off Highway 99, but I would sit in the restaurant section and have a glass of wine. I looked at José.

"What do you think?"

"I think we need to talk to Sam," he said.

"Come on," I said to Sam. "We'll give you a ride."

We exited and headed for the car across the street. As we stepped off the curb, Sam stopped us.

"I really didn't know who else to contact. I know we're not good friends, but I couldn't let them call my wife."

"Come on," I said. "We can talk at Farucci's."

The restaurant was not far away, tucked behind Starbucks, but for the four minutes it took us to get there, no one spoke.

CHAPTER 43

To say I didn't care much for Farucci's would have been an understatement. In its heyday, it was probably a great place to pull off the highway and have a hamburger or fried chicken. But the décor hadn't changed since it opened and a few of the booths sported duct tape while they waited to be repaired or replaced. Many of the Formica tabletops were chipped at the edges. A long counter with red vinyl–covered stools ran up and down the interior and glass cases behind displayed various pies and desserts. Faux paintings that resembled the old paint-by-number products dotted the paneled walls, and the carpet was frayed at the edges. More importantly, it was in serious need of a deep cleaning.

Only a handful of people were dining so we slid into the cleanest booth we could find, José and I on one side and Sam on the other. A server appeared and offered us menus.

"No thanks," I said. "We're just here to have a drink."

José and I ordered Chardonnays and Sam his usual scotch and soda. We sat in silence until the drinks arrived. Sam hoisted his glass.

"Cheers."

José and I reciprocated, and after a sip I launched into the conversation.

"What the hell were you thinking?"

Sam dropped his head. "I told you before, sometimes the urge is just too great."

"Sam, look at me," José said, his voice soft but firm.

Sam raised his gaze and for a moment I detected a slight glistening in his eyes.

"You know you're in big trouble," José continued, speaking in that same voice. "There's no way you can keep this from your wife now."

Sam looked out the window at the vehicles whizzing by on Highway 99. "I just don't know what I'm going to say."

"Just tell her the truth," José said. "That's all."

Sam turned his attention back to us. "You know what Reed said to me? He asked me if I knew Sergio Ramírez or Robert Márquez. I recognized those names. They were the first two victims last week."

"And?" I urged him to continue.

"I told him I had never heard of them until they made the news." His gaze darted back and forth between José and me. "He showed me photos. Asked if I'd ever seen them. He was fishing to see if I killed them! How the fuck did I get here?" He buried his hands in his face.

"Sam, listen to me," I said.

He wiped away a tear and straightened himself. He downed his drink and then signaled the server for another.

"Let me get one more before you talk," he said.

We waited until his drink arrived. He gulped down a mouthful, and then I spoke.

"You need to get off DikMe." My voice was forceful, authoritative. "If you did nothing wrong, then Reed can't do anything to you."

He nodded.

"And you need to get help. You need a professional who can guide you through this part of your life."

He drew in a deep breath. "I, I know."

"Jake will help you with the legal stuff, but you need a therapist."

"I know some people in Fresno," José said.

Sam bit his lip. "Shit. Fifty fucking years old and we're talking about therapy."

"Yes," José said, "but think of it more as help. You and your wife will need it. Think of her."

José called the server over and asked to borrow her pen.

"Here." He wrote down some names on a paper napkin. "These are two people I know who will be sympathetic to your situation. They are great people. You can look their numbers up."

He handed the napkin to Sam, who read the names and then folded it and stuffed it into his shirt pocket. He sucked down some of his scotch and soda.

"I don't know how to thank you. I really didn't have anyone else who would understand."

He downed the rest of his drink and called for the bill.

"Time to go home and face the music. My wife must be wondering where I am."

We all stood and made our way to the cashier.

"This is on me," Sam said.

He paid and we pushed our way through the double glass doors and out into the waning sunlight. I stopped Sam before we stepped off the front steps and into the parking lot.

"Don't lie to your wife. Tell her the truth. Start now."

"Could I ask for your number?" he asked. "Just in case I need some support before I see about these guys in Fresno."

"Sure. But I'm no substitute for someone professional."

We traded phone numbers and then Sam said goodbye and trudged toward his car.

"I wonder if he'll make it," José said.

"I don't know." My gaze was locked on Sam as he got to his car, opened the door, and then moved into the driver's seat. I turned to José. "One thing is for sure. His life will never be the same now."

• • •

AFTER DINNER, JOSÉ and I snuggled on the sofa to watch a rerun of *The Golden Girls*. Rose had just brought home a piano-playing chicken, one that plucked out "Old McDonald" with its beak and talons. My phone pinged an incoming text.

"It's from Sam," I said to José.

> Talked to the wife. She cried, said she suspected something. She's in the bedroom by herself. Not sure what to do.

I thumbed a reply.

> Go to her. Put your arm around her and tell her you love her. Tell her you both will get through this. Tell her you have the names of some people to contact.

"That's a great response," José said.

"Well, if she suspected something, then she's not in as much shock as she could be. At least she didn't go after him with a knife."

"Maybe things will be okay for him in the long run."

José put his arm around me and pulled me in. "Things always work out the way they're supposed to."

And I thought, *Yes, they do. Except for Sergio, Robert, and Luis.*

CHAPTER 44

OVER MORNING COFFEE, José asked me if I'd heard anything more from TastyDaddy.

"No," I said. "I asked him where he lived, and he disappeared."

At that point, José reached over and drew his index finger across the top of my lip.

"Latte foam mustache," he said with a wink.

"I was just thinking." I set my coffee cup on the counter. "Last week, we had a slate of three murders. Just like that. This week, it's been quiet."

"But that's a good thing. We don't want any more." José stood. "I need to get ready for work. By the way, any news from Sam this morning?"

"Nope. I guess things are okay there for now."

He planted a kiss on the top of my head and hustled upstairs. While he showered, I stayed in the kitchen, staring at my coffee and mulling everything over. The killer had all but disappeared. José was right that it was good that things were quiet this week, but unease gnawed at me. Where did the killer go? Why was he all of a sudden lying low? And what about TastyDaddy? I hadn't heard from him since the morning before. And as if on cue, my phone chirped. It was a message from him.

> Still interested. Tell me
> what you want.

Oh, what the hell. I thumbed a reply.

> To suck.

Sounds good to me.
When?

> You tell me.

Tonight?

> Maybe.

There was a lull in the chat. From upstairs, I heard José turn off the shower, the glass door closing behind him. I looked at the oven clock. 7:30 a.m. It was rather early for TastyDaddy to be online. But then, being DL, he probably had to squeeze in messages when he was alone. I imagined him in the bathroom at home, also getting ready for work. He'd be alone and he could text to his heart's content while his wife was somewhere else, maybe getting breakfast together for the kids, thinking her hubby was busy grooming for the day. A chirp let me know he was back.

Maybe?

> Yeah. Maybe. I have to see.

Are you a tease?

> No. Just busy. Send another pic when you can.

I didn't really want another pic, but I had to say something to keep him interested. I put down my phone when I heard José's footsteps on the stairs.

"I was going to see my parents tonight," he said as he entered the kitchen. "Do you want to come?"

My phone chirped. *Shit.*

"Is that who I think it is?" he asked.

I ignored the phone and stood. "Possibly." I straightened his tie. "Do all store managers have to wear ties?"

"No. I just like to. You know, makes me look like the big boss. It's a psychological thing." He enveloped me in his arms. "So, what do you think? Parents?"

I nodded. "Yep. Parents." I kissed him.

"Okay. I'll swing by and pick you up after work. Oh, and bring a change of clothes. We can spend the night at my house and come back in the morning."

I offered a military salute. "Yes, sir!"

He shook his head, smiling, and made his way to the front door. I locked it behind him, then dashed back to the kitchen and picked up my phone. The message wasn't from Tasty-Daddy but from some guy with the screen name "DL Bi." His profile said he was thirty-one, bisexual, and into bottoming. His text was a simple "hi." I decided not to respond. I sighed, then slumped onto a stool. I tapped on TastyDaddy's profile, staring at it, having already seen it a number of times.

Who was he?

I stood, grabbed my coffee cup, and trudged upstairs. Instead of a bike ride, I thought about a nice four-mile walk. That would give me time to mull over everything, think about whether I needed another strategy. Yeah, a nice long walk. But before I could even get my shoes on, my phone chirped. TastyDaddy had sent me another message.

Let's meet tomorrow night.

I stared at the text. My heart fluttered and I swallowed hard. This was it. I was going to commit to meeting this guy.

I'd need to tell José, of course, keeping my promise about not doing anything without him. I texted a response.

> OK. Where and how will I know it's you?

Text you later.

And then the little green dot disappeared.

CHAPTER 45

I N THE AFTERNOON, I met my sister at Starbucks. As usual, the staff greeted me when I entered, like I was Norm on *Cheers*. Of course, given their ages, none of those employees had probably even heard of that sitcom or how every time Norm walked into the bar people shouted "Norm!" The thought reminded me of my age. Sigh.

My sister was already seated, so I hustled over to the table. "Couldn't wait for me?" I said.

"Shut up and get a coffee so we can shoot the breeze."

I made my way to the counter and ordered my usual from Bobby.

"And no, I'm not talking to strangers," he quipped as I passed my app under the scanner.

"Ha-ha. Just remember we care about you."

He held his hands up. "I get it. I get it."

I winked at him and then went to sit with Laura while I waited for my drink. There was only a handful of customers inside, but a line of cars snaked out from the drive-through window, keeping the baristas bustling. There must have been a number of requests for cold drinks because the crash of ice into containers and the whir of blades on the blenders drowned out any noise from the espresso machines. Gigi called out.

"Will! Your latte's up!"

I fetched my drink and thanked her. When I sat down, my sister was staring at me.

"What?" I asked.

"You didn't take my call the other day and we've hardly talked. Too busy with your new boyfriend?"

I waved her off. "Stop being dramatic. Yes, José and I are seeing each other every day, but I'm more preoccupied with this murder stuff."

She licked latte foam off her lips. "Spill."

I gave her the rundown on my latest thoughts about the murders, and she listened with narrowed eyes, hardly interjecting, the wheels in her head turning. Finally, she sat back and said, "I don't like that you're this involved."

I sighed. "Laura, it's okay. First, I'm not going to do anything stupid. Second, I will get the police involved before anything gets out of hand. I just have to do this, don't you see?"

"I told you before," she said, "you've always been like this. You can't let go of something once you start." She paused. "And I understand even more now."

She was referring to Carlos, of course. I looked down at my coffee. I willed away the image of him lying on the field at school. I took a deep breath and then sipped on my coffee.

"There's more."

I told her about the memorial service and that smiling face on a very much alive Sergio Ramírez, age twenty-two. "If you'd seen that photo, watched his family, you'd feel the same as me."

She shrugged. "Maybe. But just remember, you're not the police. Did you ever stop to think that maybe they have information they're not sharing with you?"

"Of course."

The truth was it had occurred to me that Reed withheld information, but I hadn't given it much thought. Now that Laura had brought this up, there was one thing I needed to verify: the possible murder weapon. I knew the victims were all bashed, but was the weapon the same in each crime? What kind of weapon was it? Wouldn't the ME have come to some kind of conclusion? I wondered if Reed would tell me. He'd answered other questions for me.

"Hello?"

I shook my head and blinked when I heard my sister's voice. "Oh, sorry. You made me think about something."

She eyed me. "Yeah. I've known you for fifty years. I've seen that look lots of times. Did something click into place?"

"Sort of." I stood. "Listen. I've got to go. I'm sorry I've been distant the last few days. We're going to José's parents' tonight."

Her eyes widened as her mouth fell open to signal *Really?*

"Yes, I'm meeting the parents. Just like you had to meet him last week. So don't give me that look." I paused. "How about we join you and Amanda for wine and cards this weekend?"

Laura thought for a moment, then smiled. "I'd like that."

I leaned in and kissed her on the cheek. "Love you."

"Love you, too."

I dashed out the door. Starbucks was only three minutes from the police station. With luck, Reed would be there.

• • •

AS BEFORE, THE lobby of the station was quiet. The receptionist toiled away on a stack of papers on her desk, and only once did the phone ring as I waited for Reed. He emerged from the door to the right of the reception window, dressed in a gray suit with a white shirt and tie.

"You have a formal party after work?" I asked.

He ignored the sarcasm that floated among my words. "Just got back from a court case. What can I do for you, Mr. Christian?"

I shoved my hands into my pockets. "Well, I was wondering, Lieutenant, about the murders. I know that both Sergio and Robert received blows to their heads."

He nodded as he listened.

"I'm assuming Luis Pérez was also killed in a similar way."

Once again, he put on his poker face, those steely eyes not revealing a thing. "You're wondering about this because?"

"I was hoping the ME report offered some idea of the kind of weapon that was used."

"Is this important somehow for...'your story'?"

His pause didn't escape me. I tried another tack. "Have you ever read *In Cold Blood*?"

He shook his head. "No. But I've heard of it."

"Well, Truman Capote conducted an extensive investigation into the murders committed by Smith and Hickock. He was so detail-oriented that he took something like eight thousand pages of notes during his research in Kansas. I hardly think my question is a big deal."

His gaze remained locked on mine, waiting for me to blink or look away. Why was he acting like this toward me? He'd said he was no longer suspicious of my involvement— and all I was asking for was some simple information. He stood there, unyielding, one thumb hooked into his belt. I waited.

"It is routine to keep some details of a crime from the public," he finally said. "In this case, I would prefer not to discuss the potential type of murder weapon. In any event, this is not a private space." He gestured around at the dull, gray lobby of the station.

I pursed my lips as I kept my gaze on him. "I understand. I appreciate your time, Lieutenant."

"You're welcome, Mr. Christian. Oh, by the way. How's your friend, Mr. Allison?"

He fixed his gaze on me in his usual style. I was almost used to it and returned the look.

"He's talking with his wife. I think they'll be fine in the end."

He nodded. "Have a good day, then." He turned and disappeared behind the door from where he had appeared earlier.

I left the station and crossed the street as I headed for my car. I knew there had to be a way to find something out about the murder weapon. Could I approach the Madera County ME? Not without Reed finding out, unless I used a different name or faked who I was, as I had done with Robert Márquez's father. As I clicked my key fob to unlock the car door, I stopped in mid-stride. I snapped my fingers.

"Yes!"

I jumped into my car, thumbed a text, and waited for a response. It came quickly.

I'm at home.

I immediately texted back.

Be there in a few.

CHAPTER 46

I PULLED UP in front of the familiar modest home painted in pale yellow and parked. I followed the sidewalk to the concrete steps and then sauntered up to where Julie Ramírez waited for me on one of the faux Adirondack chairs. She waved from her shaded spot as I approached, a wan smile on her face. I sat on the other chair next to her.

"How are you doing?" I asked.

"Okay. Would you like some iced tea?" She gestured toward a plastic thermos dispenser flanked by plastic cups on the small table next to her chair.

"No, thank you. I'm good."

She took a sip from her cup, then pushed back a few errant strands of hair that taunted her forehead.

"How are your parents holding up?" I asked.

"As well as can be expected. I didn't tell them you were coming."

I pressed my lips together. "They're still grieving. There's time for them to talk to me later."

"What did you want to talk about?"

I leaned forward, resting elbows on knees and clasping my hands together. "I don't want to dredge up anything painful, but it's important for me to ask some questions. You buried your brother soon after he was killed, right?"

She nodded. "My parents wanted the burial separate from

the memorial service. His body, his face..." She searched for words. "He wasn't in a condition for public viewing."

"I understand. Were you with your parents when they made the arrangements?"

"Yes, why?"

"By any chance, did the mortician make a comment about the wound your brother had suffered?"

She tilted her head and looked up at the overhang on the porch. "No. I don't think so."

"Are you sure?"

She nodded again. "Yes."

"Did the police ever say anything to your parents about how your brother was killed?"

A tear gathered in the corner of her eye and started its slow descent. She brushed at it. "Just that he received a blow to the head."

I reached for her hand. "I'm sorry, Julie, to ask you to remember this. It must be awful to think about how your brother died."

She cleared her throat, then sipped on her tea, caressing the cup with both hands. She seemed so frail, so delicate. "I never saw his body. I'm kind of glad, you know?" She looked at me, her gaze probing me to see if I really did understand.

"I do know," I said. "I've seen dying people. I've seen dead people. My mother. My grandparents. A good friend I knew when I was bit younger than you. I saw your brother in that field. It's better to remember them as they were in life."

"Yes. Yes, it is. I keep Sergio's photo by my bed. The same one we had at the service."

I smiled. "That's the way I want to remember him, too." I paused. "I have one final question. Who was the mortician who prepared your brother's body?"

"We used Weldon's Memorial Chapel."

Of course. That was the one and only place in town that did such work. Otherwise, the next closest places were in Madera and Merced. A voice from inside the house called out to Julie.

"*Hija, ¿qué haces? Ven a ayudarme.*" Her mother wanted to know what she was doing, saying she needed help with something.

"Coming!" Julie responded.

We both stood and I wrapped my arms around her in a gentle hug.

"I'm still here if you ever need me."

"Thank you," she said, pulling back.

We said goodbye and I started down the steps. She called out to me.

"Do you think you will?"

I turned. "Will I what?"

"Find the man who killed my brother."

"I told your dad I would."

She offered a small wave goodbye—the way a child might—and slipped inside the house, gently closing the door behind her. I turned and hurried to my car, pulling out my phone to check the time. 4:00 p.m. Did I have time to run by Weldon's and make it home to freshen up and change for an evening with José's parents? I got into my car and started it up. I drummed the steering wheel as I mulled my options. Then I threw the car in gear and pulled away from the curb.

• • •

WELDON'S MEMORIAL CHAPEL sat on a side street off of Ryan Boulevard, the main thoroughfare in downtown

Mañana, just a few blocks from the church where Sergio's service had taken place and not far from the police station. Like a number of establishments in our town, this chapel was once a private home. From the street it looked like all the other houses in the area: single-story, white with pale green shutters, and a porch that hugged half of the front of the house. Its distinguishing feature was the sign out front—along with the tall pole topped by the American flag flopping limply in the slight breeze that teased the hot afternoon. I pulled up in front of the building and hustled to the front door.

I entered an area that had once been a living room, now converted into a reception area. A bell announced my arrival as I opened the door. The room was as white as the exterior of the building; even the fireplace had been painted over. A gray leather sofa and two armchairs offered seating for clients, and a small desk and chair sat off to the side equipped with a phone, a small desktop computer, and several notebooks. I caught the scent of lavender and noticed that on the mantel above the hearth two candles glowed with soft light. A man in his forties, medium height with graying temples, and dressed in a short-sleeve button-down shirt and blue Dockers, appeared from around the corner.

"May I help you?" he asked, his face offering the slightest of smiles.

"Yes. My name is Will Christian."

"Nice to meet you." We shook hands. "I'm Frank Weldon."

"You're the owner?"

"My family owns the business, yes." He gestured toward the sofa. "Would you like to take a seat?"

I begged off with a wave of my hand. "Oh, no. I won't stay

long. I understand your chapel attended to the body of Sergio Ramírez."

The man's smile disappeared, and color drained from his face—the look of someone haunted by a memory. "Yes. We did. In fact, I took care of him personally."

"I'm a writer working on a piece about the recent murders here in town, and I was hoping you might answer a question for me."

"What is it?"

"Did you happen to examine the wound on Sergio's head?"

He narrowed his eyes. "Mr. Christian, I'm sorry but—"

"Please. I'm not just a writer. I have a connection with Sergio. I was the one who discovered his body in the field that day. It's an image I will live with forever."

He mulled on that. "I see. Yes. What I saw when they brought him in has stuck with me." He closed his eyes and then opened them.

"Then you understand my sense of connection."

He stroked his chin. "You'll need to speak to the police or the ME to get actual information."

"Yes, I understand. And I will."

"Well, I'm no expert, but I've seen head wounds in the past. A fellow was bludgeoned with a hammer once and I remember the wounds. His skull had several small craters, like what you might see on the moon."

He used his index finger to point to several places on his head, illustrating as though I weren't able to imagine the injuries on my own.

"And Sergio?"

"His wound was different. The entire side of his head was

caved in. He must have been hit with something much bigger than a hammer head."

"Would a golf club have done that?"

He tilted his head from one side to the other as though thinking my question through.

"Not likely. A putter head is small. That damage would look more like what a hammer would cause, I think. A driver is larger, like a small fist." He balled up his own hand to show me. "What I saw, though, seemed bigger than that, and longer."

"Longer?" A sickening feeling gathered in my stomach. I knew where this was headed.

"Yes. Like something struck him across the entire side of his head, from the corner of his eye to the back of his neck. Again, I'm no expert. But I might say the poor boy was bashed with a baseball bat."

I froze as the feeling in my stomach moved up into my throat.

"Mr. Christian, are you okay?"

"Oh, sorry," I said. "I, uh, I just remembered something, that's all. I won't take up any more of your time, Mr. Weldon."

I shook his hand once again and took my leave. I hurried to my car, climbed in, and started the engine. I took several deep breaths, my mind a whirl of thoughts. I fumbled for my phone and opened DikMe. I tapped on TastyDaddy's profile. There was no face, no identifying photo. Just the image that I had seen the other day.

A baseball cap.

• • •

Sometimes I wonder what my life would have been like had I left Mañana. I used to watch the trains down at the tracks, thinking about where they'd come from, where they were headed. I'd sit with my back up against a post and imagine what it would be like to hop a freight car, like people did way back when. I think the trains that pass through here go all the way to Los Angeles. Now, that would be a switch from Mañana.

[pauses]

Do you think small towns are bad for people? That we should get out and see the world, maybe leave the nest and carve out a different space? Maybe small towns have a way of breeding small thinking. I looked this up once. There is something called small-town syndrome. It causes a sense of entitlement and makes the outside world irrelevant. People engage in clique behavior and rely on gossip and innuendo. I think I even read that some psychologists call it toxic. Have you ever heard of that?

[pauses]

I don't know. I think we are what we are. We take that with us everywhere, small town, big town. I remember my uncle saying something like that. It's in our nature to do what we do. I doubt I would have done anything different had I lived somewhere else. But then, if I'd lived somewhere else, I may not have been put in the situation I was put in.

• • •

CHAPTER 47

A FTER MY VISIT to Weldon's I needed a shower to clear my head. I let the warm water cascade down my body, wishing it could wash away the jumble of emotions in me. Weldon had said Sergio might have been killed with a bat. TastyDaddy's image was a baseball cap. Was this coincidence or was I on to something? Maybe TastyDaddy was dangling a clue in plain sight, smiling as he teased me virtually from the comfort of his home.

I'd just stepped out of the shower and was drying off when I got an incoming text. It was from Sam.

> Made some phone calls.
> Going to see someone
> tomorrow.

I texted a reply.

> Great. You can do this.

As I pulled out clothes from the closet, I heard the ADT ding signal that the front door opened and closed. I'd given José a key the day he brought clothes over, along with a gate opener so he wouldn't have to stop at the guard shack each time he came.

His voice floated up from downstairs. "Will. Where are you?"

"Up here, getting dressed. I want to look nice for your parents."

José appeared at the doorway to the bedroom just as I was pulling a polo shirt over my head. He waltzed over and kissed me.

"I just heard from Sam. He's got an appointment lined up for tomorrow, it seems."

"Good for him."

"Do you want to change?" I asked.

"Nah. We'll stop by my house and I'll put on something fresh. Did you pack for the night?"

I nodded and pointed to a backpack lying on the bed. "My best nightgown and slippers."

He chuckled, then went over to the bed and picked up the backpack. "I'll wait for you in the kitchen." He disappeared and bounded down the stairs.

As I pulled on socks and shoes, my stomach fluttered. I was going to meet José's parents. Was I nervous? Just a tad, and I wasn't sure why. Of course, if I'd really examined my feelings, I was a bit anxious because I cared so much about José. This was no casual relationship—and although we hadn't been together long, I saw the potential for something very long term. At least, that's what I hoped. He'd already joked about proposing to me. And we were, for all intents and purposes, living together, with him spending nights here and me now spending the night at his place. So, yes, meeting José's parents was a big deal. What if they didn't like me? But, then, everybody liked me. I had a way with people, could converse on just about anything. I smiled at that thought.

My phone chirped a DikMe alert. *Shit. Not now.* I needed to let go of the murders for the evening, make José's parents the focus of my attention. But I knew myself, my curiosity, and my compulsion. What should I do? I grabbed my phone and looked at the alert. I sighed with relief. Some thirty-year-old had sent me a nudge to indicate interest. I could ignore that. Yet, my gaze drifted on the screen to my saved conversations with TastyDaddy. The image of his ball cap floated before me.

No, no, no. Back burner. Leave that on the back burner, Will.

• • •

WE ARRIVED AT José's parents' house at six thirty and his father greeted us at the door with a huge smile. He was seventy with graying hair and a mustache to match, and was exactly the same height as José. The father-son resemblance was clearly there: the same square jaw and dark eyes with thick lashes.

"*M'hijo*, so glad you're here!" he said, hugging his son.

José pulled away. "Papá, this is Will. Will, this is my father, Pedro Torres."

I extended my hand. "A pleasure to meet you, Mr. Torres."

"Ay, no, no, no!" he said as he shook my hand vigorously. "Please, call me Pedro."

He ushered us into the living room, and it looked just the way I'd imagined it for two retired teachers. It was not particularly large, and a sofa sporting a floral pattern sat opposite two armchairs, with a Mexican tiled cocktail table perched in the center. A wooden mantel clock flanked by several Lladró figurines ticked in the background. The two floor lamps and the one table lamp behind the sofa cast warm yellow light about the room.

Another "*M'hijo!*" sounded out as José's mother entered,

wearing an apron. She was a good five inches shorter than her husband and José had already told me she had just turned sixty-eight a few months back. I surmised she dyed her hair to keep it close to its natural dark brown and she carried a few extra pounds on her. She had a twinkle in her eye as she swept into the room and extended her arms out toward José. She enveloped him in a maternal hug and then turned to me.

"You must be Will," she said, reaching for my hand. She grasped it in both of hers. "You are as cute as José said you were."

I blushed. "Thank you, Mrs. Torres."

She flapped a hand at me. "We're not so formal in this family. Please call me Teresa." She gestured for us to sit down as she removed her apron. "Pedro, why don't you get us some wine to drink?"

"Be right back," he said, and he disappeared around the corner into what I presumed was the kitchen.

"So," Teresa said, "tell us about yourself, Will."

"Well, I used to be a university professor, but I made a major career change and left to write full time."

She nodded to indicate interest. "And what are you writing?"

"Mostly I edit and do some freelance work."

"Don't be modest, sweetie." José nudged me with his elbow. "Tell her about your novel."

She raised her brow. "A novel?"

I blushed again. "Yes. I'm working on my first novel. It's about two strangers who meet, a man in his thirties and another in his later years. It's kind of a buddy novel but the twist is the old man thinks he's an angel, sent to Earth to help people."

Just then Pedro returned with wine.

"That sounds interesting," he said and then he lifted his glass. "To our son, José, and the new man in his life, Will."

We toasted and then Teresa asked me about my family. I gave her the basics: where I was born, that I was of Mexican heritage, that my parents had already passed.

"I have one older sister. She lives down the street from me."

"Will actually moved back to California just to be near her," José said.

"*Eso está muy bien*," Teresa said, saying that what I had done was a good thing. "*La familia siempre es importante.*" Family is always important.

"*Sí, lo es*," I said in agreement. "*Y mi hermana y yo tenemos una relación muy estrecha.*" My sister and I have a very close relationship.

"So nice to see José with someone who speaks Spanish," Teresa said, sipping on her wine. "Not like that gringo you went with in San Jose."

Pedro patted his wife on her knee. "Now, now, Teresita, we don't need to talk about that in front of Will." He turned to me. "She's very protective of our sons."

"Well, I never liked that guy," she added, her chin jutting out.

I shot a glance at José who used his eyebrows instead of his shoulders to shrug.

"I think you'll like Will a lot, Mom," he said. "He's smart, polite, and he's a really good cook."

She arched a brow.

"But not as good as you, I'm sure," I quickly added. "Whatever you have prepared smells wonderful. I can smell green chiles. Poblanos?"

"Very good," she said, wagging her finger. "I made chiles rellenos because it's one of José's favorite dishes."

My eyes widened to show I was impressed. "Those take a lot of work."

"Speaking of work, I need to get back to the kitchen and finish a few things." She stood.

"May I help?" I offered.

"Oh, no, no. You're a guest. It'll just be a few minutes." She retreated to the kitchen with wine in hand.

"So, Will, how far along are you with your novel?" Pedro asked.

"I'm about a third of the way through. It's been slow going because—"

A DikMe chirp cut me off. Red-faced, I shoved my hand into my pocket.

"I'm so sorry. I forgot to silence my phone."

I yanked it out, switched off the sound, and thrust it back into my pocket. Pedro just smiled, but José looked at me expressionless. Was he irritated? *Damn!* I reached for my wine and took a sip. I was about to finish answering Pedro's question when Teresa called from the kitchen.

"Pedro! Can you come help me for just a minute?"

He stood. "Excuse me. I think we're about to have dinner."

José turned toward me, his posture stiff. He kept his voice low. "You couldn't turn off your phone? This night is about my parents meeting you. Not about DikMe."

"I'm sorry, hon, I forgot!" I reached for his hand.

He relaxed a little and let out a small sigh. "It's okay. I'm overreacting." He offered a slight smile. "Just do me a favor and don't bring up the murders."

I nodded and then crossed my heart while mouthing "I love you." Just then Pedro reappeared.

"*A la mesa,*" he said, telling us it was time to take seats at the table.

And on that, José and I both strode into the adjacent dining room. Teresa had set out her best china, it seemed, along with polished silverware—all waiting for us on an ecru-colored damask cloth. A hutch in the corner told me my observation was correct: plates were missing from their stations inside. I smiled at how she was trying to impress me, and I took in the aromas of chiles and spices as they drifted from the kitchen. But my mind went elsewhere as I turned to look at the other side of the room. I stopped and stared. On a wall above a sideboard was a brass plaque on wood, some kind of award. I couldn't make out the lettering, but I did see José's name as the largest engraved print.

Pedro must have seen me looking.

"That's from José's senior year in high school," he peacocked. "He was the top hitter in the region. More homeruns than anybody."

Mounted underneath the plaque was a baseball bat.

CHAPTER 48

T HE ROOM AROUND me spun as thoughts and images
tumbled in my mind like clothes in a dryer.

The sound of bat against ball.
Estimated times of death.
My conversation with Weldon.
Sergio's body.
Buzzards ripping at flesh.
TastyDaddy's baseball cap.

I shook my head and the dining room came back into focus.

"You okay, sweetie?" José asked.

"Yes. Yes. I'm fine." I half-smiled.

The eyebrows on Pedro's face drew together. "Maybe you
would like some water."

"No, no. Really. I'm fine. I'm sorry. I just, I was just feeling
a little lightheaded." The thoughts receded; my head was
clear. "I wonder if this heat is catching up to me. I was running around all day doing errands."

"That could be," Pedro said. "I know as the day goes on all
I want to do is sit around and not move, it gets too darned
hot. But of course, I'm an old man." He offered a slight
chuckle to lighten the mood. He gestured for us to sit.

Teresa swept in with a platter of a dozen chiles rellenos, all
arranged in a circle with a garnish of cilantro in the center.

Placing them in the middle of the table, she said, "Pedro, would you get the side dishes, please?"

She had not seen what had just happened, and I smiled as I examined the dish before us. Pedro disappeared into the kitchen while Teresa sat opposite her son.

"My mother's chiles rellenos are the best," José said. He smiled at his mother.

"Well, they smell delicious," I added.

Underneath the table, José placed his hand on my knee and squeezed gently. I cleared my throat.

"Teresa, you were a middle school teacher, I understand."

"Yes, for over thirty years," she said, a hint of pride behind the affirmation. "I taught Spanish, and I loved being with students. It was hard for me to retire, but Pedro and I manage to occupy ourselves and not get bored."

"And Pedro?" I asked.

"He taught high school biology. He was Madera teacher of the year twice," she crowed.

"Impressive."

Just then her husband reentered with two plates—one with black beans and the other with avocado and tomato slices drizzled with olive oil and seasoned with salt and pepper. Teresa took the plate of beans from him and placed it on the table while Pedro did the same with the other. He poured us each some wine and then sat down.

"Go ahead," Teresa said. "*Sírvanse, por favor.*"

José started piling food onto his plate and I followed suit. Soon we were all eating and steeped in conversation about everything from José's childhood to the state of education in California to vacation spots on our bucket lists. Things shifted when Pedro's father mentioned the murders.

"I assume you've been following the news," he said to me.

José remained quiet as he bit his lip. I took the hint. "Oh, yes. Everyone's appalled by what's happened."

"What do you think?" Teresa said as she dabbed at her mouth with a napkin. "Are they hate crimes? Why Latinos?"

"And all gay, too." The words just slipped out. I avoided eye contact with José.

Teresa looked puzzled. "I didn't know that."

I couldn't help myself. I cleared my throat again. "Well, that's what I heard, anyway."

Teresa looked at her son. "*M'hijo*, you are quiet all of a sudden."

He looked at her. "Sorry. I just don't like thinking about these things. It saddens me deeply."

"Just be careful," Teresa said. "Both of you. I still remember what that gringo did."

Pedro reached for his wife's hand. She looked at him and he shook his head slightly.

"I'm sorry, Pedro," she said, "but there are some things I just can't forget—or forgive."

I turned to José and furrowed my brow. What was going on? What was Teresa talking about? Did she mean José's previous boyfriend?

"Mom, I haven't talked to Will about that part of my life yet."

Teresa pulled her shoulders back and pushed at the back of her hair, her lips pouting slightly. I couldn't tell if she was embarrassed for bringing something up that she shouldn't have or if she was defiant and wanted to talk about the issue then and there. A few seconds ticked off, tension seeming to mount as silence hung in the room. The only sound was the distant tick, tick, tick of the mantel clock in the living room. José turned to face me.

"There's more about my life in San Jose than I told you. We'll talk later."

"Well," Pedro said, "shall we retire to the living room?"

He and Teresa stood, while she began gathering platters and dishes.

I picked up José's plate and mine. "Let me help you."

She clucked. "No. No."

"I insist." I turned to José. "Go with your dad."

Pedro put his arm around his son's shoulder and ushered him out of the dining room. In the kitchen, I placed several plates on the counter. I marveled at how clean the area was after Teresa had prepared such a great meal. She must have been one of those cooks who cleaned as she went, not wanting to leave a big mess for afterward. As I turned to go fetch more, Teresa put her hand on my arm to stop me.

"I'm sorry," she said. "I shouldn't have brought up anything about José's old boyfriend."

I placed my hand on hers and squeezed gently. "That's okay. I'm sure he'll tell me later."

But she didn't release her grip on my arm.

"Just promise me," she said, "that you'll never hurt him. Never touch him."

Touch him?

Her gaze locked on mine, probing me to see my reaction.

"Teresa, I love your son. It's only been a short time, I know, but I do love him. I don't know what's happened to him in the past, but whoever that other guy was, I'm not him."

She dropped her gaze and released her grasp. "Of course. Of course you aren't." She looked back at me and smiled. "Okay. Let's finish clearing the table and then we'll take some flan out to the living room."

"Wow. You made flan, too? And I was wondering how you were going to top such a great meal!"

She laughed and flapped her hand to wave away my compliment, then took me by the arm to walk back into the dining room. But in the back of my mind, I wondered about what she'd said.

Never touch him.

CHAPTER 49

Back at José's house, I pulled off my clothes and climbed into bed after the usual ritual of washing my face and then brushing and flossing my teeth. The room was bathed in soft, warm light from the nightstand lamps. I pulled the crisp, white sheets up to my waist, impressed that they were wrinkle free. José must have ironed them. I smiled.

As I waited for him, I contemplated Teresa's comment: *Never touch him.* Something terrible must have happened with José's last boyfriend, and I realized I knew so little about that part of his life. Curiosity tugged at me.

José emerged from the bathroom, pulled back the covers, and slipped between the sheets. Both naked, we scooted next to each other and I wrapped my arm around his shoulder. I caught the light scent of sport deodorant on him as he nestled into my embrace.

"My parents really liked you," he said. "My mother pulled me aside on the way out and said you were a keeper."

"Well, I liked them, too. You're lucky to have such a great mom and dad. Maybe I'll meet your brothers someday."

"Fourth of July is coming up. We usually do a big barbecue." He reached up and tapped my nose.

All in all, it had turned out to be a great evening. The food was delicious, his parents were great conversationalists, and they entertained well. It was clear to me how much they loved their son and what a happy home they must have made for their three boys. It made me reflect on my own broken home and how what José grew up was a part of life I never had.

My thoughts drifted to Sergio. He had hidden his sexuality from his parents, only for them to find out in the most horrific way. On the other hand, José's parents accepted him with loving arms, and in my own family, being gay was never an issue—at least not with my mother. And of course, not with Laura, being a lesbian herself. Poor Sergio.

"Hey, why are you so serious all of a sudden?" José asked.

"Oh, just reflecting. Hon, do you want to tell me about San Jose?"

He traced the outline of my lips with his index finger. "What about it?"

"There's more to the story than infidelity, isn't there?"

He turned to settle on his back, looking up at the overhead fan, and clasped his hands on his chest.

"His name was Eric. I moved there to be with him. And no, it wasn't just infidelity. Turned out he had a drinking problem."

I propped up on my elbow to better look at him.

"He got violent with me. Twice. The second time, I had to call the police."

"It was that bad?"

"Yes. He'd gotten my baseball bat and came after me. I thought he was going to kill me."

"What did you do?"

"He was drunk enough that he wasn't as quick as he might have been. I maneuvered around him and grabbed the bat on both ends."

I remembered that day in Starbucks when José had done the same to Sam Allison, how he had deftly gotten behind Sam and twisted his arm up.

José stared straight ahead. "I pulled the bat up and pressed it hard against his throat. He started to choke. When I realized what I was doing, I let go. He was gasping for air. Just then the police arrived."

I gently brushed some hair away from his forehead. "Then what happened?"

"They took statements. He was hauled away, and I pressed charges. I didn't know he had an outstanding DUI, too."

"Did you have to go to court?"

José nodded. "Because he didn't actually hurt me, he was convicted of simple assault. Given his DUI record, he got the maximum of six months in jail and a $1,000 fine, along with mandatory rehab. His driver's license was revoked as well."

I leaned in and pulled José toward me. "I'm sorry that you had to go through that."

He half-smiled. "Live and learn."

I kissed him and then lay my head next to his. Guilt washed over me for even thinking that José could have been involved in a crime. Instead, he had been the victim of one. I hadn't yet told him about my trip to Weldon's, what Frank had said about Sergio's wounds. He did not need to hear anything more about baseball bats.

We lay in silence.

• • •

AFTER JOSÉ DROPPED me off at home in the morning, I checked DikMe. The events of the night before had completely consumed me, and I'd forgotten all about the chirp alert I'd received at Pedro and Teresa's house. Sitting at my kitchen counter with a steaming latte in front of me, I tapped on the messages tab, and sure enough, TastyDaddy had sent me something.

> Tomorrow night. Meet me
> for some car play.

I texted a reply.

> Time and place?

He immediately texted back.

> 10:00. End of the cul de
> sac behind the Regent
> School.

I stared. *Shit.* That was right near where I found Sergio's body. And ten o'clock was close to the estimated times of death for Sergio, Robert, and Luis. I swallowed hard. My thumbs trembled as I wrote a response.

> Need pic. Want to see
> what you look like.

I waited. Seconds ticked off. Nothing. I was about to put my phone down when the notification chirped: "Photo Received." I tapped. A message accompanied the photo.

> No face pic but here's my
> body.

It was, indeed, a full body shot, taken from the neck down. His torso was bare, displaying a lightly fuzzy and muscular chest along with defined abs, but the rest of him sported Levis and cowboy boots. I didn't need to see the face to recognize who it was. My mouth fell open as I stared at his waist. It was encircled by a one-of-kind belt with a large turquoise buckle.

The one I'd seen on Tim Shakely a number of times.

The lieutenant's cousin.

● ● ●

I'm divorced now. Makes sense. The day after I was convicted, I got the papers. I signed them, of course. I would never have been able to attend a hearing, and what was there to contest? After all, I am stuck here until I die. I wonder how long that will be. Male life expectancy is late seventies. But in here, who knows? I read a statistic that for every year of incarceration, you lose two years of life expectancy. The reasons aren't clear, though. No matter. Probability is I'll die in here sooner than I'd die out there. And no, I'm not expecting sympathy. I'm just stating facts. So don't think that you've found some hint of remorse after all.

[pauses]

If you would have asked me when this all started if this was where I'd be right now, I would've said, "Hell no." After all, I had the perfect plan, the perfect cover. It was all neatly figured out. I probably should've stopped after number three. Coulda, shoulda, woulda. The famous threesome. Just like the Holy Trinitiy, the three little pigs, three men in a tub.

[chuckles, then pauses]

I'm sure it has occurred to you that you were on your way to being number four. Ever think about how you might have died that night? And you would have, too.

● ● ●

CHAPTER 50

I STARED OUT of the kitchen window at the large olive tree behind my house, focusing on the leaves as they rustled slightly in the gentle morning breeze. Ideas started to build on each other in my head, one on top of the other, like the limbs and branches of the tree that held my gaze.

Tim's profile pic was a baseball hat.
He coached Little League.
I'd seen the equipment in the bed of his truck.
I watched him carry bats off the field after practice.
He had a truck. An easy transport for a body.
The ME and Reed spoke the day I found Sergio's body.
The ground should be soaked with blood.
He was killed somewhere else, then dumped here.
Tim had happened to be driving by and stopped.
Some killers like to insert themselves in the investigation.
Gives them an extra jolly.

At our initial encounter, Tim had been distant, even hostile. Was he pissed that I had found the body? Maybe he wanted to pretend to find it. Call it in. His cousin would never suspect him. But I had ruined that plan, taken away the extra thrill.

And there he was on DikMe. Looking for young Latino males. Is that why the phones were missing from the bodies?

Had Tim taken them so that the police wouldn't see his messages and rendezvous arrangements, wouldn't see what I saw? A lanky cowboy-like body with a big turquoise belt buckle. A profile that could be traced back to him.

My phone buzzed a call and I jumped, dropping the phone. I fumbled for it. The caller ID displayed Laura's name.

"What's up?" I asked.

"Amanda and I are going to Whole Foods in Fresno. You wanna go?"

"Uh, no. I need to work."

There was a pause. "What's the matter?"

"What do you mean?" I asked.

"I can hear something in your voice."

"I just told you. I need to get some work done."

Another pause. "Well, text me if you decide you need something."

Alone in the kitchen, I pondered what to do. Go to Reed? And what? Tell him I suspected his cousin of the murders, that he was on DikMe trying to hook up with me—well, not with me but with what he thought was a twenty-four-year-old hottie. All I had was a set of ideas and assumptions—what anyone could see was circumstantial. But why did I feel in my gut that I was on to something? Then it occurred to me. Who else might recognize the cowboy body in the photo?

I hopped in my car and headed south to Madera.

I hoped David would be working

• • •

I PARKED MY car and climbed out. The Walmart lot was only half-full this time of day and I hustled inside. I raced past the corral of blue shopping carts and headed toward the back part of the store. A small child darted in front of me, his mother in tow—yelling for him to stop running. I sidestepped them and continued toward the electronics section. I was in luck. David was behind the counter and there were no customers in sight. He closed a cabinet behind him, then turned and chewed on a fingernail. I caught my breath and then strode over to him.

"Hi, David."

He smiled when he saw me, nervously pulling the finger away from his mouth. "Oh, hi. Will, right?"

I nodded. "How's it going?"

"Okay, I guess. You need help with something?"

I leaned onto the counter with my elbows and lowered my voice. "Actually, I was hoping you might answer a couple of questions for me."

He swallowed hard. "Is this about Robert?"

Again, I nodded. "You said he liked older guys, right?"

He looked around to make sure no one was in earshot. He lowered his voice as well. "Yes."

"How old?"

"I dunno. Over thirty-five, I know that."

"Any fifty-year-olds?"

He shrugged. "I'm not sure but I think maybe, yeah, he mentioned one guy."

"He didn't happen to mention his name, did he?"

"He never told me any of their real names." He dropped to an almost whisper. "He always referred to them by their DikMe names or he gave them nicknames."

Then I saw him look up. I followed his gaze and spotted the reflective globe that housed a hidden security camera.

I winked and pointed behind him. "Pretend to show me that Fitbit."

As he pulled out a box from the locked cabinet, I asked, "Did he ever mention someone named TastyDaddy?"

David scrunched up his face. "Maybe. I'm not sure."

He handed me the box and I pretended to examine it. I shook my head, suggesting this wasn't the product I wanted. Then I whipped out my phone. I opened DikMe and showed the photo I'd received from TastyDaddy.

"Act like I'm showing you a model I found online," I said. "Ever see this photo before?"

He leaned in and peered. "No."

"So Robert never showed it to you?"

"No. Never."

Damn. So much for these guys having been close buddies. I would have thought Robert had been eager to share his exploits with David, showing pics and saying, "Hey, check out this hot guy." I was wrong.

He pulled out another Fitbit device and pretended to show it to me. I shook my head. "No, that's not what I want, either," I answered, playing my part.

I pulled back, pocketing my phone. "Thanks, David. I really appreciate the time."

As I started to leave, he called out to me. "Will, you aren't just writing a piece about the murders, are you?"

I tilted my head. "What makes you ask that?"

"Well," he said, "you kind of ask questions like a policeman."

I shrugged. "It's my nature."

I turned and hurried down the aisle and out the sliding front doors. I stopped in the shade and pondered my possibilities. I surveyed the parking lot, not sure why, maybe hoping inspiration would strike me. *Of course! Why didn't I do this first?* I'd put too much faith in the bonds of friendship and had ignored the one person most likely to recognize Tim on DikMe. I grinned as I pulled out my phone and texted.

> You free?

I waited for a response, but I didn't wait long.

> Going to Rite Aid then
> Starbucks.

I thumbed a response.

> Great. Meet you for coffee
> in 20 min. Urgent.

I rushed to my car and was soon speeding my way back to Mañana.

CHAPTER 51

I PUSHED THOUGH the entrance to Starbucks as the fly blaster above bathed me in rushing air. Employees called out to me amid the usual cacophony of blender whirs and milk steamers.

"Hey, Will!"

I waved and then looked around. *Damn!* Not there yet. In fact, hardly anyone was there. I headed for the counter.

"The usual?" Bobby asked.

I said yes and paid with my Starbucks app. The coffee appeared as I pulled my phone away from the scanner. Gigi smiled at me, sliding the cup gently toward me.

"I saw you pull into the parking lot," she said.

"Nothing like being a regular with a regular drink," I responded. "Thanks."

I sat at a small table in a corner by the front of the store. I leaned my elbow on the tabletop and rested my chin in the palm of my hand. The overhead music faded into the distance as questions eddied in my mind, along with the photo from TastyDaddy—Tim's photo. Was I really on to something? Or was Tim just another closeted married man in the Central Valley and I was relying too much on coincidence? I could have been headed for another Sam Allison episode. The fly blaster announced Julie Ramírez's arrival. She saw me, waved, and came over.

"Can I treat you to something?" I asked.

"Oh, thank you. A sweetened iced tea, please."

I got up, ordered, and paid. As I walked back to the table, Gigi handed me the drink at the pickup area.

"Boy, you are super on the ball today," I said.

She chuckled. "Both of you always get the same thing. Makes it easy on me."

I handed Julie her drink as I sat down. She coaxed a straw from its paper wrapper and inserted it into the cup, then sipped, pushing strands of long dark hair behind her ear.

"You said it was urgent. What did you need?" she asked.

I leaned forward, cradling my drink in my hands. "Did Sergio ever talk about the man he dated? The one you told me about?"

"A little. Why?"

"Did he ever mention his name?" I tried to contain my anticipation, hoping this would not be a repeat of my conversation with David earlier.

"Yes," she said, moving the straw up and down in her drink.

My heart leapt. *Yes! Yes!*

"But only his first name. He wanted to keep their relationship secret. I think because the guy wasn't out." She lowered her gaze. "I began to suspect he was married."

"Julie, there's no need to be embarrassed. Like I told you, Sergio wasn't the bad guy in all of this." I let a few seconds tick off before I asked the question. "What was his name?"

"Tim."

My pulse quickened. "Are you sure?"

"Yes." She looked at me, lips pursed. "Why are you asking?"

I pulled out my phone and held it up for her to see the

snapshot of the Levi-clad cowboy body with the big turquoise belt buckle. "Did Sergio ever show you this photo?"

She nodded. "How, how did you get that?" Then her eyes widened and she brought her hand to her mouth. "You, you think he might be involved in Sergio's death?"

"I don't know." I put my phone down. "I think he might know something. Julie, listen to me. Will you do me a favor?"

"What?"

"Please don't talk about our conversation with anyone. Not your parents, not the police, not your friends. No one. Do you understand?"

She nodded again.

"I need to track this guy down and talk to him, but if anyone else finds out, it may ruin our chances of knowing what happened to your brother."

"You don't think the police should know?"

I shook my head. "I can't tell you why, but no. Do not talk about this Tim guy to anyone. Do I have your promise?"

"Yes. I promise."

I smiled as I relaxed into my seat. "Thank you."

"Now I'm sure you will." Her voice had lowered. She looked down at her drink then up at me.

"I will what?"

"Find Sergio's killer."

CHAPTER 52

THE CLOCK IN my car read 11:15 a.m. as I headed home. Thinking about lunch, I pulled into the Save Mart parking lot and dashed through the exit doors. They were closest to the checkouts and service area, where I hoped to find José. Cool air enveloped me, and I wondered what the electric bill was for something like a grocery store. Between thousands of square feet, refrigeration, and air-conditioning, I could only imagine.

I surveyed the area, but José wasn't there. Kenny saw me and gave me a head bob as a greeting.

"Looking for José?" he asked as he approached.

"Yeah. I was hoping he'd be out front."

"I'm not sure where he is."

Kenny marched over to the nearest register and picked up a phone. He punched in two numbers and his voice came out through the overhead speakers.

"José, please come to the front."

Kenny gave me a thumbs-up and headed for the customer service area where an elderly man waited.

"Thanks!" I called out.

I waited by the register closest to the door, watching several cashiers as they dragged items across the scanners, the familiar beeps registering prices into the computers. Marisela, one of the checkout people, called out a "hello" to me and I waved back. A woman was piling items onto the moving belt and a carton of eggs slipped from her grasp. It landed back into the cart, upside down.

"Ah, shit!" she said.

I covered my mouth to hide my chuckle.

"That's okay, sweetie," Marisela said to the customer. She turned to the young person who was helping her bag. "Go get her another dozen, would you, please?"

The bagger was off and running. Fortunately, nothing leaked from the carton, so the woman handed Marisela the container and its contents of presumably cracked eggs. Just then, José emerged from the liquor aisle.

"Whatcha need?" he asked, looking at Kenny.

Kenny pointed to me. José turned in my direction, smiled, and then jogged over to where I stood. I blew him a kiss.

"Hi, sweetie," he said. "What's up?"

"Are you taking a lunch break today?"

"Yes. Why?"

"I need to run something by you."

He furrowed his brow. "Something serious?"

I lowered my voice. "It's about TastyDaddy."

We agreed to meet at the Panda Express in half an hour. I used that time to hop in my BMW and drive to where I'd found Sergio's body. Remaining inside my car with the comfort of the AC, I scanned the field and tried to picture what might have happened that night. I imagined Tim's six-foot frame hauling Sergio's smaller body off the bed of the truck and carrying it out into the field, then dropping it onto the ground with a thud. Then a sick image of him smiling and whistling as he walked away from the corpse floated before me.

I closed my eyes to clear these thoughts. After all, maybe this was all fanciful thinking. Maybe Tim wasn't involved at all. Could someone else have targeted gay Latino males and Tim was just a guy who Sergio had been seeing? But I couldn't ignore the fact that he'd pulled up to this spot that morning I'd found the body. I couldn't dismiss his initial hostility toward me. I couldn't shake the image of him trudging off the Little League field with baseball bats.

"Too much coincidence," I said out loud.

My thoughts turned to the evening, about what I should do. I needed to prepare. I shifted into drive and pulled away, heading for the Rite Aid. I had a few minutes before meeting José for lunch, and Rite Aid would have what I needed.

I grinned at my own cleverness.

• • •

THE PANDA EXPRESS was just over the highway from Save Mart on a side road, and José and I managed to beat the lunch crowd. After we ordered and sat down, a line of ten people snaked out from the counter. The sound of cooking utensils scraping against woks filled the background and the odor of hot sesame oil hung in the air. Seated on a hard plastic benches at one of the smaller tables, I dug into a plate of lo mein while José enjoyed kung pao chicken.

"You're pretty handy with chopsticks," he said to me.

I shrugged. "Long story but it has to do with a Japanese family I lived next to when I was a little kid."

"So, tell me about TastyDaddy."

I took a sip of my Diet Pepsi. "It's Tim Shakely."

His eyes widened. "The lieutenant's cousin? From Little League practice?"

I nodded. Then I launched into a summary of my meeting with Weldon the day before, my interchanges on DikMe, and my conversations with David and Julie. José listened intently, gesturing with his head and eyes to let me know he was following along, compiling the information.

"Anyway," I said, but I didn't get to finish my thought.

"Wait," José said. "This Weldon guy says the killer may have used a baseball bat?"

"Uh huh."

He fixed his gaze me. What was he probing for?

"That's what happened last night," he said after a few seconds.

"What do you mean?"

"At my parents, when we went to sit down for dinner. You froze for a moment. It was the baseball award with the bat, wasn't it?"

I looked down at my drink, rolling the fountain cup between my thumb and fingers. "Yes."

José didn't say anything. After a beat, he went back to his food. God, I hoped he wasn't thinking that I had suspected him at one point. I wanted to say something. Words formed in my mind, but a feeling told me to let it go, to say nothing. Instead, I pulled out my phone.

"Here. Look at this," I said as I held up Tim's photo from DikMe. "See that belt buckle?"

He nodded as he shoved a forkful of chicken into his mouth.

"I've seen him three times now with that belt on. The first time I met him, one time at Starbucks, and that day we ran into him at La Viña winery."

José scrunched his face. "Oh yeah. I think I remember it, too."

"Believe me, it's the same buckle."

"Right. You and your excellent memory."

I tapped my temple. "It all fits."

José put down his fork and sat back. "What are you going to do? Go to Reed?"

I shook my head. "Can you imagine trying to tell him his cousin is on the down low on DikMe and I think he might be involved in these murders, might be the killer? Plus, as you have reminded me, I am committing fraud." I paused. "And what if I'm wrong? I was wrong before."

José placed his hands behind his neck and drew his arms back, stretching with a slight grunt. As he released, he said, "You were premature with Sam. This time, there's just too much to be coincidental."

I took my last bite and tossed my chopsticks to the side. "I need your help, hon. I'm supposed to meet him tonight."

José went to say something but stopped short when my phone chirped. I tapped and there was a message from Tasty-Daddy.

"It's him." I read the message out loud.

Still on for tonight?

I looked pleadingly at José. After a pause, he nodded in silence. I thumbed a reply.

See you at 10.

I set my phone down.

"So," José said, "what *are* you going to do?"

I pulled one side of my mouth up into a smirk. "I was hoping you'd want to go for a little outing tonight."

And then I laid out my plan.

• • •

I'm not a natural born liar. I wasn't good at it as a kid. My mother could sniff a lie on me like a dog trained to find drugs. Once I took five bucks from her purse so that a friend and I could go down to the Dairy Queen. It was a classic hot Mañana summer day. All I could think of was how much I wanted an ice-cold float. Nothing like that when the temperature hits the upper nineties. When my mother asked me about the money, I said I didn't know what she was talking about. Shouldn't have been a big deal. It wasn't like I was taking money to buy anything illegal. Shit, I was only seven at the time. Know what she did? She stood there, still as a statue, staring down at me. She locked her eyes on to me like a lioness on its prey. After a bit, she pulled back and said she knew I was lying and to never forget that the eyes reveal everything. I took her word for it and never lied again. At least, not to her.

[pauses]

You can develop lying, get better at it. Must be the years of experience hiding feelings, desires, and all the stuff we don't want people to know about us. We even keep things from the people closest to us. Behind every smile, behind every kiss, lies and secrets lurk. Remember that.

[pauses]

So, like everyone, I got good at lying. Fooled you right up until the end, didn't I?

• • •

CHAPTER 53

STOOD AT the kitchen counter, staring at the oven clock. 9:00 p.m. One hour until rendezvous time.

"Are you nervous?" José asked, coming up from behind.

"A little." I turned to face him. "I wasn't when we were going to meet Sam Allison, but this seems different."

He put his arms around my waist. "I think with Sam it was more like a game. And maybe you weren't sure about him. But you've moved beyond that. Three people have died. You're deeply involved, especially with Sergio's family."

I looked into those chocolate-drop eyes, trying my best to communicate how much I adored him. He kissed me gently on the lips.

"Maybe I should have contacted Reed," I said, pulling back just a bit. "This could all be a mistake."

He pressed his index finger against my lips. "I won't let anything happen to you." He slipped his arms around my waist once again. "I have an idea. Let's dance."

"Huh?"

"Let's dance."

José swayed rhythmically from side to side. I rested my forehead on his and fell into time with him, matched his movements, wrapping my arms around his back.

He began singing Bette Midler's version of "Do You Want to Dance?" his voice low and breathy. I smiled and for several minutes we rocked in each other's embrace. When he finished singing, he pulled back.

"Feel better?"

I nodded.

"Then let's get everything ready so you can go meet this asshole."

● ● ●

AT 9:55 WE pulled into the dead end behind the Regent School. It was marked off by a white fence and red reflectors so that cars wouldn't accidentally drive into the field at night. The area was far enough from the school and its low-pressure sodium lights so that if there were any security cameras, they weren't picking up where we'd parked. I turned the engine off and looked at José.

"A kiss for luck?" I asked.

He leaned in and pressed his lips against mine.

"You know where I'll be." He slipped from the car and disappeared into the darkness. I waited in my car and drummed the steering wheel with my fingers as I bit my lip. Headlights came down the street that led to the school.

"Showtime."

A truck pulled up about ten feet away and the driver's door opened. Tim Shakely stepped out, looked at my car, and then leaned against the vehicle. It was dark enough that he couldn't make out that it was me, but his own silhouette was unmistakable. He even sported the cowboy hat he'd worn the first time we met. I opened my door and gingerly stepped out. The slight edge from nerves I'd experienced back at home was gone. I had José on my side, and I knew who this killer was.

"Hello, Tim."

He straightened, his frame stiff against the backdrop of his truck. "Will?"

"What's up?" I asked. "Out for a little stroll?"

"What are you doing here?"

"I'm here to meet someone. You?"

There was silence. Then he said, "Just came out for some air."

"Really? All the way out here? Sure you aren't here to meet someone, too?"

By now my eyesight had adjusted to the low light and I could make out his expression. His mouth parted slightly as his lower jaw jutted forward. He hooked his thumbs into his pockets.

"You?" he asked, his eyes widening.

"Yep. Little ol' me. LatinoHot4U." I hoped he could see the cocky smile on my face.

"Is this blackmail or something?"

"No, Tim. You see, I figured it all out."

"Figured what out?"

Before I could respond, another car's headlights signaled its approach. Who the hell would come out here at this time of night? Then it dawned on me: Tim had an accomplice.

Oh shit. What had I gotten into?

The car pulled in on the other side of his truck. I recognized it immediately and knew who would emerge. The door opened and a familiar voice spoke.

"Mr. Christian. This is a surprise."

It was Lieutenant Reed.

CHAPTER 54

M Y JAW WENT slack. Reed strode over and stood next to his cousin, a toothpick twitching between his lips. He pulled it out and tossed it to the ground.

"I think you've been catfished," he said.

"Looks like it," Tim replied. "What're we gonna do?"

Reed turned and reached into the bed of Tim's truck. He pulled out a metal baseball bat and slapped it against his hand. My mouth went dry as I eyed his movements.

"Mr. Christian, I was hoping you'd go away, but you didn't. I was hoping you'd keep me informed of what you were doing, but clearly you didn't. And now, here we are. I told you early on: curiosity killed the cat."

Oh fuck. I reflected on my meetings with him, how he seemed not to make progress, how he at first chastised me for interference. Then, suddenly, he embraced me for my snooping. Now I understood. He wanted to keep tabs on me. See if I was making progress. If I'd gotten too close, I would have been targeted and been just another in a string of victims. And that poker face of his. He knew all along the victims were gay. He knew everything I'd learned. God, was I dumb! He'd been covering for Tim all along.

"The phones," I said.

"What?" Reed asked.

"It was you. You kept the phones. No phones were

returned to any of the families with the victims' personal effects. You knew they had evidence on them."

"I said it before," Reed replied. "You would have made a good detective."

I looked at Tim, trying to keep my voice calm. "So, what happened with Sergio? I know you were seeing him." I walked an internal tightrope suspended between scared and pissed off.

"It got messy. Stupid kid fell in love with me." He spat onto the asphalt.

My heart sank. Poor Sergio. So he had succumbed and thought it was love—just like I'd told his sister often happened with kids like him. Tim had been using him for sex, stringing him along as he cheated on his wife. I conjured the image of Sergio's photo, that smiling face, all that promise in a twenty-two-year-old. I pushed down on the roil of emotions in my gut. Rage was overtaking fright.

I looked at Reed. "Did you know your cousin was a closet case?"

Reed shrugged. "I suspected, but I didn't care. As long as everything was on the down low."

"Why couldn't you just walk away?" I said to Tim.

"He wanted me to leave my family. Said he'd tell my wife. I couldn't have that."

"You killed him for that?" This time, anger slipped into my words.

"No," Reed said. "I did."

My heart skipped a beat as my jaw dropped. "You?"

"I couldn't let that little shit ruin our family."

Then I remembered what he'd told me when we met over a week ago. "Tim's dad was police. He hired you."

"Yep," Reed said. "He was more of a dad to me than my

own." He slapped the bat against his palm again. "Tim came to me two weeks ago. Confessed everything. I couldn't let him get into trouble. I knew how to take care of it."

Never rule out anyone in a murder case. He had practically confessed that day in his office. I'd been too dumb to consider it.

"And the others? Why them?" I asked.

"Actually, you gave me that idea."

"What do you mean?"

A small smile played about Reed's lips. "That day at Starbucks. You said I could be dealing with a hate crime. What better way was there to cover up the motive for Ramírez's death than a string of murders of Latino men? And Allison, in his MAGA hat, with all those witnesses around. Easy setup."

I reeled internally. He was laying the blame for the murders of Robert Márquez and Luis Pérez at my feet! Had I planted the seed in his head? No! I wouldn't accept that! My stomach burned with acid.

"So that night Sam got arrested. You pretended to be interested in him as a suspect. Why? To make it look like you were actually doing an investigation?"

Reed just smiled, gripping the baseball bat.

My stomach continued to burn. "Let me get this right. Tim here lures them out and you bash them. Then you dump their bodies somewhere else, take their phones. And all this time you pretend to be working on the cases but not making any real headway."

He tilted his head as he twisted his mouth into mock frustration. "Lots of cases go unsolved."

His hand twirled around the large end of the bat, like he was caressing it, warming it up. Tim crossed his arms and stood with his legs shoulder width apart. My gaze went back and forth between the two of them. My pulse picked up and I knew what was coming. I sucked in a deep breath as I backed up against my car, having left the door open. I slowly reached behind me onto the seat.

Reed squinted. "What're you doing?"

"Oh, just fighting the schoolyard bullies," I said, trying to mask my nervousness.

I grabbed one of the balloons that I'd brought and, as fast as I could, I hurled it squarely at Tim's chest. It exploded and for a moment he stood there stunned. Then he laughed.

"What? A fucking water balloon?"

But the smirk on his face evaporated as he began sucking air.

"I, I can't breathe!"

"Water?" I said. "Try some chloramine vapor, asshole!"

He clutched at his throat, his eyes wide. He fell to the ground. Just then, José appeared. While I had Tim and Reed distracted, he'd slunk around behind Tim's truck.

He rushed with his baseball bat poised to hit a home run. Reed was too focused on his choking and sputtering cousin to see my boyfriend barreling toward him. José's swing met with the side of the lieutenant's right kneecap. He cried out in pain as he dropped the metal bat, sending it clanging to the asphalt underneath him. He reached for his knee and then crumpled, writhing on his side.

"You motherfucker!" he screamed.

José was lightning fast as he dropped his own bat and pulled a roll of duct tape from the back of his shorts. He flipped the screaming lieutenant onto his belly, then yanked his arms behind him and taped his wrists together. Then he did the same to his legs.

I waltzed over to Tim. He lay there, gagging and coughing.

"You'll survive," I said. "And you." I turned to Reed, whose screams had subsided into moans. "You were right. My boyfriend does have a good swing." I pulled my lip up into a smirk.

José plopped onto the asphalt and wiped sweat from his forehead. He held out the duct tape for me and I went to work on Tim. From behind me I could hear cars approaching. Lights flashed and two armed police rushed toward us, guns ready.

"Either of you José Torres?" one of them asked.

"That's me," José answered, pulling himself up with a grunt. Then he gestured with his head toward the two men on the ground. "There they are."

I looked at José, wide-eyed. "You called them?"

"Yeah," he said as he wiped debris from his butt. "While I was waiting to make my move."

One of the officers hurried to inspect the two men. "Holy shit! It's Reed!"

"Lieutenant Reed?" the other asked. I assumed he was the officer in charge.

The first one nodded. He spoke into his shoulder mic, calling for EMS.

The officer in charge looked us over. We were unarmed. He holstered his gun, hooked his thumbs in his belt, then said, "Okay. Start talking."

I pulled my phone from my pocket. "I think this will speak for us."

A wire traveled from the phone up inside my polo shirt to a microphone I'd attached to the collar. In the dark, Tim and Reed wouldn't have seen it. I pulled up the recording I'd just made and the officer in charge listened intently. When it was done playing, he looked over at Reed and Tim, then back at us.

"My God. I don't fucking believe it."

The sirens of the EMS split the air as they raced down Avenue 28 and then turned onto the street leading to the school. Within seconds they treated Reed and his cousin, then loaded them up to cart them off to Madera Community Hospital. The other officer got on his mic and called in for police to be waiting for the ambulance.

"I'm going to ride with them," he said. Then he climbed into the back of the EMS truck and it sped off.

"Okay," said the officer in charge. "We're going to need full statements. How about a trip to the police station?"

"Sure. You can follow us," I said.

José and I climbed into the car. As I started the engine, he turned to me.

"They might try to cover this up, seize your phone, put us in jail for assault."

I smiled. "What do you think I was doing while you were trussing Reed up like a Thanksgiving turkey?" I turned to him. "I backed everything up to the cloud. And today, I downloaded all my DikMe conversations to my desktop and uploaded those to the cloud, too. And I contacted a reporter in Fresno this evening. I bet there's going to be more than police waiting for Reed and his cousin at the hospital."

He grinned. "I love you."

"I know." I leaned over and kissed him. "Thank you for rescuing me again."

CHAPTER 55

T HE NEXT DAY proved to be a circus. José and I were interviewed in the morning, and by noon we were breaking news on the local channels. The same reporter who had come out the day I discovered Sergio's body stood with us in front of the Regent School and began the segment.

"I'm standing here in front of a local school in Mañana where two citizens broke the case regarding the recent murders here and have become instant heroes as they tracked down and subdued two men now charged with those murders."

It was hard not to beam in front of the cameras, but José and I both contained ourselves and remained calm and collected during the segment. The neighborhood alert system posted a blurb about us with the heading "Murders Solved!" and people organized a small parade of cars during which they honked as they passed in front of my house whistling and shouting. Lanny led the way in his Escalade.

"Yay, Will Christian! Yay, José Torres!"

José and I stood on the front porch waving and smiling. He put his arm around me and pulled me in close. Later, he received a phone call from the corporate office congratulating him and wanting to know if he would consider a move to become a regional manager.

"Only if I can work from here," he replied as he winked at me.

The VP who'd called said he thought that was doable and they could talk in a few days.

I received a phone call from an agent in Hollywood wanting to "buy my story" for a possible movie project. I asked him how he got my number.

"We have ways," he said. "My staff monitors police alerts and the news for good story lines."

"I don't know," I said. "I'm an aspiring writer, and this would make for a great book."

He didn't hesitate. "I'll represent you. Get you a publisher and make sure we keep the movie rights. You can do the screenplay."

I said I'd think about it.

We also received a call from the mayor.

"This city can sleep better now, thanks to the two of you," he said.

He wanted us to come to city hall during the week and receive a special award, so we said we'd call his office early in the week and set up a time.

And, of course, my sister had to stop by.

"I've got to hand it to you," she said, bulldozing her way through the front door. "You guys did it!"

She'd brought homemade tamales for lunch and so we sat around the kitchen counter eating while she grilled us on the details of the night before. When we finished the entire story, she asked us how we felt.

"It's kind of overwhelming," I said. "All this attention."

Then she turned to José. "You're good for my brother. I think he should keep you."

I winked at José, who responded, "Actually, *he's* the prize."

• • •

IN THE MIDAFTERNOON, José and I went to Starbucks for a caffeine pick-me-up and were greeted with applause and cheers from the staff. Some of them banged on the metal pitchers they used to steam milk while others clanged the insides of blenders with spoons. Marta, the manager, walked out with Bobby. She addressed the dozen or so customers in the store.

"If you've been watching the news or getting alerts on your phone, you probably know who these two men are. If you haven't, they are Mañana's heroes. They solved the recent murders and have helped to put the killers behind bars."

Whistles and more applause broke out as she and Bobby reached for our hands and raised them in victory. José and I smiled and bowed our heads slightly.

"Your money is no good here," she said to us. "Your drinks are always on the house."

I clasped her hands and thanked her. Staff and strangers lined up to take selfies with us. After things quieted down, we ordered our coffees and sat at a corner table.

"I was thinking," José began, but he didn't finish because my phone pinged a text.

The message was from Sam Allison. I smiled, then showed it to José.

> You did it! So proud! And thanks. That could've been me. Working with a therapist in Fresno. Learning how to deal with my situation and my marriage. Thanks for all your help.

"Well, good for him," José said.

I thumbed a reply.

> Good to hear. You know
> where I am if you need me.

I put my phone away. "You were saying?"

"Oh yeah." José reached for my hands. "I have softball practice later today. You can come watch if you want. I think the bats are all safe there."

He grinned at his own joke and I just shook my head.

"You're sick," I said.

"But that's not what I wanted to say," he continued. "Tomorrow's my day off. I was thinking of taking Monday and Tuesday off as well. I think the company wouldn't mind their hero skipping out for a few days. How about that trip to Carmel?"

I interlocked my fingers with his. "I'm already packed."

Bobby came from around the pickup window to tidy up the condiment and napkin station. Looking at us, he rolled his eyes and said, "Oh, please. Get a room."

I turned to him. "That's exactly what we're planning."

Bobby chuckled and went about his cleaning.

"Listen," I said to José, "there's one thing I'd like to do before it gets late. I'm hoping you'll come with me."

"What is it?"

• • •

WE PULLED UP in front of Sergio Ramírez's house at 3:30. José and I sauntered up the walk and climbed the few steps to the front porch. I knocked. The door opened and Mr. Ramírez appeared.

"It's you! We saw the news earlier," he said, pulling me into a hug. He called out to his family to come. "*¡Vengan! ¡Vengan todos!*"

Mrs. Ramírez hurried to the door, asking what the matter was. Julie was in tow with her little brother. When she saw us, she let go of her brother's hand and flung her arms around me.

"I knew you would do it." Happy tears flowed down her cheeks.

"I made a promise," I said.

I pulled away and introduced José. Mr. Ramírez shook his hand vigorously. Mrs. Ramírez dabbed at her eyes with a tissue and thanked him.

"*Que Dios te bendiga*," she said, asking God to bless him.

José turned to Sergio's sister. "You must be Julie."

He extended his hand and she gently grasped it.

"Thank you for helping Will," she said.

Mrs. Ramírez made a gesture, beckoning us. "You must come inside. Please. Have something to drink."

"We don't have much time," I said. "José has ball practice." I turned to him. "Hon?"

"Sure," he said.

"Just for a little bit," I added, speaking to the Ramírezes. Then I bent over and spoke to Julie's little brother, who couldn't have been more than six years old. "And what's your name?"

"Carlitos," he said.

The nickname for Carlos. I smiled, even though I could feel my heart melt a bit.

"I like that name. I had a very good friend who was also a Carlitos." I reached out and he slipped his hand into mine. "It's a pleasure to finally meet you."

He grinned and then pulled back toward his sister, burying his face in her hip as he clutched at her thigh and peeked at me out of the corner of his eye.

José and I followed everyone into the house, and as we entered the living room, I caught the smell of vanilla-scented candles again. I spotted a lone votive, flickering on a side table. Behind it was an eight-by-ten framed photo of Sergio smiling out at me.

ACKNOWLEDGEMENTS

I'd like to thank first and foremost Mark Spencer for his critique and guidance as I finished this book in one of his courses. His continued encouragement has meant a lot to me. I also need to thank my friends in the Writerie and Chowchilla writing group—especially Glenna, Wyatt, and Nancy. Thanks are also due to Michael Rehder for his wonderful cover design and to Phillip Gessert for his interior design and layout. Ryan Quinn, you did a great job editing and catching all my mistakes. Thank you. Finally, I need to thank my childhood. As part of my escape from a dysfunctional family and the bullying from my extended family, I learned to love the public library where I discovered all kinds of books, including mysteries.

ABOUT THE AUTHOR

B ILL VANPATTEN IS the author of *Seidon's Tale*, recipient of the Klops-Fetherling Silver Phoenix Award for new voices in fiction in 2019, and two collections of short stories—*Dust Storm: Stories from Lubbock* and *The Whisper of Clouds: Stories from the Windy City*. He also writes fiction in Spanish for heritage speakers and second language learners. He left a very successful career in academia to pursue both fiction and nonfiction writing and currently lives in the Central Valley of California. This is his second novel. You can find out more about him at www.aliasbvp.com.

Made in the USA
Monee, IL
07 February 2023